Other Fires

Other Fires

A Novel

Lenore H. Gay

SHE WRITES PRESS

Published 2020
Printed in the United States of America
Print ISBN: 978-1-63152-773-9
E-ISBN: 978-1-63152-774-6
Library of Congress Control Number: 2020908138

For information, address:
She Writes Press
1569 Solano Ave #546
Berkeley, CA 94707

Interior design by Tabitha Lahr

She Writes Press is a division of SparkPoint Studio, LLC.

To Sasha and Cy

FAILING AND FLYING

*I believe Icarus was not failing as he fell
but just coming to the end of his triumph.*

—Jack Gilbert 1925–2012

Contents

Author's Note

CAPGRAS MISIDENTIFICATION SYNDROME was first discussed in medical literature by the French doctor Joseph Capgras (1873–1950). His psychiatric theory of its origin was later updated by brain research to be the results of a closed-head injury. The visual cortex relays information through two routes. One route to the temporal lobe, which is linked to facial recognition, and one to the limbic system, which registers emotional reaction. With Capgras Misidentification Syndrome, the route from the visual cortex to the limbic system is damaged, but the lobe is unharmed. The person looks like "mother," "wife," or "husband," but the patient has no emotional response—hence the patient believes he/she is seeing an imposter.

Chapter One: Terpe

ACRID SMOKE BURNED TERPE'S NOSE and stung her eyes, jerking her awake. On the first and second floors of the house, smoke alarms shrieked. Her backyard was filled with thick smoke.

She ran downstairs and jumped on her parents' bed. "Fire! Get up! Get up!"

Mom sat up, dazed. "The baby! Get the baby!"

Terpe ran across the hall to Geline's room, scooped her out of the crib, and grabbed a blanket. When she turned, she remembered Dad was sleeping upstairs. Holding the baby tight to her chest, she took the stairs as fast as she could. The den door stood open. Mom stood by the pullout bed, yelling at Dad and shaking his arm. "For God's sake, Phil, can't you hear the alarms going off?"

"Okay, okay," he mumbled.

Mom screamed, "Phil, the house is burning! It's burning!"

His feet hit the floor.

Her parents stumbled into the hall. "Goddamn! Goddamn!" he yelled.

With the baby cradled in one arm and her free hand tight on the railing, Terpe hurried down, heading straight for the front door, Mom coming close behind.

2 | Other Fires

Dad stood at the top of the steps.

Terpe turned to look at him.

Cracking sounds as two boards hit him and slammed to the floor. He shouted, swayed, grabbed the banister, and crept down slowly. He let out one long scream that didn't stop when he hit the bottom step.

A terrible smell of burning hair.

Mom threw her bathrobe over his head, grabbed a scatter rug, and dropped it next to his body. "I have to roll him!"

With Geline on her hip, Terpe grabbed the hall phone and dialed 911. She repeated their address.

Mom patted his head to put out the flames. "Terpe, run! No, help me! No, take the baby and run!"

Terpe froze by the open door when a rush of fresh air hit her. She bolted down the front steps, threw down a blanket, put the screaming baby on it, and ran back inside. Mom wrestled with Dad's body, pulling and tugging. But Dad stood at six foot two and probably weighed over two hundred pounds.

"Take his head. I got his feet," Terpe yelled. They dragged him onto the front porch. "I'll get water. His hair stinks. It's still burning."

"No! I put it out. Where's the baby? She's crying. Where's the baby?"

Terpe ran into the yard, scooped up her sister, and yelled, "She's fine. I put her down to help you." She rubbed Geline's back, but the baby kept crying. Terpe walked in tight circles, trying to sing and calm her, but soon sirens drowned out her singing. Red lights flashed in the driveway, two fire trucks followed by an ambulance.

Mom swung her arm and yelled, "Over here. Here!"

While firemen pulled hoses, two people rushed out of the ambulance and ran toward her parents. They loaded Dad on a stretcher and rolled it into the back of the ambulance. Mom jumped in behind him and shouted, "Get help at the O'Tooles'!"

Terpe nodded. Her mind jumped to their new roof. Maybe burning tree branches spread sparks onto the roof? She rushed to a man holding a hose. "What are those shingles in the back made of?"

Over the roar of water, the man waved her back. Her head throbbed, and she moved the baby farther from the smoke. She sat by Geline and watched her house burn. Flames shot out of the back of the house. Finally, at eight, she'd had an upstairs bedroom. Now it was gone.

A silhouette came across the yard. The familiar voice of their next-door neighbor, Mrs. O'Toole, rushing toward her.

Neighbors gathered in the street, watching the monster gobble everything.

One man shouted, "Who's in the ambulance? Who's hurt?"

"Boards fell on Dad. He got burned, too. Mom went with him to the hospital."

Mrs. O'Toole asked, "What happened?"

"I don't know. It happened fast."

Mrs. O'Toole said, "Let me get my purse and go to an all-night and get milk for the baby. You and Geline will stay at our house tonight." Without waiting for an answer, Mrs. O'Toole crossed the yard. A few minutes later she drove off.

No more fire, but with the smoky air and the back and top of her house burned away, it felt like something happening in another place, like on a TV show. Terpe tried to talk to a fire-man, who said in a mean voice that some detectives would come soon, maybe tomorrow. He asked if she had a place to stay. She told him she'd go to the next-door neighbors.

She walked around the yard, clutching the baby, who wouldn't stop squirming and crying. A neighbor from down the street asked if she wanted to stay at his house; he handed her a business card. She thanked him. After the man walked away, she cried. The man often jogged by her house, but they didn't know each other. From now on she'd wave to him. No

one had ever given her a business card; almost nine and only
a third grader.

Car lights swooped across the yard. Terpe grabbed the
blanket off the grass and followed Mrs. O'Toole into their house.
Their house had a similar floor plan, but they had way different
old-fashioned furniture. Mrs. O'Toole emptied three shopping
bags on the kitchen counter. "Here, the baby essentials."

Besides food, sleep, and air, Terpe wondered what else
could be essential.

Mrs. O'Toole took Geline. "Terpe, my dear, you go right
on upstairs and climb into bed. You're welcome to take a shower,
if you want. You're exhausted. I'll feed Evangeline and take her
to our room. She likes sleeping in our old cradle."

In the guest bathroom, Terpe washed off the soot covering
her face and arms, then drank two cups of water. Her feet, black
with dirt, ached with cold. She lay on the bedspread, shivering.
Restless, she rose and opened the curtains to see what remained
of her house. She could only see one side. The big trucks were
gone. Her neighborhood felt quiet, empty, and dark.

What was essential? Her mind flew to worrying about Dad,
who'd always been essential. She felt glad they didn't have a dog,
even though she'd been nagging her parents for a big dog to
go with her on adventures down by the creek. But a dog might
have burned up. They'd have another terrible thing. How long
would she have to stay at the O'Tooles'? When would she see
Mom again?

She crawled under the covers. Pictures jumped in and out
of her mind all night. Sometimes she bolted up in bed; maybe
her parents were coming back. But when she checked outside,
the streetlights revealed nothing new, only the side of her house
and an empty street.

In the morning her body felt sore; maybe she'd never slept.

At breakfast Mrs. O'Toole said, "Your mother called. Your
father broke a rib and got some burns on his head that aren't

serious. They're watching for something that happened in his brain. For now, he's stable."

Either Mom or Mrs. O'Toole was lying. Dad could not possibly be stable. His head had been sticking out of the rug, small flames shooting from his hair. Wrong. Did flames really come out of his head? Did the fire eat him up, like a giant sticking a boy into a bonfire, turning him, roasting him, and gobbling him up?

Mr. O'Toole came into the kitchen, carrying Geline. His wife fixed a bottle and handed it to him. He settled in a chair, slipped the bottle into the baby's mouth, and grinned when she began sucking.

Terpe smiled at Mr. O'Toole, but couldn't talk. Her face muscles felt stuck. She rubbed her jaw until it unclenched.

This trouble came because of Mom. If she'd let Dad sleep in their bed downstairs, like always, they both could have escaped. Why had Mom been yelling and fighting with him three nights in a row before the fire? They probably thought she was sitting at her desk in her bedroom studying, but she'd hid on the patio, listening. Mom yelled that he could not sleep in her bed, that it would never be their bed again.

They stayed at Mrs. O'Toole's all day on Sunday. Mom stayed a long time with Dad at the hospital. She came home Sunday night. Monday morning in the kitchen, Terpe asked if she should go to school or stay home and take care of the baby. Mom didn't answer. Her face looked all puffy and her long hair was all messy.

Finally, Mom said in a distracted voice, "You go to school, that's your job. Buy your lunch. I didn't have time to make it." She picked up her purse, rummaged through it, and shoved a five-dollar bill at her. When the bus rounded the corner and stopped for a group of kids, Terpe raced to catch it.

Mom would visit Dad every day until he got well and came home. This worried Terpe. If she missed the school bus, she'd be stuck at home all day, by herself. Probably Mom would take Geline to day care. Terpe enjoyed riding the bus and liked the driver. When the seat behind the driver happened to be empty, she sat there and talked with him.

In English class, the teacher, Miss Pink, called on her to name three characters she'd picked from an assigned book. They were supposed to read a paragraph that told a lot about each character. Terpe picked up a blank sheet of paper and stood beside her desk as they were required to do. She leaned her hip against her desk, but when it was certain she had no words, some girls giggled. Miss Pink stood at the front of the room. Terpe tried to read the blackboard behind the teacher. With a scowl, Miss Pink took off her glasses and with long strides moved along the rows of desks, glaring, trying to make all giggling stop. Miss Pink's expression caused everyone, even the boys, to giggle louder. Finally, Terpe joined in.

Miss Pink repeated the question.

The blackboard looked blank, no help at all. Terpe's mouth felt glued shut. Her jaw locked. The teacher told her to take her seat. She fell into her chair. Since she had no friends, she examined the floor.

More than school, she dreaded staying home. No more searching for Princess Roway's water kingdom or climbing mountains with her special friends. Her real quest now would be to figure out why the house caught fire. Wind had probably carried burning branches onto the roof in the back where the roof lay flat, not peaked like the front of the house. In December the ground stayed dry, usually, so which trees would be dry enough to ignite?

Mom warned her not to go upstairs until the mess had been cleaned up, but the next morning, Terpe snuck upstairs to her stinky bedroom. Her room and the den smelled smoky, and the rugs were damp and squishy from the fire hoses. Yet her room was only a little burned, the walls sooty in places. She leaned out a window and studied the flat roof built out of something like wood. Broken glass covered the bathroom floor. Her sleeping bag didn't smell like smoke, so she brought it downstairs into Geline's room. She'd stay there until her room got fixed.

The room next to hers had been turned into a den with bookshelves, a desk, chairs, and a file cabinet. That's where Dad had been sleeping on the old sofa with a double pullout bed.

.

Chapter Two: Adam

ADAM'S MORNING PAPER LAY UNDER the mail slot at the bottom of the stairs. The same flight of stairs he used every morning to grab his paper and get his mail. For a few seconds, he tried to recall why he'd opened his apartment door, muttering reminders about the latest football scores. Coffee smells drifted from the kitchen.

His foot didn't connect with the top stair. He stumbled, reached for the banister, and missed. Groping for the rail again, he found himself half sitting, three steps from the bottom.

The left side of his face throbbed. From football days, he knew how to check his shoulder. With a gentle motion he inched his shoulder up and down and massaged it. Each finger moved without pain. No dislocation. Worse pain shot through his foot, but his shoulder hurt too much to reach down and examine his ankle.

A familiar pain in his foot. *Do not think about it. Do not think about those days in the butcher shop with Papa. Stop.*

The empty foyer, with the familiar dirty white tile and dull yellow walls, smelled like garlic and tobacco smoke. Through the front door's frosted glass, he watched some bundled-up people blur and weave along the sidewalk toward the bus stop and subway. He wished someone would come in or out and find him with a hurt foot. He pictured two or three old people sitting in front of their TVs or dozing in their La-Z-Boys. Even with nothing to do, they weren't the sort of people who opened their doors to some injured person.

He inched up the steps, pulling on the railing with his left arm. At the top, he turned to study the images passing by the frosted door glass. The outside world felt far away, all muffled. Lonely.

The newspaper still lay under the mail slot. Never mind. He had to get inside before someone saw him.

Most dreams floated away, but he thought over this morning's, which felt like grabbing handfuls of mist. He shuffled to the kitchen and poured a cup of coffee. Falling had been his own fault, or rather the dream's fault for distracting him.

A winter Monday, a week until Thanksgiving, with him hobbling around on a bad foot. He hadn't been drinking when he fell. Mama would give him sympathy. A busted ankle, another excuse not to get back to work. He had mixed feelings about work. Sometimes he loved his job.

His empty gin bottle had sat for weeks on the floor by his easy chair. Another dead soldier on his bedside table, and an empty pint hidden behind the toaster on the kitchen counter. Mama refused to touch his bottles, refused to buy him liquor, or beer. In a gruff voice, she declared alcohol a poison. He tuned her out when she acted like an old nag.

An ice pack in a dish towel, balanced on his ankle, would do the trick. In his chair with a cup of coffee and the remote, he felt ready for a whole day of TV. He fiddled with changing channels, hoping to find a show about rock climbers; nothing ever looked clumsy or impulsive about those folks. On edge the whole time he watched, he studied the ascents and descents, fascinated by their courage. Wishing he were courageous.

Not brave or agile enough, Adam couldn't climb a boulder, much less a cliff, except on his dream island. Though wide-shouldered and well-muscled, a former center in football, he couldn't imagine lugging his own weight up the side of a cliff, even when he was younger and fitter.

Finding no climbing shows on any channel, he switched to an animal show. He liked programs about woolly mammoths and other animals. Mammoths once walked the earth, and he suspected they still did, but nobody had found them yet. The program narrator explained how mammoths had lived lives of vigorous exercise, full of challenges. Without outside enemies, mammoths fought for sport, or food? Humans sure did.

Working for Papa in the butcher shop had been Adam's worst challenge. His father hurt him for sport. Adam had watched his father's face; sometimes Papa looked almost happy when he came after him. Waldo turned into the enemy Adam had to survive when he turned twelve.

Birthdays were important in Adam's family. Since his thirty-second birthday, Adam wondered what challenges to take on. The first thing was to get back to the gym, lift weights, and run on the treadmill to build up his body again. Too many chocolate chip cookies, beers, and bourbon shots. With a few weeks of hard training, he wouldn't walk everywhere; instead he'd run again. If he started drinking again, the plan would fall apart, as usual. He couldn't recall getting more bills from the gym, but his memory stopped being reliable when he drank. One thing he could trust: if he still owed money, new bills replaced the old ones.

Electrical work meant good money; he collected the same day he finished the work. If he knew and liked the customer, he might take half the amount and send a bill for the rest. But he kept lousy records. If he couldn't find his notebook, he scribbled figures on envelopes. Maybe this time he'd swallow his pride and ask Mama to show him how to keep records.

When his ankle stopped hurting, he'd visit his old boss and get back to doing his own electrical, save up until he could rent his own place. He should have somewhere important to go to every day, with people who wanted to talk with him. Not any friends. His three friends from high school were still around, but no new friends since he graduated high school.

Three days with an ice pack on his ankle did the trick. The fourth morning he flexed his foot with a growl of pleasure. His thirst came back. Just a few beers to celebrate his mended ankle. Where would a few beers lead? Nowhere good.

To steer his mind away from hooch, he hunted for empties and tossed them in a black trash bag. He braved the rickety fire escape, crossed the weed-filled yard, and yelled "Aah!" when he tossed the trash bag into a can. In his room he changed the month-old sheets and opened the window to get fresh air.

He mopped his bedroom floor, found his silver cowboy shirt balled up under the bed. Beer-stained and too tight in the arms, but still his beloved shirt. He hung it in the closet. A minute later, he took it off the hanger. The pearl buttons weren't chipped, and they sort of shone under bar lights; he bought the shirt in better times when money came rolling in. Someday his moving out west could happen. He wanted to take a shot at rodeo riding on real bucking horses, hanging on for the golden eight seconds, whooping and hollering.

Sometimes he hollered at rowdy neighborhood kids walking home from school. Only younger kids—he didn't want to hurt them, just laugh and yell. Not exactly true. While strong enough to beat the crap out of older boys, he could end up in jail. He reminded himself he didn't resemble his father, who probably got in bar fights all the time.

Adam reminded himself he'd stopped that shit. He slid his silver shirt into a paper bag. Did a thirst for excitement explain why he longed for a shot of bourbon this minute? Why did he yell at kids when he sat on the stoop on quiet afternoons? Did he find yelling that exciting? Could he be afraid of getting caught by some angry father? Papa sure loved to yell. He held the yelling championship in the family.

Adam tucked his shirt under his arm and negotiated the front stairs with care. His car still sat around the corner where he'd left it. Three days without a single parking ticket. A good omen. Not many of those in his life. He dropped off his special silver shirt at the cleaners. The walk from there to the grocery store felt longer than usual. Inside the store, his foot felt hot and throbbed, forcing him to clutch the cart handle with both hands and lean forward to ease the pain.

Not his favorite grocery store, but Mama liked it. In front of the rows of grain bins, he picked out nuts, scooped about a cupful, and dropped them in a baggie. Right away he noticed they didn't sell Cokes or the good kind of potato chips. He grabbed more baggies and loaded in raisins, granola, and brown rice. What did this rice taste like? Maybe he'd eaten it and forgot? He pocketed a card with preparation instructions. A jar of peanut butter, eight cans of beans, and two cans of peaches went into his cart. He picked out a twelve-pound turkey. Eggs, sugar, and flour were for his Thanksgiving pie. Milk and cream for coffee.

Adam stood on one leg to relieve the throbbing while he bagged oranges and collard greens. Eyes on him made him turn. A woman with hair dyed black stared at him with a smirk. He turned away and ran his hand through his hair; yep, his hair felt thick and greasy, and he was kinda dirty.

Passing shelves of wine and beer, he headed to his new reward, coffee. He smiled when he dumped two brands of coffee in the cart. One of the large bags was called "French Roast." He hoped it would taste exotic, something new for a morning wake-up. Sometimes he woke up feeling so sad, he wondered how he'd get through the day without coffee.

As usual, he paid with Mama's credit card. At the door he stopped, put down his groceries, and hobbled a little way down the first aisle to check which beer might be on sale. He picked up a six-pack, liking its familiar heft. Stop. For sure, he didn't need that crap.

He picked up the grocery bags. Maybe tonight he'd make a peach pie. Since he was a kid, he and Mama talked about cooking. Her knife skills made her a natural for chopping vegetables and potatoes. She demonstrated chopping and taught him to make soups, and stews with various cuts of meat. Also, cookies and pies. The front stairs felt steeper than usual, causing him to creep like an old man. It took two trips to bring up the groceries. He hobbled around the kitchen, putting everything away.

Had it been two or three months since he had any electrical work? Probably. His inside voice nagged him about still living with his mother when he felt way too old, and past time to rent his own place. After she got used to living alone, he intended to buy a better truck and head west. He pictured himself at the wheel, wearing cool sunglasses and his silver cowboy shirt.

He dumped clutter off the dining room table into a trash bag, and stacked dirty cups and glasses on the countertop. Then he wiped crumbs into his hand and dumped them. While wiping and polishing the table, he put himself in various situations: greeting electric customers with a confident handshake, depositing their checks at the bank, and giving the bank teller a big hello, maybe a wave while walking out.

In the shower he wondered if he had bothered to cancel a new customer's appointment from a week or so ago, when he was still hitting the bottle. No, he hadn't canceled. A scrap of paper said he had scheduled it for tomorrow. He'd keep the appointment. From her call, the job sounded simple, something about a basement dryer that wasn't an emergency. This customer would help him get back in the work groove. After he finished at her house, he'd get over to the high-rise building site and catch up on some wiring he'd promised the contractor he'd do. Of course, he agreed to do the wiring a while back. He hoped the contractor hadn't hired someone else.

Constant winds scour the dream island, stirring up a storm. Sharp wind burning his face and hands, white sky and land down to the ocean, angry waves a roaring white. Land torn and scarred by jagged rocks that rip open his feet. Over his shoulder, his own bloody footprints follow. His legs fly out from him: enormous legs and feet turn into balloons helping him soar. He flies on his back and imagines the land below. He drifts into a pile of snow. On all fours, he pushes his way out.

Distant noises, dogs or wolves. Dark shapes make a wavy line against the horizon. Gradually the line separates into shapes. Sled dogs? His body halts, paralyzed. Five or six dogs race toward him, their wide chests heaving and dark tongues lolling out their mouths. His question of why these animals don't attack flows into another scene. The dogs pile on and force him into their furry heap. They lick blood off his feet, startle him with bright blue eyes; their rough tongues take away his numbness. Their thick fur comforts him. He's safe, no human can yell at him or kick him. The dogs heal his wounds.

Adam surfaced from beneath his blankets. Slivers of sunlight leaking between slats in the blinds. The clock read seven. He wouldn't leave his bed until he thought more about the dream. He had rules so he wouldn't get scared. He couldn't let himself consider the whole dream, only parts about the terrain and dogs. The Alaskan Iditarod on TV inspired this dream, yet any thought of running without shoes over icy rocks and snow made him cringe; he never took off his shoes outside, except at the beach.

Adam drove to his customer's house. His dirty hair stuck to his head, like he'd been sweating at a construction site, except he hadn't gone to the site. His eyes, usually his best feature, were bloodshot, a painful surprise in the truck's rearview mirror. The customer's back steps were steep, and he took them as if he had an arthritic back.

When he walked through the kitchen door, the woman wiggled her nose.

"Sorry it took me so long," he said. *Which excuse? My truck's-in-the-shop excuse.*

The customer held up her hand. "That's okay, I found another electrician. The job's done."

He gave her what he hoped was a friendly grin. "Anything else need fixing? I'm pretty handy."

She shook her head.

"I understand." He cleared his throat. "Can I have a glass of water?" He wanted her to put ice in it. He wanted to lie in a tub of ice. He sat at her kitchen table. She gave him tap water, leaned against the sink, and crossed her arms.

He sipped the tepid water. "You know, it's too bad people don't get along better." He choked a little, not sure where the words came from. He felt pissed at her, which must be it.She frowned, walked to the back door, and opened it.

He gulped down the water. "Thanks. I gotta get downtown to the site."

She stood by the door.

In his truck, he tried to clear his head. He should have gone to the customer's house, maybe three days earlier or maybe a week earlier. *Get on down to the construction site.* They depended on him.

He pulled into the parking deck and found a space almost at the top level. Few cars and trucks were parked up this high. Close to ten, plenty of time to walk over to the site. He got out of the truck, stretched, and walked to the edge. Across the street, the new construction stood like a skeleton. Just a few sips from the pint of bourbon before he went over to the site.

Hot as an inferno, itchy and wet, Adam woke. He focused on his cell phone next to him on the seat, took the key out of the ignition, and slid out. When he reached back to grab his phone, he slammed the door on his thumb. "Goddamn, fuck, fuck!" He kicked the fender. Using his left hand, he fumbled with the handle until he managed to open the door. His thumb burned, blood oozing around his nail. Half a pint lay on the seat. He had to drink all of it for this shit. The liquor went down fast, but his thumb still hurt. He stumbled to a corner in front of a car and peed. God, he hated to see people pee in public. No class at all.

A nothing guy, a big sweaty guy with a smashed thumb. He felt like crying at the lonely quiet settling over the construction site across the street. Voices drifted from across the way. Most of the guys had probably left for the day, and the rest were packing their tool boxes.

Tires screeched overhead. Brakes gone out a floor above? A truck came barreling down the ramp.

"Slow down, man, slow down!" Adam yelled and flattened himself against the wall near his own truck. The truck careened around the corner aiming straight at him, but it lumbered to a stop about twenty feet away. A skinny guy slid down from the cab, a wad of tobacco under his lip. He carried a shovel and spat tobacco.

Adam exhaled. "Hey, man, you handled that real good. Your brakes are shot. I'll be glad to give you a ride. I'm getting ready to take off for the day."

The guy's laugh sounded like some ghoul in a horror movie.

Adam had nowhere to go. The shovel swung toward him. He couldn't move fast enough. When he woke, his mouth tasted like blood and his skull drummed. His thumb had a pulse.

Lights for the yellow level winked on. The guy's truck still sat about twenty feet away. Adam's own truck had disappeared. That old 150 Ford was all he had.

Adam tried to stand. He swayed while he stood on the concrete floor, wondering who to call. When he breathed through his mouth, his chest felt better. Who could help? No one. Working guys were drinking buddies, not reliable. His three old-time high school buddies had real work; no matter, he couldn't call any of them. Mama didn't have a cell phone. Old Waldo was rotting under dirt.

Don't think about him. Even the thought of Papa could make Adam puke. Memories rushed back: He lay on the familiar cold floor, feeling terror, Papa standing over him, about to whack him again. Adam would stay curled up; through half-closed eyes he'd follow his father's thick legs, his hairy arms, and his black hair greased back to cover his bald spot.

Papa's grumbling turning into a roar when he swung his fists. "Boy, if you don't mind me, you know what's coming!"

Papa ran his hands over his bloody butcher's apron. Big hands kept wiping blood on the apron from the time the shop opened until it closed at sunset. That clean apron at dawn always bloody by dusk.

Adam shook his head to get rid of Papa. He limped over to the side where some guys were walking away from the construction site. He recognized two of them, waved, and yelled down, "Hey, some guy hit me with a shovel and stole my truck. Can you give me a ride? I don't live far."

"Oh, sorry, dude, my wife's waiting because we're taking our kids out to eat. These guys are with me. I got to drop them off. No worries, a bus will come along soon. They run a lot of buses this time of day." The four men got into a truck and drove off.

Adam climbed down the inside staircase to the street at the edge of downtown. He walked through a few blocks of falling-down rooming houses. On a bleak corner, he felt eyes watching him limp along because now his ankle ached. He felt bad he had no one to call. Three miles to home would be good exercise. He settled into a slow pace and tried not to notice the neighborhoods he passed through. Finally, he felt happy to see trees and newer apartment buildings. The four o'clock afternoon sun irritated his eyes without sunglasses. His whole body hurt.

The pain reminded him of Waldo's butcher shop. When he turned twelve, Papa announced that he should help out at the shop. Later Adam whispered to Mama he didn't want to go, but she stood with her arms tight across her chest. She wouldn't help him or protect him. Not this time.

"You go and work with your papa," she said. "Do you good to help him and learn the business. You might want to take up butchering. You don't do much on Saturdays anyway, except watch those cartoons. You're too old for cartoons." Her tight mouth told him she wouldn't discuss it again.

He coulda picked a fight with her, insisted he liked fishing, nature, and survival shows best of all. But he didn't fight with her. Without her to soften up Papa, he'd be in bigger trouble.

Waldo's voice turned oily as soon as the bell over the shop door jingled. Sometimes he kicked Adam's leg, a signal to hurry to the counter to wait on a customer. But if Adam had a bloody lip, he hid behind a pile of boxes in the back room. Not good for customers to see the kid's messed-up face.

When no customers were in the shop, Waldo cut meat and took phone orders. His eyes hardly left Adam, waiting for a mistake. Adam's insides trembled like a rabbit's, yet he faked confidence while he wiped counters, scrubbed meat trays, and swept wide floorboards.

Adam watched for trash on the sidewalk, any reason to hurry out and sweep carefully, tending every inch in slow-motion escape. If his father looked distracted, Adam spread out the trash and swept it again. A grown-up or a cute girl might pass by and wave, sometimes even say hello. If he turned his back to the shop, he could sneak in a smile and say a few words. Fresh air, sunshine, even rain, he loved the outside world. He wanted more friends. But through the plate glass window, he always felt his father's evaluating eyes.

When shadows shaded the puny trees out front, Adam took his jacket off a hook and put it on. Often, he refused to ride home with his father, hopping on a bus instead. While the bus rolled along, he thought about the six days of relief before he had to go back.

He brought himself out of the bad memories of Waldo's shop. The important worry still remained: his truck. Where had that creep driven it? His insurance agent became the most important person. There should be enough money to buy another truck. He hoped he could afford a newer 150. He should report the guy who bashed in his head. But screw it. He didn't want to talk with any police. The people who ran the parking deck could deal with that problem if they wanted.

When he got home, he called an insurance agent and left a message. His message sounded forceful: he had to have a truck for his electrical business. The agent needed to get on it right away and call back this evening.

Adam was napping the next afternoon when his cell rang. His ankle and thumb hurt, and the inside of his head made banging sounds. When he saw the insurance agent's number pop up on his phone, he picked up and tried to act cheerful.

"Mr. Werther, tell me what happened."

"I parked my truck in the parking deck, across the street from the construction site. I had to catch up on an important job. When I came back, my truck had disappeared. The guys on the work site had stuff to do, so I couldn't hitch a ride. I had to walk home, 'bout three miles. Sir, I got to have a truck. Right away. I know my truck isn't worth much, but it ran good."

"Why didn't you call the police right away?"

"Well, first off, I felt hot and tired. My cell phone had a dead battery. I wanted to get home and sleep. I should've reported it when I got home. I'm sorry."

He did feel sorry. He'd made a mistake, for sure.

"I'll get back to you, Mr. Werther. I'll have to check police reports. Perhaps your truck has been found."

Adam moved to the side of his bed. Thirst had kicked in, and he debated whether to walk to the kitchen and run cold water in a glass. "Can you do that now? So's I can get a truck right away?"

"I'll do my best."

"Can you call back tonight? I'll wait for your call."

"I'll do what I can."

"Thank you, thank you a lot."

At age ten, he first encountered a woolly mammoth at the Museum of Natural History in Washington, DC. An enormous African bush elephant stood in the museum lobby, but Adam and his parents didn't linger at the elephant. Eager to take in everything, Adam first spotted an enormous mammoth. The sight made him halt.

Papa came up beside him. "Son, how about that?"

Adam didn't answer. He felt joy rise in his chest at Papa's kind tone of voice. While inspecting the huge creature, Papa moved around it like a huge and powerful beast himself. He read the sign in front of the display and asked Adam questions about the information posted on it.

Mama watched them from a bench. Later, Adam turned to tell her something about the mammoth, but her bench was empty.

Adam asked Papa if mammoths grew a second pair of ears to make their hearing sharper so they could hunt prey. Did they develop extra eyes?

"Good ideas, Adam. But think about it, creatures living in extreme cold would have small ears so they wouldn't lose too much body heat. African elephants have big ears to cool off in the heat, just the opposite. We didn't study these animals in school. You have to research them."

"Oh," Adam said, "I wonder if they had extra eyes."

His mother's footsteps came up behind. Adam turned. "Where did you go?"

"Three museums are too many for one day." Her voice came out in a soft whine of discontent. "I put my feet up in the ladies' room and read a magazine to give you boys some time with the animals."

He and Papa grinned at each other. They were standing close together, and it felt good. They didn't do much together anymore. Adam could still feel the sensation of the day's happiness moving from his belly into his chest. Three days after their museum visit, his first island dream arrived. Since the first dream, he'd visited the island four or five times a year.

He flew above rugged land, wearing a huge unfamiliar body. His sight went above and below at the same time, impossible in real life. A herd of shaggy beasts moved across the island through a blizzard, heading to the valleys. Did the island exist in this world? Could he find it in an atlas?

By the kitchen window with a cup of coffee, he considered islands. Scientists would disagree, but he thought about the mammoths' slow migration south from the Arctic. Probably less than half survived the journey, but enough to reproduce. Huge and mean, they had no natural predators.

He hoped his own dreams told his future.

Like a two-faced planet, the other side of the island had a beach where creatures came to swim and sun themselves. Snowmelt ran down the mountains, making a lake in the island's middle. Fog drifted over water. Animals drank from the freshwater lake. If he stood in the middle of the island and faced the tall mountains, he felt winter's chill. When he turned, the island resembled spring, smelling of fresh air, except during the three terrible months of cold when animals moved slowly, and the moon rose and turned the color of milk.

He watched when the animals came to drink. Near sunrise, small and weak ones crept to the shallow end. Later, larger animals lumbered to the lake. Fights broke out if they couldn't avoid each other. Males saved face by moving away; the rare fights lasted until one of them lay dead. The bloody mess lay in the snow, but not for long cause birds and smaller animals feasted. He made a list of the animal tribes on the island. At the top were woolly mammoths. Next foxes, wolves, hyenas, mountain goats, and bears.

The first man on earth had been Adam, his own middle name. When he turned eleven, he told his parents to call him Adam.

When Waldo turned fifty, he suggested to Mama they buy an RV and travel during their vacations. She considered his idea, but spending time in close quarters with him scared her; maybe short trips, close to home. She must have almost convinced herself he would become more relaxed once he retired at sixty-five.

But at fifty-four, Waldo keeled over from a heart attack. He and Mama had been married thirty-three years.

When Papa died, Adam had already rented his own apartment, in the same neighborhood as Mama's. Right after he got her call, he jumped in his truck and drove to her place. She stood at the kitchen counter slicing roast beef. Without a word, she arranged the meat on a serving dish and quickly dumped two handfuls of pasta into boiling water. She pointed to a mound of vegetables. He chopped them and dropped them into the steamer.

He grabbed a bigger knife and held it to his throat, pretending to slit it, with a swashbuckling grin. They burst out laughing, and it felt great. What a relief—his father was gone.

Mama's face didn't look sad. "The doctor said your father's heart might've been enlarged. Enlarged? He had a small, bully-heart. But that doc never met Waldo. He stared at me. I cursed him in German."

Adam hooted. "I would've too."

She grabbed his hand and kissed it.

On funeral day, Adam picked up Mama in his truck, which had developed a noisy muffler, but she didn't mind.

He mumbled, "I called him Old Waldo when I was little. We wrestled sometimes if he felt good. Back then Papa liked his nickname."

Her hands moved on her lap. "Waldo suggested we have more children. He never found out I had my tubes tied. A kind doctor helped me. Now you're strong and not drinking."

The church parking lot appeared to be less than half full. Adam pulled into a spot and scanned the cars. "Maybe I'm not happy he's dead, but I am relieved."

"Let's get this over with." She pushed open her door.

Later at her apartment, Adam helped her put out food and sodas. Six or seven neighborhood women and their husbands brought cakes, pies, jars of pickles, and casseroles. He hadn't seen any of them at the funeral.

Adam stood in a corner with a glass of soda. He swirled it and poked at ice cubes, hoping for kind words. He waited.

Mama's friend Edith turned to her. "The real Waldo under that big guy bluster? Yeah, he turned on the charm, but he often had a smirk-face. Every time he thought you said something stupid, he made his nasty face. Just a jerk deep down."

Conversation stopped.

Adam considered blasting the woman, when a man interrupted. "Edith, have some respect. Adam's father just went into the ground."

But Edith's mouth kept flapping. "Lydia, you were always on guard around your own husband. We all saw it." Several of the women nodded.

Adam moved to the table. His voice shook. "His death has been hard on us. Papa was still a young man. Now he's gone." He focused on Edith, a gossip he'd never liked. "Not today. Do not say anything else. Not today."

His neck and cheeks felt hot.

He put his hand on Mama's shoulder. "Can I fix you a plate?"

She grabbed his hand and held tight. "No thanks, son. I'm fine." She didn't look at him.

He wanted everyone to leave this minute, but they stayed and stayed. The conversation turned to higher grocery prices, what to do with a bunch of feral cats living in the alley, and how to get the city to trim the neighborhood trees.

Years earlier when Adam told her about the beatings, Mama said she should've seen the evidence and figured it out sooner. She should have taken him and left Waldo, or made him leave the apartment. If he wouldn't leave, she would have made him sleep on the couch until he left. She did tape a note to the bathroom mirror. After Waldo read it, she took it down and showed it to Adam. The note said: "Waldo, if you lay another hand on Adam, I'll call the police. If you hurt him for telling me, I'll call again. Your son is not a stray dog to kick around. You hurt him again, you can forget having sex."

Adam felt sure she hadn't told anyone about the beatings; it had taken him a full year to work up the courage to tell her. After that, every Saturday evening when he came home, she examined him with her eyes. He'd shake his head. His father still yelled, but Adam shrugged off the commands.

The years with Waldo wore Mama down. She kept telling his father that only terrible fathers beat their children. Later she'd have to listen to Waldo rant about the beatings his own father gave him and how they had turned him into a man.

Waldo's death handed Mama her freedom and a nest egg. She planned to sell their shop when she turned sixty-five and took Social Security. Until that time, she'd keep it open five days a week, but only four hours Saturday morning and closed all day Wednesday and Sunday. While Mama made out her new schedule, Adam sat with her at the kitchen table and made suggestions. He wanted her to close the shop on Sunday and Wednesday, and add Monday. She showed him the schedule written in her neat, careful hand.

"Good thinking, Mama! Though I wish you saved Monday for yourself. I'll be happy to help out when I can. So, what about Monday off, too?"

"Let me think. See how it goes."

"Okay. I don't wanna push you."

Without Waldo spoiling the air, she and Adam talked more. Her friends would have been surprised to learn that her brother Bernard wrote her once a week and she answered. She showed Adam the only photograph she had. It was old and creased with blurred faces that were barely recognizable of Bernard and her little brother and sister.

"I wouldn't recognize them, scattered all over Europe, growing old. This photo is hard for me to look at."

When they were kids, she said, Bernard always protected her and the younger children until he couldn't stand any more fistfights with his stepfather. He ran away from home in the middle of the night. Mama never told their parents that she knew Bernard would leave home, even after he disappeared.

Adam sensed Mama never told him everything about Bernard's middle-of-the-night getaway. If Adam ever met Bernard, maybe he'd hear the whole story.

Adam's grandmother, still alive in Germany, was always a real hag, Mama said. "She never answered my letters, never wrote to your father, her own son." Mama called the old woman when Waldo died. They talked a few minutes. "The old bitch said nothing about Waldo, like she didn't care. Adam, you must never hurt your children. Never, never. Hear me?" Mama paced around the kitchen, flinging her hands in the air. Her usual gesture when she got really upset.

Two weeks after the funeral, Adam's island came back in a dream. Summer fog covers the flat land without a horizon, and in the distance red dust keeps rising from it. A fast-moving shape comes closer, revealing itself as an enormous red horse that stops and nuzzles Adam. When he reaches to pet the horse, someone shrieks. The horse's black-clad rider. A bony hand pushes back the hood of the cape to reveal a woman with wild orange hair.

Open mouth dark and full of rotted teeth. She holds up a sword, and the horse whinnies and lowers its head. Adam strokes the horse's head, and it sends these words into Adam's mind: "You are the first man. Strong and powerful, born from dirt. You are made for adventure."

The woman's sword flies off and lays on its side hovering in midair. A thread of light bursts from the sword and flies toward the sky. She whips out a jagged knife and lunges at him.

He lurched from sleep. A strange woman had invaded his island, but he didn't want her in his dreams. What if he had to keep her horrid images in his mind?

Four days after his truck had been stolen, the insurance guy finally called back.

"Mr. Werther, I can put a check in the mail today. Since it's a Friday, you should get it Monday, Tuesday at the latest."

"Already been four days. I'll come pick it up. Where's your office? Are you on a bus line?"

"We're a few blocks from a bus stop. It's our downtown office—2016 Main Street. I'm going out for a late lunch, so I'll leave the check with my secretary. You'll receive a letter with my recommendation that you consider adding coverage to your policy. If your truck is stolen again, or you're in an accident, you'll be able to rent a car while your car is being repaired, or replaced. Another thing. Since it's Friday, our office closes at four thirty. You'll have to hurry."

Adam threw on jeans and an ironed shirt while gulping down coffee. He stomped all the way to the bus stop. The buildings, trees, and honking cars—really everything in his path looked like crap. The whole world stank, but at least he'd get a drivable truck.

Chapter Three: Joss

WAITING IN PHIL'S EMPTY ROOM, Joss dug through her purse, pulling out old slips of paper: shopping lists and ideas for her current manuscript. She added a few manuscript ideas, but couldn't keep focused. Her wait stretched out until she longed to bolt and run around the block screaming.

Finally, rattling sounds came down the hall. She stepped out to give the orderlies space to transfer Phil into bed. Two tubes in one arm and another in his chest; part of his head covered with bandages, but not his eyes. She reached to hold his hand but pulled back. Bandaged pitiful hands. She couldn't touch his hands since she might hurt them. She lifted the sheet and thin blanket and checked his body. Tape covered his chest, all around broken ribs. There, a swath of exposed skin.

A tube disappeared down his throat and a urine bag hung off the bed, half full of dark liquid. She turned away. Urine bags were for old, dying people, not a young, healthy man. What did this dark urine mean? She waited for inspiration, for something kind and profound to say, certain he could hear her even if he didn't respond.

But his injuries were his own fault. If he hadn't been sneaky and unfaithful, he would've been with her in their king-sized bed downstairs, not on the lumpy pullout sofa upstairs. Fury drenched her. Her hands shook.

If she told him she loved him, he'd take her declaration to mean she forgave him for the affairs, which she had not. She did love him, still. But. So many buts now. A spoiled philanderer. Phil the Philanderer. Married how many years? Sixteen? Her concentration kept slipping away, and the number of years made no difference.

Could she tell him how much she loved him? Could she say soon the nurse would take off his bandages and pull the tube out of his throat? But that might not be the truth. She wanted to tell him they needed to talk. She felt some guilt for ignoring him in the days before the fire. Evenings when he didn't come home for dinner, she confronting him, until finally she demanded that he sleep in the den upstairs.

How many months since they'd discussed anything important? How many months without sex? Not often since Geline's birth, and none of it memorable. They'd become the cliché of a deteriorating marriage. Maybe he didn't want a wife anymore. Nothing exciting had happened between them, until the fire, a horrible kind of excitement.

On the other hand, the father of her daughters deserved compassion. She and Phil could sort out their problems later. She laid her hand on some exposed skin and whispered she loved him. They could get through this and talk it all out when he got back his health.

He didn't move. She closed her eyes and did nothing to stop her tears. She had an overwhelming desire to get away from the incessant beeping. A nurse told her what the numbers meant, but she didn't write it down; she couldn't remember which numbers meant improvement. Light filtered through the window. The clock in the nurses' station read five. No wonder the beeping was making her nuts. She'd been sitting with him since midnight. She must have dozed off.

Joss had given the ICU nurse his medical history. He'd had the usual childhood illnesses without complications, and when he turned twenty, his appendix burst, and he had emergency surgery to remove it. He'd started smoking around fourteen and smoked a pack and a half a day. He tried to quit three or four times, but couldn't make it for long. When she said the pulmonologist's name, the nurse explained that the pulmonology practice had a contract with the hospital, which meant Phil would be examined by his own doctor.

"Good, a familiar doctor." Joss nodded.

"Your husband has an advance directive. The doctor will talk with you about having a DNR, Do Not Resuscitate. If his heart stops, or he has a breathing crisis, this form gives us permission not to revive him. That's if your husband's condition is deteriorating. His lungs were damaged by smoke. His vent's taking over for his lungs, so he's in a medically induced coma.

"We don't know the extent of the brain bleed. We'll wait and see. He couldn't tell us anything, he'd lost consciousness. But he's a young man.

"You're his medical power of attorney. With that and an advance directive, you've done more planning than most your age. The doctor will talk with you. Go home and rest. If something should happen, we'll call. Any questions?"

"He's basically healthy. Yet if the doctor thinks I should sign this piece of paper, I will. I'm going to the cafeteria. Here's my cell phone number."

The nurse wrote the number in his chart. Joss hurried to the elevator. She must remember to ask the nurse again what the beeping numbers meant. Her mind had turned into a sieve.

Maybe he wouldn't recover. If so, he had a right to know his condition. She wouldn't know how much he understood, but she wouldn't lie to him.

In the cafeteria line, the sight of eggs, bacon, and oatmeal made her stomach lurch. She needed stamina, so she poured two large coffees and added real cream. At a table, she played with the spoon and thought about her daughter, Terpe. She must be careful to keep information from her. Remain optimistic. During the chaos, her daughter had been a real trooper. The child deserved some peace of mind.

A man sat across from Joss. He nodded at her and dug into a plate piled with eggs and bacon. She feared she'd vomit. Coffee cups in hand, she hurried to a restroom. In front of the bathroom mirror, she talked to Phil. "My mind is jumbled. I guess we'll try to start over and talk about the woman you've been sleeping with behind my back. And for how many months? I don't know if we can get through this. You're such a liar!

"I thank the gods that Terpe woke up. If she hadn't smelled smoke and kept yelling, you would've died of smoke inhalation or burned to death." She wouldn't say it out loud, but she wondered if her life would improve if he did die.

Chapter Four: Terpe

TERPE HAD A PLAN FOR MONDAY afternoon. When she got off the school bus, she'd go to the O'Tooles' first. She had to figure out more about the fire.

When the detectives drove up the driveway, she was watching the man and woman through the foliage from the O'Tooles' side of the hedge. When she felt confident, she pushed through the hedge into her own yard. She introduced herself, gave them her back door key, and followed them inside. Upstairs they looked around the bathroom, her bedroom, and the den. They climbed out on the roof. The two inspected the window frames and what remained of the glass blown out by the heat. The woman asked if the room next to the den had been her bedroom.

"Yes, the smoke woke me up first since my room's in back. Flames were coming from the backyard. I ran downstairs and woke Mom, ran and grabbed Geline, my baby sister. I took her out the front door. Mom ran upstairs to get Dad. He had to sleep on the pullout sofa."

Terpe followed the detectives, hoping to hear their conversation while they finished looking around upstairs, but they were silent. When they went back outside, they poked around in the dirt around the blackberry canes, shrubs, and small trees.

The man put dirt samples into baggies, like the ones Mom used for her school lunches. Terpe waited, but still no conversation.

She followed them to their car. "I have to ask questions. It's my job since Mom couldn't be here. She's at the hospital with Dad. Do you think someone dropped a match or cigarette in the bushes? Why would they do that? Why did the back of the house burn so fast? And why didn't the front of the house burn?"

Their eyes skittered around. The woman detective said, "One of us will call your mother with our report."

Terpe glared at the woman, trying to make her say more, but the two got in their car and drove away.

She'd learned a little about arson from TV. Their fire must not be arson because the detectives didn't spend much time at her house. Wouldn't they ask more questions if they thought it could be arson? But who'd want to burn down their house, anyway?

The fire had come on so fast that she still couldn't fit the pieces together. Pictures in memory didn't help, they were only like snapshots. Now that she was awake, she felt far away from the action. The night didn't feel as real as a nightmare, but more like she'd made up the whole thing.

Back at the O'Tooles', she watched an animal cartoon on TV. Later Mom knocked on the door, and Terpe ran to open it. Mom grabbed her and held her a minute. Her body shook, and Terpe guessed she'd drunk four cups of coffee, maybe five.

In the kitchen, Mrs. O'Toole stood by the stove.

Mom said, "His blood work is a bit better. He's still in ICU. They put him in a coma because he's intubated. It's standard procedure. We'll know more when they reduce his meds and allow him to wake up, but that won't be for a while. He needs to heal. The nurse said we have to be patient."

"I want to visit Dad. Please?"

"Sweetie, not yet. He's not good. He needs more time."

"Mom!"

"Perhaps." Mom turned to Mr. O'Toole, who came into the room holding Geline against his chest.

Mom stood. "Thank you for taking good care of my girls. How did my baby do?"

"I waltzed her around the living room and she conked right out. Would you like us to keep the baby longer?" Mr. O'Toole patted the baby's back.

Mom nodded to both of them. "You two have helped so much already. I need to take care of my daughters. Try to restore routine."

Back home Mom reminded her not to go upstairs because of the water, fire, and smoke damage. Her bedroom and the den were the worst, but the bathroom floor sparkled with window glass and still smelled smoky. She didn't tell Mom that she'd already gone upstairs.

The contractor told her mother to move out before construction started, but Mom refused a hotel. "I won't further disrupt my daughters' lives. I'll be changing my schedule. We'll be gone most days and won't be in your way."

The contractor had worked for the family before. Terpe guessed he knew not to argue with Mom.

Mom made a good decision for them to stay in the house. Plus, Mom liked their next-door neighbors, who always helped out, making it easier on Mom. Over the years, they'd almost turned into grandparents and lots nicer than her real grandparents. Mom would start picking her up from school, and if she had free time, they could go to a coffee shop before getting Geline from day care.

On the following Monday, Mom waited in the pickup line in front of school. When Terpe closed the passenger door, Mom asked, "How did school go?"

"Okay. The teachers know about the fire, so they leave me alone, at least sometimes they do."

A history book propped open in front of her made it appear she was studying when Mom walked by the dining room table.

In a hidden notebook, Terpe drew mermaids and horses. She wouldn't make more worries for Mom, not even about a small thing like homework.

She felt relieved Geline went to day care. She loved her baby sister, yet she'd go crazy if she had to take care of a baby all day, plus sleep in the same room at night.

Still a secret from Mom, she'd found her first real friend, named Zoe. Her friend rode a school bus in another direction, but they could talk on the telephone as long as they wanted because Mom only used her cell phone. Once she overheard Mom say the best place to talk on her cell remained her parked car. No one could nose around in her business. What business could her mother have? Terpe thought of her as an ordinary mother.

Except one big thing wasn't ordinary: Mom had a book contract and a deadline in the fall. Terpe wanted to brag to girls in her class that her mother had already published a book. And she'd been twenty-six. But no one wanted to hear about that. Bragging made kids hate you more.

On a cold rainy afternoon, her mother picked her up from school. "Let's go to our coffee shop where it's cozy."

"I'll try to get us a table." Terpe liked Mom calling this place theirs. It made her feel grown-up while she pushed through the crowd to their favorite table in the back. A man sitting there stood. She inched closer and shifted her feet while he packed up his computer and put on his coat. The second he left, she dropped her backpack in one of the chairs and sat. Too cold to take off her jacket, she rubbed her hands. Finally, her mother pushed her way through people, holding her latte and Terpe's hot chocolate.

Mom tried to smile. "Today turned out sort of good. The doctor cut back on the sedation and your father woke up. He moved his head and smiled. He looked at the nurse."

"He smiled because he felt so happy to see you." Terpe grinned and waited for her mother's response.

"Actually, no. He didn't act like he recognized me." Her mother stared at her coffee.

"He's been out of it for nineteen days. Maybe his eyes have smoke damage. Tomorrow he'll recognize you." The hot chocolate burned her mouth. She put down the cup and sucked in air to cool her tongue.

"Strange." Mom shook her head. "Your father gazed at me like he had no idea who I was. He turned to the nurse. I knew he wanted to ask the nurse, except he couldn't talk because of the tube."

"How much longer on that thing?"

"The ventilator? They plan to try to take the vent out today or maybe tomorrow." She glanced at her watch. "They could be trying right about now. They'll watch him to determine what's next. If he can't breathe well, they'll put the tube back in. After dinner I'll go back to the hospital. If the vent's out, he should be able to whisper."

Mom sipped coffee. "Some good news. The crew took down the walls that needed replacing and have hauled off most of the debris. The contractor will send an electrician to install new wiring upstairs. It shouldn't take long. Soon you can pick out new furniture for your room."

"Great. Plus, I'll get to sleep in my own room again." She didn't tell Mom that she'd overheard her telling the contractor to throw her books and old toys into the big trash bin in the backyard. Terpe had gone into her closet where her damp clothes smelled awful. But they could be bleached and washed. Her bow, arrows, and quiver were okay, except the feathers stuck together. She picked up eight favorite books and put them in the back of Geline's bedroom closet. She threw her stinky clothes into a laundry basket and did three loads. Except for tennis shoes, the rest of her shoes were ruined.

In a short time, Mom had turned old and tired. In the light, her skin looked thinner and her hands shook. If Mom caught her watching, she put her hands in her lap and faked a smile. A sad, trembling smile.

Mom had stopped wearing her wedding ring a few days ago.

Terpe hoped her voice sounded nice. "I'm okay staying in Geline's room. I'm there if she needs anything. She makes funny, gurgling noises. It's cute how she grabs the bars and pulls herself up, like she's climbing a tall building. After I move back upstairs, I'll try to still get up early to get her ready for day care. It's fun. Sometimes."

Mom sighed and covered her ringless hand.

"Mom, you're really tired."

"Even when I come home at eight, get in my nightgown, and turn off the light, I keep waking up, half the night. Once I'm on the worry train, I can't get off."

"You used to give me a warm bath and tell me a story."

"A bath's a good idea." She glanced at her watch. "Time to get Geline. While I'm cooking, I have to compose a group email to update people about your father. I've already emailed Jacks, but I haven't heard back yet. He's out on some river with tourists. They're fishing, or maybe he's guiding hikers on some trail. He'll call back when he gets home. Always does."

"Oh, do you think Jacks will come see us? That would be so great. Go email everyone. I'll cook the spaghetti and steam the broccoli. And defrost some meatballs."

Mom patted her hand. "I don't know if Jacks will be able to come east now. But I hope so, too! And, sweetie, you have been a real help these days."

Terpe felt happy that Mom thought she was a help because she was having big trouble with her classes. Classrooms blurred, and the teachers' voices fell away, and she couldn't hear anything. Sometimes she couldn't even recognize her rooms by the kids. Looking at the blackboard became a way not to feel lost: The large map and big globe meant geography and history; the long tables lined up with microscopes were obvious.

Quotes from Shakespeare or Keats on the blackboard meant English class, also her homeroom. Gym became the worst class; of course she recognized the gym, but refused to change clothes. She felt too tired to run around the gym. Feeling exposed, she tried to hide in the locker room, but usually she got caught and had to change into her ugly shorts and T-shirt.

The morning Terpe met Benjy and Declan, a cloudy sky hung low in chilly mist. In her special place, down the hill behind her house, she walked along the creek, considering a spot for her tree house. She wanted Dad's help building it. They would have fun. To show bravery, she'd sleep there for a few nights. If she had to use the bathroom, she figured she could climb down the ladder, sliding over the ice, searching for a place, her tennis shoes filling with snow and an icy flashlight freezing her hand. She knew she could do it.

Voices. Two boys stood on the creek bank, throwing stones. They aimed for the other side, and argued over whose stone went the farthest. The one who landed a pebble on a wide tree stump won. A stupid competition because this creek measured three feet across. Like her, the boys wore jeans and down vests over sweaters with holes and winter caps with ear flaps. They were athletic and about eight years old, her same age.

She asked, "What's your name?"

The boy with brown hair falling in his eyes answered. "Declan. And don't tell me the name's weird, I know it. This is Benjy," he said, pointing to the shorter boy. "He's Benjamin, but nobody except old people in his family call him that."

"Welcome to my woods," she said in a strong voice. "What are you all wanting for Christmas?"

Benjy announced, "A robot that spits fire and two Transformers, almost as tall as me. A real bow tie, not a stupid clip-on."

"What about you?"

"Another set of colored pencils," Declan said, "a grown-up easel, not the kid kind with wobbly legs. And most, I want a paint box with all the colors in the world."

"Write Santa. Make sure to read it to your parents." Her voice sounded bossy, but she didn't care.

Benjy grinned. "Great idea."

Mom's voice, calling her for lunch. She must be calling from the patio.

Terpe shouted, "Mom, don't come down, I'm coming."

"Gotta go." She ran up the hill. Had Mom been spying on her?

The next morning, Terpe put a reminder flyer from her homeroom teacher on the kitchen table for Mom to see. But a day later, on conference night, Mom didn't go, and Terpe didn't remind her. The next morning Mom apologized, and Terpe acted disappointed, even pouted a little to make it more believable. "Oh, don't worry. Everyone understands. When Dad gets better, you can meet with my homeroom teacher."

Mom came the last day of school before vacation. Everyone marched to the auditorium to watch a Christmas play. Later they sang carols as the music teacher banged away on the piano, her head looking bigger with pounds of hair on top of her head that bounced in time with the music. When she got to the booming end of "Jingle Bells," her hair rolled itself into a brown ball that spun right off her head and grew four legs. The fat mouse danced across the auditorium to "Jingle Bells." The mouse made Terpe giggle.

A few days later, she ran down the hill behind her house. Declan and Benjy were crouched by the creek. They wore jeans and sweaters with holes. Benjy had on a brown wool cap, but it didn't have flaps. Declan wore his ball cap backward. His big ears stuck out and were all red.

"Remember me? I live in that house up the hill. You guys have Christmas trees?"

The boys nodded. Declan said, "Presents everywhere." He rubbed his nose. "Got a Kleenex?"

She shook her head. "Blow your nose on a leaf."

Declan rubbed his nose with the back of his hand and quickly wiped snot on his jacket.

"Plenty bushes with big leaves." She swung her arm around, pointing at the bushes.

"Why so sad, Terpe?" Declan kicked some leaves.

She looked at the ground. "No Christmas at my house. No tree. No wreath. No turkey. Oh, one good thing. My uncle Jackson sent me a great book about Alaska with lots of animal pictures. He always remembers Christmas and my birthday. This year even the wrapping paper looked pretty." Her voice sounded hoarse, probably because sometimes she talked to herself inside her head, which made her voice rusty-sounding.

She turned to Declan. "You should wear a real hat. Maybe one with flaps. It's so cold. Don't your ears hurt?"

Declan covered his ears. "I guess so."

The wind picked up, rustling trees, bringing a fresh smell of snow. They stood by the creek, getting used to each other. She threw rocks to get the boys in a good mood, and Benjy told jokes. Stupid jokes, yet when he or Declan finished telling one, the other two threw back their heads and stomped in hysterics.

When it came to her turn, her throat hurt. "Something else. Right before Christmas my house burned up, well, it burned halfway. My dad got hit by some boards and is in a coma. Except for Uncle Jackson remembering me, my Christmas wasn't anything, even if Dad doesn't die."

"I hope your father won't die," Declan said. "At least your mom gave you some stuff?"

"A pair of shoes. Not a usual kind of present. All my shoes, except tennis shoes, got ruined."

"Your mother is a good person." Benjy nodded. His mouth drooped. "That's for sure."

"Yes, she is." Terpe forced a smile. "I gotta help with dinner. See you. Bye."

Walking up the hill, she thought maybe joke telling could be another way people became friends. Talking ugly about someone they both knew could work, too. But, mean. If you and another person hated or liked the same person, you had something to talk about, even if it wasn't always true. She wanted to make some real friends in her class.

Terpe thought back to the fire and when the family made the TV news. Two times. Did the kids in her homeroom worry that bad things could happen to their own families? The newspaper printed an old picture of her parents holding hands, all dressed up, at some fancy dinner. It must have been when Dad tried to run for Richmond City Council. He ran twice but didn't win. He wouldn't ever win, Terpe thought. Dad told her he didn't like people that much and didn't like to shake hands and talk much.

At school, the fire probably made people's opinion of her family bad. If one of your parents died while you were in third grade, it meant everyone in your family could be infected with death. Right now, their house stood out on their block, with a giant blue tarp across the roof. Even though a company had cleaned the house, her bedroom sometimes stank like smoke if she shut the door for long.

She imagined sitting by Dad's grave wearing a black dress and a fancy black hat, like on TV. When the picture felt too real, she stopped and told herself everything would turn out fine. She had to keep hoping.

Except for Zoe, nobody at school liked her. They met in gym class but didn't have any other classes together. They didn't eat in the cafeteria at the same time, either.

Loud whispers from girls followed Terpe down the halls. She could still remember her first day back after the fire, when girls at her lunch table didn't move to make space for her.

Pretending not to notice, she sat at an empty table. Soon the table filled with unpopular kids. Ones who didn't have a group. She didn't know their names. Were the girls more afraid of her because they thought she tried to burn down her own house? Maybe. But that didn't make any sense. She thought of herself as a good kid, usually.

At least boys didn't bother with her. Unless a boy had a sister he had to talk to, he ignored girls. At least boys didn't usually act mean.

Her teachers, even her homeroom teacher, acted polite, yet she could tell by their sad looks no one wanted to talk to her. Before the fire, she had raised her hand and answered questions. Even if she got an answer wrong, that didn't bother her. While she had the teacher's attention, she could ask other questions. Sometimes she did ask more. But now she never raised her hand.

During class she also drew magical tree houses, like a place where fairies could live as long as people weren't around. Would Princess Roway give up living in water and live in air? Terpe wrote spells to make Roway's big fin disappear and some to grow fairy wings. She stretched out her arm and pointed her index finger at the drawing. She mumbled, "Big fin go away. Away go fin big. Away, away! Let the fairies come. Come fairies. Let the fairies come!"

She waited for Roway's transformation. Nothing happened while the teacher droned on and on. Terpe made another drawing that took up two pages; the first page showed a flock of mermaids flying over her house, landing in her backyard. The second page showed the mermaids nesting in a cluster of tree houses. Her own face stared at them out of her new bedroom window.

But no matter how many spells Terpe cast, Princess Roway didn't transform or talk. This made her frustrated and sad. One more thing that didn't work out.

She showed Mom some of her drawings, but Mom told her to stop drawing and do her homework before she read for pleasure. In Mom's opinion, Terpe needed to learn more about the world, specifically how the world came to be. Her mother's suggestion started her wondering about people in other countries besides Greece. Mom had told her lots of Greek stories. Her favorite became the myth about Daedalus and Icarus. Daedalus, a master craftsman, made wings for himself and his son, Icarus, to escape Minos's maze. But Icarus didn't obey his father and flew too close to the sun. When the sun's heat melted the wax holding the wings together, Icarus fell into the sea and drowned.

Mom said Icarus's fall gave a warning to humans not to fly too close to the gods. Terpe supposed it also meant for kids to listen to their parents about dangerous stuff. Mom explained that early people told each other stories because they didn't write words. They memorized stories.

Mom said not to worry about learning everything at her age; still, a child without a good education couldn't decide which story held the most truth. When she grew up, she could make up her own mind. But her mother said that now should be the time for her to begin developing critical thinking skills.

Terpe had already decided one thing. The story that said the world had been created in seven days couldn't possibly have happened. Did the Bible's words mean something that she couldn't yet understand? Maybe the words were mysterious on purpose.

Saturday after lunch with the O'Tooles, Terpe left the baby with them. She walked around their backyard, stood on tiptoe, and peeked through the hedge, hoping she couldn't see into her own yard. She didn't want her neighbors watching her patio or looking through trees and down the hill to the creek. They'd be asking the reason Terpe kept jumping around, talking to the air. Or to herself.

The hedge hid her. She giggled to herself.

Safe in her own backyard, she sat beneath a tree, closed her eyes, and called Benjy's and Declan's names. The boys came running up the hill.

She felt happy. "Last year I got a new bike with pink streamers on the handlebars. After the fire, Mom had the contractor build a new toolshed." She pointed toward the shed.

"I wish we had one." Declan pouted.

"Let's meet there when it gets colder." Benjy said.

"She should charge us." Declan blew his nose.

"I can pay. We'll make it a clubhouse. Fifty cents a week?" Benjy looked at Terpe.

"A tightwad. That's what my dad would call you. You brag about being rich, but you're poor." Declan looked at her for agreement.

"We can talk about that later," she said. "My teachers don't call on me anymore. I don't do assignments. Mom doesn't know."

Declan snorted. "I'm sick of your whining about school. Do your damn homework!"

"But you're nice, Declan. How dare you say that! You're jealous because your parents make you do your assignments? You're stupid."

"I like numbers. I'm not stupid, but I don't read good. Something's in my brain makes it hard to recognize letters. The teacher and my parents agreed. I get extra lessons."

Declan looked on the edge of crying. Terpe's stomach clenched. She'd hurt his feelings, and she liked him the best.

Benjy pointed a finger at her. "Did you stop doing homework before or after your teachers stopped calling on you?"

Benjy must be planning to be a lawyer when he grew up.

"I stopped homework after the fire. My mind isn't on it."

Benjy pointed at her. "You're missing an opportunity. Your parents pay money for your school." He held his nose like he smelled something stinky.

She wanted to slap him. With her back to them, she crossed the patio and went inside her house. She pulled a can of Pepsi from the fridge. From the living room, she gazed through the big windows at the trees and front yard. Some grassy spots were still scorched from the fire. Yet she felt safe in her house and the peaceful neighborhood.

Worry slammed her back into the living room. Her mission remained solving who had set the fire. How did it happen? She'd walked through her backyard three times, inspecting bushes and trees like the detectives had done, hoping to find something they'd missed. But she hadn't seen anything new. What sort of clues would she need? A motive, a person? But who and why? She felt stumped.

In Geline's room, she picked up dirty baby blankets and a tiny sweater off the floor. She wiped drool and sticky goo off the crib bars and the wall behind the toy chest she'd noticed a while ago. Sometimes cleaning helped her relax. She could tell herself she'd accomplished something, yet this time it didn't help her mood. She stalked the house searching for something to distract her.

She pulled her sleeping bag and pillow out of Geline's closet. Lying on top of the bag, she thought about what Benjy had said about wasting an opportunity. She pretended she didn't care, but he'd said it right. She'd fallen behind in schoolwork, couldn't concentrate, and didn't want to think about the fire, but she had to think about it.

Maybe Caroline, a girl in her homeroom, could be a friend, too? When the girl wore this light purple dress with smocking, Terpe thought the smocking looked sort of pretty. But Terpe would need ten dresses and a cuter pair of shoes to get popular. The next day, Terpe suddenly couldn't stand Caroline's green dress, which looked like the lavender one. Furious, Terpe tore a piece of notebook paper out of her binder. She held her hand funny so Caroline wouldn't recognize her handwriting.

"Caroline, your hair is ugly and you smell like mold. Everybody says it."

At recess, she pretended to have a headache to get excused from the playground. She sat at her desk with her head down, waiting until Caroline and the others went outside, and slipped the note inside her desk. If Benjy had been there, he'd say she hurt Caroline because of the baby, not because of stupid dresses. Benjy reminded her of Jiminy Cricket. She already knew she'd written the note to the baby.

Someone must have watched her put the note in Caroline's desk. Right away every girl in the class knew who did it. Maybe everyone liked Caroline and her dresses. She imagined Caroline's expression would be puzzled and hurt because the girl never got angry. None of the other girls would forgive Terpe. She hadn't forgiven herself. One more terrible thing.

At home pots banged in the kitchen. Without a clock in the baby's room, she had no idea how long she'd slept. Her mother's voice, talking on the phone. She brushed her teeth and combed knots out of her messy hair. Instead of going into the kitchen to help, she stood in the hall and listened.

Mom said, "Dreama, my visit? What a bizarre scene. He acted like he didn't know me."

Silence. Then Mom's loud voice. "No, really. Don't joke about something like this! He turns away or glares at me like I'm his enemy."

More silence and finally she said, "Yes, yes, the tube's back in, so they sedated him again. Off the vent less than a day before they put him back on. He must stop smoking. One doctor said the longer he stays in ICU, the higher his risk for infections. In his weakened condition, an infection could kill him. They'll try again to take him off the vent, but it could be a while.

"Yeah. Of course, I'm going back tomorrow." Mom stirred something in a bowl. Terpe peeked and saw the phone resting between Mom's shoulder and ear. "Yeah. Of course I'm tired. It's hard to think straight. Rain or shine, he'd stand on the patio and smoke. Sometimes he stank like an ashtray. This isn't helping his recovery.

"I'm glad things are good with you. While we've been on the phone, I've been cooking. Gotta get off the phone and flip pancakes. In this crazy house, sometimes we eat breakfast for dinner. Let's talk soon."

Terpe wondered if the person on the phone could be a new friend. Or did Mom stick that name on top of an old one because she disliked the real name? Mom's sort of thing. Her friends laughed about it.

She went into the kitchen. "Who were you talking to?"

"Know what Dreama means in Greek? It means 'joyous music.' That fits Gertrude better. I mean who wants to be called Gertie? Ugh."

"You were talking to Gertie? Why didn't you name me Dreama? It's cool. I wouldn't get teased at school with that name. It's your fault kids hate me. Your stupid PhD in Greek. Euterpe means 'one who gladdens.' That sounds ridiculous. And my stupid middle name. Eunice means 'victorious'? Why did you think I'd be either one of those things?" She put her hands on her hips and tried to stare her mother down.

"Even Geline's name isn't as bad. 'Good news.'"

Terpe thought the nickname Geline sounded okay. Would kids at school like her baby sister better? Maybe, if Geline didn't tell anyone her middle name, Elodie, "marsh flower." Just another reason a brother would have been better.

Mom's mouth fell. "I love those names. It's not my fault you get teased. We've talked about this. You have to act friendlier and smile at school, not act sulky. You are Terpe in my mind. Remember that Euterpe means 'one who gladdens.' Go wash up for dinner."

Terpe wouldn't have the nerve to rename a friend. No matter, since she didn't have any, except probably Zoe. But they hadn't been to each other's houses yet, and everyone knew a sleepover meant they'd become real friends. Mom would ask her to call the girl to invite her for a sleepover. But Terpe didn't want her new friend to come until their house quieted down. The house must be fixed up, and it couldn't smell like smoke. Zoe shouldn't see her family in a mess.

Clouds from the sky, which Terpe, Declan, and Benjy called "the over-blue," drifted down. The clouds made them shiver, as their wet bodies were halfway bare beneath their green cloaks with golden circlets on their heads. Wind blew from the north, meaning more snow. The three waited for Princess Roway to rise from the water, like she had most days since two-legged creatures had walked on dirt. The three were the only warriors their tribe could spare for the welcome. They spat out arguments about whose turn it was to speak the welcome and ask the princess to grant one wish, okay, maybe more, if the princess said yes.

Of course, Terpe would have the honor. Crouched on boulders, they rocked on bare, calloused feet like forest animals; they huddled to make heat and rubbed each other's hands that were blue with cold.

Roway rose with a splash, tall as a pine tree, with shiny gray skin. The princess didn't have a mouth. Terpe wondered what no mouth meant. Could she put spells on kids so they couldn't talk, drag them underwater, and make them part of her kingdom?

Terpe lay on her stomach and spread her arms. Once in church, a man wearing a white dress had lain like this on a polished floor. Someone told her it showed humility. She wanted to look humble before the princess. But she couldn't make her voice strong lying on her stomach. She sat cross-legged and put her hands together. "Welcome, Roway."

Roway's voice squeezed out of her pores. "What's your wish?"

"We want you to stay on our land. Give us a task. A journey?" She kept her head bowed. When she saw green light, she lifted her head. The green illumination had come from inside Roway. It shone around her; everything, even creek water, turned green.

"Princess, please stay here on our world. Please, give us a task."

"No," oozed out of the princess's body.

Terpe bit her lip. "Not even a small adventure?"

Roway put her hands together, flipped them left to right, left to right again. Her movements made a whirlpool. She dived straight down, vanishing into green bubbles.

Terpe ran to the boulders where she had left Declan and Benjy. The boys weren't hiding; they were gone. Alone, without an adventure. Again.

At school Terpe overheard awful words when she walked down the halls: "weird" and "strange" in loud whispers; but this hurt her the most: "Stay away from that girl with the weird name."

During class, Terpe drew tree houses to help her decide among different shapes. She'd ask Dad if it should tower high on the other side of the creek or face the hill? Should it sit on a strong branch with a tall ladder, or should they build it wider, close to the ground? When Dad got better, they'd decide.

Princess Roway and mermaids had purple, green, and blue fins, so she drew them that way. While her hands stayed busy, she waited for the teacher to say something interesting. Why did teachers go over how to add and subtract, information she'd known before she started school? She wanted to learn something new.

After school, she hurried down the hill behind her house. No boys. Ice covered the ground, and her feet made crunching noises. She moved to keep warm. Bright gray sky shone through tree branches. She tossed her hair and hummed like she didn't care whether either boy showed up, in case they were watching, hiding behind bushes. She spit. "To hell with them," she muttered loud enough for them to hear.

Her house felt toasty warm, but what about killing an animal to make a fur coat to keep her warm outside? Last summer she'd used Dad's knife and carved a bow, quiver, and some arrows out of sticks. She'd hidden them in the back of her closet where her mother never cleaned. Firehose water had ruined them and she'd thrown them away. Now new ones:

"Bow, I call you, and I call you, quiver, and I call you, splendid arrows." Her bow appeared in her hand. At her feet lay a quiver and a pile of arrows. She filled the quiver, slung it on her back, and walker deeper into the woods. A small animal, like a ferret, scurried out of the brush. She'd have to kill too many to make a coat. She threw her bow, arrows, and quiver on the ground and stomped on them until they disappeared into the dirt.

She needed the boys' help to travel to catch a big beast, to help her kill, skin, and dry it. This would turn into a better adventure than bowing to stupid Princess Roway, who couldn't even talk right.

Terpe paced, thinking up nasty words to say to the boys. Twigs snapped. The boys crashed through the woods and stood nearby. With hands on her hips, she stood tall. "You're late. I've thought of an adventure, and we have to get started." They probably expected her to talk nice because she was a girl. Did they realize she could kill an animal as well as they could?

"This is the plan. We'll shoot a big animal. I'll make bows and arrows for us. I'll shoot first. You all will have turns. You two will skin, clean, and dry it. No blood and guts can stink up my coat. It should look like the fur coats in stores on Main Street."

"You're spoiled rotten," Benjy said. "We need another girl in our group. One who won't boss us and act like a prissy-pot."

"We do not need more girls. There are three girls and one dad in my family. Besides, I'm a tomboy."

"I'm not messing with blood and guts." Benjy stuck out his tongue.

"I'll help," Declan said. "If you find me a good gut-scraping knife."

"With a knife, our problem should be solved expediently," Benjy said. "Let's send ourselves to the mountains. The biggest animals live up high."

Declan walked faster than Benjy and led the way through the woods. Terpe thought Declan knew geography the best. In fact, geography might be his only good subject, besides art. She wouldn't ask, not wanting to hurt his feelings.

"Where should we go?" she asked.

Declan's hand sliced the air. "Mongolia, on whose plains all horses are short, yet strong. Shaggy because it's really cold. We'll steal three and race for miles until we find the biggest animals. Or maybe send ourselves to Nepal? Montana? Big animals will be sleeping in dens if it's terrifically cold. We'll disturb their hibernation, and they won't like it. Maybe we'll kill one quick."

"The word Montana means 'mountain' in Spanish," Benjy said. "Montana has over a hundred named mountain ranges and sub-ranges. Spruce and Douglas firs grow at the top. Lots of bears, mountain lions, and goats. Let's go to the Rattlesnake Mountains. Eight thousand feet, high enough."

Montana sounded fine. She and Benjy outvoted Declan, who said he didn't care.

She wondered how Benjy could lift his head—it seemed so crammed with words.

"We'll land on a valley floor, and we'll have to climb rocks and boulders." Benjy rubbed his hands.

They made a pact: if one of them got lost, they'd stop and search for the lost one. In a circle and holding hands, Benjy muttered jumbled words. They ran around in a circle and let go, spinning so fast, Terpe fell, and her hand twisted under her. She jumped up.

"We're at a perfect spot," Benjy pronounced while she held her wrist and shoved it in her pocket.

They climbed. Declan let out a whoop. "Lean over, it'll make the air warmer. Sideways steps might attract mountain goats. We could grab one of those."

She held her nose. "Phew, goats stink. Walking straight

up's hard enough. You think I want to walk sideways? Or wear a nasty coat stinking like a goat?"

Fussing, they climbed. White birds, each with two sets of wings flew close. When the sun shone on their giant bodies, the undersides of their wings flashed yellow and green.

Declan hollered, "Watch out, Terpe, one of those birds might swoop down, pick you up, and carry you away!" His voice rose. "Watch out. Really! Something's flying your way."

She stopped when a giant cone hit her, punching a hole in her jeans. "Teeth!" Rows of tiny brown teeth. More cones flew toward her, jabbering in screechy voices. "How do they fly without eyes?"

Benjy said the cones sensed their approach because children had special sound waves. He translated their warnings: "Walk no farther."

"Let's pile them up and set them on fire." She dug in her coat pocket for matches.

Benjy hurried toward her. "Walk away. I'm serious, no joke."

"We should've gone to Mongolia," Declan whispered. "We'd be racing across those steppes on those horses, or maybe riding camels."

"If they're Bactrians, they're worth riding," Benjy declared. "Two years ago, my parents and I visited Saudi Arabia. The dromedaries just had one hump."

"No time for stories. We've got gobbling cones and giant four-winged birds after us!" Terpe said. Benjy sounded like her father. Get Dad on a subject at dinner and you could forget asking him to pass the chicken. Terpe would walk around the table to grab a serving dish and serve herself.

Benjy spun around. "Hear it? I'd say the thing's big. Walk faster."

Behind a boulder, two deer butted antlers. She said, "They aren't big enough to make that kind of racket. Probably a tiger, a hyena?"

Benjy said, "Dummy. No hyenas here."

"Your new favorite words? Dumb, dumb yourself." She glared at him.

"You don't have powers," Benjy groaned. "This adventure isn't real. It's in your imagination. If you say dumb things, Declan and I will leave you in Montana. Your adventure will end up being figuring how to get home alone."

Declan tugged her arm. "I won't leave you, no matter what."

"Benjy won't leave me either. I'm in charge."

"What do you expect when you stare into the beast's eyes?" Declan's face scrunched up.

"Something cruel," she said. "Like that creepy feeling when you wake from a nightmare."

A thing burst through the bushes, its shaggy coat dragging the ground. It froze, staring at them. It slunk toward them, smelling like rotten eggs.

"Run," Declan spat. They took off down a trail, stinky eggs behind them. Partway down, she glanced over her shoulder. The boys weren't behind her. She stood by her dim creek, the setting sun fading through the trees. Walking up the hill, she thought about Declan, a kind boy, a lot of fun. She liked Geline now, but before the baby was born, Terpe would have traded the baby sister for a brother. For Declan.

Chapter Five: Joss

IN THE EARLY DAYS OF PHIL'S injury, Joss called the ICU first thing in the morning. While the coffee dripped into the pot, she talked with the night nurse to find out if he had a good night. A hurried breakfast for Terpe, who had to run to catch the school bus. Joss ate toast, took Geline to day care, drove to the hospital, looked in on Phil, talked to the nurse, ate something unremarkable in the cafeteria, visited Phil for a few minutes or longer, rode down in the elevator, got in her car, picked up Terpe at school, picked up Geline at day care, and drove home.

Tonight her watch read almost seven after their pancake dinner. She bathed Geline and talked with Terpe while loading the dishwasher. She handed the dirtiest dishes to Terpe to rinse off first, despite her daughter reminding her that rinsing had become old-fashioned.

Mrs. O'Toole arrived to sit with the girls. Joss poured coffee into a travel mug, hugged Terpe, and pulled on her coat. On the drive to visit Phil, she wondered whether if she kept her hands off the steering wheel, the car could drive itself to the hospital. She let out a bitter chuckle. She hoped to only stay a half hour or so. Her own mother used to say: "I'm dead on my feet."

Three weeks passed without change in Phil's condition. Joss slept later, put on her winter coat, and took her coffee to the patio to watch the sky lighten. *Think about anything except him,* she told herself. At times ceaseless worry panicked her.

The sun rising over the trees slowly set them glowing, but with the rushed days, Joss felt nothing except the urge to sprint to the driveway, get into the car, and race through her routine before speeding home in darkness to appear once more in this scene: same patio, same coat, same coffee in a travel mug in her hand.

During the hours she sat in Phil's room, she sometimes tried to fit together the pieces of her own parents' marriage while trying to create a map of some exotic place using the cracks in the ceiling as an outline of this new world of fire and injury. She felt too scattered to think about her parents' marriage and divorce.

No matter how long she gazed upward, her eyes kept straying back to the monitors. The endless beeps still hurt her head and jangled her nerves. She feared she'd have nightmares triggered by these incessant sounds.

A few days later, more thoughts about her parents' marriage came to her. As a child Joss had eavesdropped on their conversations and fights. Her mother had changed her ways quickly once Daddy began earning more money at the racetrack. She insisted that she'd used enough of her own money, and now she wanted to spend more of his. First, the family moved to a larger house with a pool and a stable for their horses. Mother insisted that in the long run it would be cheaper than boarding all the horses.

Soon after they moved to the bigger house, Mother lost interest in managing and refused to do much to settle them there. Sally, their longtime maid, told the movers where to place furniture. Uninterested, her mother disappeared for hours: bridge club, clothes shopping, tennis matches at the club, and cocktail parties. At least that's what she claimed.

Joss looked up at Phil, still motionless. Only the machines made noise and moved. The minutes crept along until Joss felt like jumping up and down and screaming.

The next morning, she stared down at the patio, holding her empty coffee cup. She promised herself that today she'd leave his room after fifteen minutes. She wanted to take a walk, clean the house, and grocery shop before picking up Terpe from school.

After fifteen minutes had passed, she waved in the direction of the nurses' station and fled. The next day she modified her schedule. After rushing Geline to day care, she hurried home. She pulled on gloves and walked fast, finally slowing to an amble. She kicked piles of leaves. With its bare trees and brisk wind, the time around the winter solstice had become her favorite. Over the years she grew tired of stifling summer heat followed by rain showers. No snap to a summer season. Late autumn and winter carried surprises, snow followed by a warm spell, later icy rain, and maybe a big snow again this year.

She leaned against a tree and scanned the sky, feeling the rough bark, but an image of Phil in a hospital bed interrupted her reverie. She took off at a faster pace. Would she have to take care of him at home? No, she'd kill herself first, not literally, but she wouldn't take care of him as long as he was playing around with other women.

She must find work, full-time teaching probably. Her second book, like her first, would have a small audience, mostly academics and students. The sales wouldn't bring an adequate income for her and the kids. The rehab staff would have to find Phil a place to live.

Stop. Don't wander into the future.

Surprising changes were evident in Terpe. Normally she was a sulky child; now she appeared happier. She usually refused to do chores or did a sloppy job, yet lately she acted without being asked. This morning she dressed the baby and packed the diaper bag before running to catch the school bus. Terpe's help lessened Joss's panic about how she'd manage all the changes in finances, and the girls, without Phil.

The morning Phil came off the ventilator, Dr. Howard met with Joss in a lounge down the hall. He talked in a low tone, saying he hoped Phil wouldn't need to go back on the vent. If he did, they would do another procedure first: a small surgery to insert a trach instead of the tube. Joss had a vague idea what all of that meant.

When she peeked in Phil's room, his eyes flew open and darted around the room. "Hi. It's wonderful you're awake. How do you feel?"

Phil surveyed the room, scowling. She hurried to the nurse's station and whispered to his nurse, "He's awake, but I think he's confused."

The nurse patted her arm. "It's the nature of the territory right now. He has a closed-head injury, has been in an induced coma, and just off the vent."

She followed the nurse back to Phil's room.

When they entered, the nurse asked, "How do you feel?"

"What day is it?" he asked in a weak whisper.

"Your voice will come back in a few days. You came here before Christmas. It's January 2017. An ambulance brought you here. We sedated you and put you in a coma so we could put you on a ventilator. You needed help breathing. We treated your head wound."

"Where's Halloween?"

"Halloween happened before you were admitted. Maybe you mean Thanksgiving? That's over, too. We're in the middle of January of a new year."

He turned toward the window. Joss willed him to turn his head and talk to her.

The nurse moved to his bed. "Your throat will stay sore for a while because of the tube. Tomorrow we'll take the feeding tube out of your nose. It's uncomfortable, but you needed it. It's a tube for food."

Wide-eyed, he turned to the nurse. "A hospital, right?"

The nurse attached a blood pressure cuff. "Let's do this right quick." Before he could answer, she slid a thermometer into his mouth and soon it beeped. She finished his blood pressure, turned to the small computer in the corner of the room, and typed in numbers.

"Who's that?" He pointed at Joss.

The nurse frowned. "Mr. Montgomery, that's your wife."

"No."

"Yes. Her name is Joss."

"She might be somebody's wife. But she's not mine." He tried to raise his arm, but it fell back on the bed. "Sort of like her, but not her."

Joss bit her lip, took a breath.

"Mr. Montgomery?"

He turned to the window and mumbled, "Something at my house."

Joss said, "That's right. A fire started in the backyard and spread to the back of the house. You and I were hurrying downstairs when some boards fell on your head. You were half-asleep and stumbled a bit coming downstairs. Terpe and I pulled you outside. The kids and I are okay. You're going to be okay. We're all going to be fine."

He didn't turn his head.

The nurse motioned to Joss. Back in the hall, the nurse whispered, "Why don't you take the rest of the day off? He needs time to sort out his memories. We've given him enough information to digest."

"Does this often happen? Do people wake up and not know their family?"

"No, not usually. But with closed head injuries, we see various responses. We need to be patient."

"How much time?" Joss tried to keep the edge out of her voice.

The nurse patted her arm. "This is a day-to-day thing. Brain injuries are the most difficult to predict outcomes. I'm so sorry."

By now, "Don't cry" had become Joss's litany.

She didn't look at Phil or speak when she dashed into his room to grab her purse and coat. Keeping her eyes straight ahead, she hurried down a short hall. She pushed open the heavy door separating the ICU from the rest of the world; the ICU felt like a planet unto itself, an out-of-the-way warren of rooms where no one wanted to be, or visit. Sometimes the hushed rooms exploded with frantic movement, rushing feet, and urgent voices. But soon everything settled back into a quiet place, with beeps and sighs in the background.

In the car she put a key into the glove box lock and pulled out a notebook. The journal kept her thoughts safe. She dug in her purse for a pen without any luck, but found a pencil and turned to a blank page.

I'm a scholar and try to be of use in a crisis. I fumbled when the kitchen flooded and didn't know what to do to fix the electricity. Just like my mother, I shouldn't have a husband or children. I love them, but I'm useless at daily problems. Should I live in a cabin? Listen to music, walk, and write? Occasionally drive to town for dinner and a night of drinking at the local bar?

Phil cheats on me, and today he claims he doesn't know who I am. If he thinks I'm going to let him get away with it, he's nuts. A few weeks after we started dating, he asked me to do his laundry and acted surprised when I refused. Now I run his frigging errands. The reasoning is solid. I have free time, but not as much as he thinks. In Phil's imagination, the baby sleeps all day while I sit at my desk, thinking frivolous thoughts and writing a line or two. He'll expect my sympathy over his injury and thinks the sympathy will turn into forgiving him for his affairs.

My life feels like a B-grade movie filmed in black and white. Floating along the malevolent river, the backs of snakes and crocodiles rising and submerging in murky water. Charred logs, maybe remnants from something big, rushing along, turning the water fetid brown.

The captain pulls out his shotgun.

A woman and two children wearing rags huddle near the captain. They have come a long way, only to land in more danger.

The captain yells, "Crocodile!" The boat lurches as the speed increases. The children fall. The woman tends to their skinned elbows and knees.

The captain shouts, "A snake of death! Thirty feet if it's an inch. We'll outrun it!"

The boat powers through logs that knock holes in the hull. The boat takes on water. Snakes and crocodiles snap at the boat. They scan the shore in search of a safe spot.

The captain yells, "When we touch the dock, run."

The family jumps onto a rickety dock and takes off running. The captain's gun echoes in the widening distance. The shots must mean all's well. The three are relieved that they and the captain are safe. They will all be fine.

But they wouldn't be fine. Phil remained a philanderer. When I discovered what I thought at the time could be his only affair, I shouted, "Your parents named you well. You are a philanderer. Your name,

Philip, came from the Greek. Philip meant horse-loving, a rich nobleman—a man who owned horses had to be rich."

"*You and your damn Greek!*" he shot back. "*What a bore."*

Later she'd rolled the word *philanderer* around while busying herself with dinner cleanup; she washed dishes by hand to vent frustration. Earlier in their life together, he'd said he admired her mastery of Greek. He often told her those words. He read five or six pages of her new book, the one she'd been working on. But just a few pages. He praised it. But his words later turned into a sword.

When problems arose, at least she tried, but Phil had turned into a petulant five-year-old. She pampered him when he felt frustrated about a piece of research, or fell ill with bronchitis. His lungs were terrible. If he were too sick to go to work, he brought his computer and books into the living room and spread everything out on the coffee table and the floor. Settled on the sofa, he whined for soup with his favorite crackers, a Pepsi or ginger ale, a bowl of pretzels with mustard. She set up the cold-water humidifier, provided clean sheets for the sofa, and covered his favorite pillows.

"Hey, Phil, you're sprawled all over. Wouldn't you be more comfortable in bed?"

"I'm a sick man. A sick man deserves kindness."

"While I heat up homemade soup, can you change the baby when she cries?"

"Can't do a diaper. I'm presenting a paper at a conference in two weeks. Didn't I tell you I planned to go away?"

She retreated to the kitchen. Banging pots and pans didn't help.

The baby's gurgles turned into crying. While she changed Geline's diapers, she wanted to scream along with her.

He got over one bout of bronchitis, but three or four weeks later, he'd run a fever again. With the second bout she asked the doctor to call in the same antibiotic. She didn't like sitting in the waiting room with Geline, fearing germs. Their internist referred him to a pulmonologist. Joss insisted on reading over his medical history before he gave it to the doctor to make sure he didn't try to minimize his deteriorating lungs. She sat with Dr. Swanson, the pulmonologist, and Phil when the doctor informed him he must quit smoking. The nicotine patch failed, and the pills made his hands tremble. While chewing nicotine gum, he also sneaked a few cigarettes every day.

Phil's family had little money, but his parents kept pretending. Joss thought his values fluctuated and were dependent on his feelings, not logic, which explained why having money confused him. Yet he remained judgmental about his parents' lies. Were the judgments about their lies or about their craving lots of money, or both? She didn't know. One thing she did know, more money wouldn't have barred his mother's sharp slaps and wicked tongue.

Phil's determination to make great money in a career not known for great money showed his ambivalence about the whole subject. His fantasy to own a successful business had been just that. In truth he loved historical research. She felt relieved and happy when his department awarded him tenure. With all his lung problems, if he'd been under contract, he might have been fired. In grad school he basked in the accolades, the prizes for his brilliant scholarship. After his postdoc fellowship, he had five or six teaching offers. Everyone in grad school thought his research had been inspired. She'd urged him to interview for research-focused positions.

Phil knew he could be impatient, yet he convinced himself he could learn to control his temper with students. He preferred one-on-one conversations, yet he often couldn't connect well with his colleagues. He assumed everyone wanted to go after him, so he picked fights over minutiae. His excellent research didn't stop his colleagues from engaging in ugly talk behind his back. Once Joss overheard gossip about him at a faculty party. The two colleagues were standing right behind her. They were calling Phil an asshole for bragging about his research, disrupting meetings with long rants, and humiliating students in front of his whole class. The two men never noticed her. She headed in another direction, retreating to the guest bathroom, feeling ashamed for Phil.

Most students disliked Phil, and his poor student evaluations proved it. Would his chair stand by him while he kept missing classes? Probably for a while. But no flowers had been delivered to him from the department, or from anywhere else.

As a teenager, Joss wrote in secret, sometimes sitting under a favorite tree or in the bathroom with the door locked. It helped her release stress about what was happening between her parents, and about her own fights with them and her brother.

But tonight, she couldn't sleep, so she crept out to the driveway with a flashlight, slipped the journal from the glove box, sat in the passenger seat of the car, and wrote.

> *While we slept immersed in our own worlds, vulnerable to the world, flames burst through Phil's blackberry canes. Content in the yard away from his books, he'd labored, planting those canes, humming under his breath, yes, even happy. He'd smile while gazing out at the yard, proud when they produced berries, yet shy about his success at something other than research and writing.*
>
> *I remembered telling him I hoped he'd keep gardening. That idyllic first summer in the new house. A few years before Geline came into our lives.*
>
> *Now a fire-breathing dragon had tracked us down. Leafy branches cracked off trees and blew from*

the force of the dragon's fiery breath. Fiery torches
rained down on the roof. Inside, burned and battered,
Phil windmilled, stumbled all the way down the stairs.
Nothing to do but wait for the high whine of the
ambulance, the miracle truck with hoses.

The following day, Joss stopped by the nurses' station before visiting Phil's room. "How is he?" The nurse motioned for her to stand behind a file cabinet. She said, "At six this morning he started reciting poetry. Anyway, it sounded like poetry. But I'm not a fan."

Joss felt her heart pound. His memory must be coming back. "If it used old-fashioned words and phrases, it's probably Restoration, or eighteenth century. His period. Probably Pope or Swift. In grad school, Phil memorized his favorites. He and two guys competed. Men can turn most anything into a competition." Joss laughed a little.

The nurse nodded, picked up a chart, and wrote.

"But Phil claimed they weren't competing, rather memorizing to relax when they took a study break. To me, their memorization sounded tedious, but he loves the literature of his period. He's always been a frustrated poet."

The nurse kept writing.

Suddenly Phil's voice sounded fuller and stronger than at first. It carried across the hall to where Joss and the nurse stood. Joss felt shaky inside and tiptoed to the door of his room. His eyes were closed.

How wilt thou tremble when thy nipple's pressed
To see the white drops bathe the swelling breast!
Nine moons shall publicly divulge her shame,
And the young squire forestall a father's name.

When twice twelve times the reaper's sweeping hand
With leveled harvests has bestrewn the land

On famed St. Hubert's feast his winding horn
Shall cheer the joyful hound and wake the morn.
This memorable day his eager speed
Shall urge with bloody heel the rising steed.

Assist me, Bacchus, and ye drunken powers,
To sing his friendships and his midnight hours!

Phil stopped abruptly.

Joss dropped her head as tears came. She knew this piece.
A favorite.

The nurse came up beside Joss and squeezed her shoulder.

"Alright, Mr. Montgomery, time for vital signs." The
nurse laid the blood pressure cuff on the bed and pulled out
the thermometer.

With her coat and purse in hand, Joss coughed to get the
nurse's attention and pointed to the door. She fled down four
flights of steps, wiped her eyes with her scarf, and bolted across
the lobby.

Strong winds blew across the parking lot. If she turned on
the car heater, it would blow cold air. She couldn't drive yet for
thinking about their college days, about how Phil's voice had
changed as he lay in the hospital bed declaiming. His cadence
had slowed, and he sounded like he had in his twenties. How
proud he looked the first time he recited a poem for her. Late
afternoon sun had been flooding the cafeteria's wide windows
where they often came for coffee two hours before the dinner
crowd descended. His shy nod before he began. His pace
remained slow, and he took probably ten minutes. When he
had finished, he drank coffee and fidgeted.

"Oh, Phil, I like it. I like it. Your voice sounded wonderful.
I couldn't memorize something as long as that."

"People memorize songs all the time. The National Anthem,
the Christmas carols we learned as kids and still remember."

She reached for his hand. "How often do you practice?"

"In the bathtub when I can't think of a song, I start on a poem."

She kissed the back of his hand. "My wonderful Philip. I love you so much."

She enlarged and froze the picture of them by the cafeteria window, hands entwined across their regular, familiar table. Had this strange scene happened? Her memory told her it had, yet the image felt distant. A static tableau of two strangers.

The next morning she peeked into his hospital room. "Hi. How are you doing? It's so cold I worried I couldn't start the car. They're calling for snow."

She stopped talking when she spotted a man in a white coat sitting on a stool by Phil's bed. He didn't stand, but smiled. "Ah, Mrs. Montgomery. We've met, I'm Dr. Howard. Nice to see you again. I've just finished some tests to measure how much function has returned. I have one more question."

The doctor turned to Phil. "Who is this person standing beside me?"

Phil turned his head. "Basically, she resembles my wife, but she's not my wife."

"All right. Thank you."

While she and Dr. Howard walked by the nurses' station, he said, "There's a conference room down the hall. Shall we talk there?" They walked past several doors to a door with a sign that said TELEPHONE. He tapped on the door before opening it. The smallish room had an old black telephone on a table and six plastic chairs.

They sat facing each other. Dr. Howard sighed under his breath, but Joss heard it. "Your husband's body continues to heal, and not smoking is helping his lungs."

Joss turned up her palms that lay on her thighs. It felt like a supplication. She forced a loving smile she didn't feel. "What about declaiming the poem? Part of his brain is functioning again. In grad school, Phil memorized poems. He and a couple of English majors made it into a competition."

Dr. Howard nodded. "Interesting. But the brain is complicated. We do know that when patients are in a coma for as long as your husband, their muscles atrophy. He came here before Christmas and now it's February. He'll need inpatient rehabilitation to regain use of his body. Learning to walk, move his trunk and arms, it'll be six weeks of inpatient care, followed by several months' outpatient. No solids yet. A choking danger, so he'll need to drink a special type of water called thick water, soups, custard."

"My biggest worry is that he doesn't recognize me," she said. "He's hateful. I keep hoping he'll snap out of it. I'm overwhelmed. A construction crew still comes occasionally for repairs. I'm up and dressed. I have two daughters. I had to put my baby in day care. My other daughter's a third grader. She rides a school bus in the morning. I pick up Terpe and the baby in the afternoon. I try to feed the kids and myself something better than fast food, so I shop and cook. For months I've been working on a book. I'm under contract with a deadline in October that worries me.

"I sit by Phil's bed, hoping he'll come back. Even when I'm home, I find it hard to write. My mind's a muddle."

"A busy woman," Dr. Howard said in a quiet voice.

"Saying it out loud makes me more tired. I need my old life back."

"I think your husband has Capgras Syndrome. It's a misidentification delusion. I've asked a colleague to examine him. I haven't treated a patient with this condition, but Dr. Drummond has. He treats Alzheimer's patients. Capgras can occur with dementia and schizophrenia. Rarely from a TBI like your husband's. A TBI is a traumatic brain injury."

"Will it go away?"

"Let's wait and hear what Dr. Drummond says. I've arranged for a consult. He's back in town Saturday, so we should have a better idea about prognosis." His confident stance didn't fool her. He acted as if he knew more than he probably did.

To get out of the tiny room, she shook Dr. Howard's hand and hurried down the hall. Despite her list of questions, Capgras Syndrome felt like the basic question. Always the same answer, wait and see. Wait, wait, and wait some more.

She hated Phil. Maybe she'd leave him here. What if no one claimed him? Could she do what some women did: abandoned their babies after delivery? She couldn't abandon a baby, but Phil? Yes. He'd already abandoned *her*. Of course, his parents would take in their beloved son. He would detest living with them, but what were his choices?

The familiar poem he'd declaimed. She tried to place it. Maybe a John Gay, perhaps something from *Beggar's Opera* or a fragment from a much longer poem. The part about getting a girl pregnant and drinking as much as Bacchus, a ribald god. Typical of Phil, wasn't it just?

Chapter Six: Terpe and Joss

AFTER FIVE WEEKS IN ICU, Phil had improved enough to transfer to a step-down unit. Weaned off the ventilator, he needed less nursing care, and the visiting schedule would be more relaxed. Nurses moved at a slower pace without the frantic feel of the ICU.

Terpe adored her father. Her temperament resembled his quiet, scholarly ways. They discussed history and he detailed complicated royal relationships and wars for her. He explained how a study of history could predict our future. He told her a phrase, which she wrote down in her notebook. Something he'd learned in high school: "History is people."

Despite her failed attempt, Terpe felt determined to try visiting Dad again. With her hands folded, she sat in silence while she and Mom drove to the hospital. Joss let Terpe approach Phil's door while she stayed back. The child stood outside the half-open door, her head bowed, perhaps listening to his voice.

She pushed open his door. "Hi, Dad!" A long silence. "Dad? How are you doing?"

Silence.

Joss waited three minutes. Unable to tolerate the silence, she rushed into the room. "Hey. How are you doing?"

Phil frowned. "Why did you come here with my daughter? How do you know Terpe?"

Joss felt a flood of relief. At least he recognized his daughter.

"Dad, remember the time Mom walked up and dropped her books on your feet because you were cute. She could've broken your foot, but she got your attention. We know she isn't subtle." She tried to look happy to be telling one of their family stories but couldn't pull it off.

When he smiled, Terpe edged toward his bed. He mumbled something. "Terpe, I can't talk with you while she's here. Soon as she leaves, we'll talk."

"But this is Mom."

His head rolled back and forth on the pillow. "I'm sorry."

Joss leaned over the bed and pitched her voice low. "You are a total son of a bitch. That is what you are." She turned and grabbed Terpe's hand. "Come on."

The lobby elevator stood empty. Mom hugged her. "Sweetheart, we have to be patient. Brain injuries take a long time to heal." She cringed, hearing herself repeat the doctors' and nurses' platitudes. Her hatred surged. If he hadn't screwed a ton of women, none of this would have happened. He would have been asleep with her in the master bedroom. A picture came of their early days wrapped around each other in their big bed, whispering and tickling each other before making love: sometimes they were rough and fast, sometimes slow that went on forever.

When the elevator doors opened, the ping brought her back to the hospital and out of her reverie. She looked around the lobby, which felt almost as familiar as her living room. An awful thought came into her mind unbidden. What if Phil had told his current lover he wanted to end their affair? What if he'd complained about being banished to the upstairs den to sleep? A girlfriend wouldn't want to hear about his marriage, unless he planned to divorce the wife. If he got mad enough to announce he wouldn't leave his wife and kids, the girlfriend would get furious. Maybe want revenge. Phil lacked savvy about women and might have blurted out details of his home life.

From far away, Terpe's tone sounded harsh. "Mom, you're standing here staring at nothing. We're in the lobby."

"Most people visiting here walk around upset," Joss said. "Except for the maternity ward, the rest isn't a happy place." Joss tugged Terpe across the lobby. They passed a woman at a flower stand, the sweet perfumes mixing with the rich smells from a coffee kiosk. In the parking lot, Joss's hands shook. She jammed the key near the ignition several times before she could get it in the slot.

"When I was little," Terpe said, "and sad, you sang to me. Later we sang together."

"I'm in no mood. Let's just sit here." Joss had her hand over her mouth so she wouldn't scream. She felt her cheeks burning and her hands cold on her face.

"Mom, let's pretend we're happy."

"Sorry, I went off on a weird train of thought."

Terpe hummed a song and launched into singing it. "*Mairzy dotes and dozy dotes, and liddle lamzy divey. A kiddley divey, too, wooden shoe?*"

Joss closed her eyes.

"Come on." She sang the verse again.

Joss forced herself to sing the silly song. With each repetition their voices rose until they screeched with a hysterical edge.

"Tell me again how old I was when I learned it?"

"You know the answer. Whenever you and I walked around the neighborhood, I sang it, and you picked up the words. You skipped ahead singing it at the top of your lungs. You can thank your grandmother you never knew for that song."

"We're better now, aren't we?"

She wouldn't scream and rant in front of Terpe. She did feel marginally better; if she could just stop thinking about that other woman.

Joss parked the car in the driveway. They headed next door to pick up Geline. To distract herself, Joss remarked that soon their heights would match.

Terpe said, "People will think we're sisters. You have to style your hair to match mine. But first, get rid of your wrinkles and those bags under your eyes."

Joss stuck out her tongue to keep from smacking her.

Terpe wore her hair chopped short, and it stuck up like a kid in one of those boy bands. But at least she combed her hair wet, using her fingers, at the breakfast table.

In the past hour, everything felt changed. They were losing a father and a husband. Even if he lived, he wouldn't be the same. Their lives were utterly changed. She and her daughter formed a team that already excluded him.

Confident Terpe didn't know about Phil's affairs, Joss feared that would change. Crises had a way of breaking a jar's seal and spilling secrets. Recently Terpe had overheard them fighting, more than once. She pictured her daughter's frightened expression when they raised their voices. She and Phil rarely yelled at each other until Geline's birth.

Chapter Seven: Joss

JOSS ROLLED OVER AND TUGGED the sheet and blanket with her. The clock read two. If she fell asleep right now, she could get five hours, not enough, but she'd often made it on five; or less, many times. She wiggled to his side of the bed. She plumped the pillow and pictured the affair, creating Phil and the bitch walking into some sleazy motel on the highway. No problem for him to have an affair with the women he'd met at the college or away at a conference. A grad student would be the most logical candidate. Some aging professors couldn't resist the lure of a pretty grad student who idolized him. How many books had been written and how many movies made on the topic? The faithful wife thrown over for a younger model.

Joss's pulse raced a thousand beats a minute. The way she felt, she might never sleep again.

She dreamed Phil's parents were standing near his bed. They wore black feathers and had long, yellow vulture beaks and sharp claws. In their huge bodies inching toward Phil, they bent over his bed, their beaks clicking. His eyes remained closed. He didn't know they were there.

Joss arrived at Phil's hospital room around noon. A new doctor sat on a stool by his bed. Young, thin, and full of energy, he vibrated. He ran his hand through his hair. She half expected him to spin on the stool.

Phil's eyes were open but didn't turn in her direction.

"Hi. How are you doing? Boy, I had to wear a sweater and a coat, it's so cold. The weatherman predicted more snow, another six inches."

Phil didn't move.

"Ah, Mrs. Montgomery. I'm Dr. Drummond. We're finishing up. Mr. Montgomery, who is this person beside me?"

Phil stayed in the same position.

"Mr. Montgomery?"

With a moan, he turned and said, "That woman resembles my wife, but she is not my wife. I'm tired of saying it over and over. Not my wife."

"All right. Good-bye, Mr. Montgomery." The doctor rose and touched her arm. In the hall he kept such a brisk pace that Joss almost ran to keep up with him. He tapped on the door to the same small room with TELEPHONE sign.

On Saturday night, she and Terpe played with the baby. Peek-a-boo was still one of Geline's favorites. They took turns while waiting for a movie to start at eight. When the phone rang, Terpe ran to pick it up in the kitchen.

"No. He isn't here. May I take a message? I don't know when he'll be home." She came back, shaking her head.

"Who was that?"

"I didn't recognize the voice. She asked for Dad."

"Did she sound young or old?"

"Young, but not as young as me."

Joss scooped up the baby. "Almost movie time. I'll put Geline in her crib." She bounced the baby, who squealed. In the midst of changing her diaper, Joss froze. The woman who called could be Phil's current girlfriend. He didn't work in a business where people made phone calls on Saturday night. How did she get their unpublished number? He must have given it to her.

Joss laid the baby on her back in the crib and tapped the mobile over the crib to make the zebras and bears dance. Geline's eyes widened, and she halfway clapped her hands. Joss laid her hand on the baby's belly. She leaned over and kissed her forehead and both cheeks. "Good night, little beauty. Sleep well. I'm turning on Mr. Froggie now." She flipped on the frog night-light and the wall turned a soft yellow.

Walking toward the living room, her heart beat faster. An angry student might torch the house. Phil's girlfriend could have convinced some boy to burn down their house, offering money or sex to persuade him. She imagined the twenty-three-year-old woman as a younger version of herself. Tall and curvy, with the thick, unmanageable hair men loved to play with. When Phil played with her hair, it was his signal that he wanted her. He'd come up behind her at the sink or when she sat at her computer, run his hands through her hair, and kiss her neck. He'd reach down to stroke her breasts.

She told herself to stop thinking about what would happen next. He didn't feel like her husband anymore.

She debated telling Terpe her suspicions. No more secrets. No. She couldn't talk to Terpe about all this mess. The whole situation felt sleazy and too much for a child to absorb. Terpe was still trying to understand why her father had called her mother an imposter. Terpe might figure out the arson by putting the phone call together with the fire. Joss checked the caller ID. A cell phone number she didn't recognize. The time stamp showed today's date, twenty minutes ago. She jotted down the phone number and time of the call and slipped the paper in her jeans pocket.

While Terpe played outside, she would be free to call the fire department.

She joined Terpe. "Geline loves the mobile. And the Mr. Froggie night-light. I'm glad you convinced me to buy them."

The contractor brought Joss his bill. "My wife sends out the official bills, but this is to let you know where we are."

"Thanks," Joss said. "I'll send it on to the insurance company when everything's finished."

"How's your husband doin'?"

"He's in the gym three hours every day, building muscles and coordination."

The contractor groaned. "Sounds like a hard road."

"He's very nervous. His anxiety is so bad he can't work out unless they give him tranquilizers before he goes to the gym. I watched his panic when they strapped him upright in this wooden contraption, but he has to learn the feeling of being upright again. He told the PT that his muscles really hurt when they are forced to move. But he works hard."

The contractor handed her a piece of paper. "Here's the name and number of the electrician. Adam has been a friend since high school. He's skilled, and his prices are reasonable."

Chapter Eight: Phil

PHIL HAD BEEN HAPPY TO leave the hospital and move into a rehab center. His excitement turned to irritation at being assigned to a small, dark room close to where the worse-off rehab patients had to eat. Irritation became indignation when they made him sit to be fed by an aide. His floppy, useless hands were humiliating, completely humiliating. Sometimes fake Joss came and fed him lunch or dinner. He appreciated a new face and having someone besides an aide for company, but he longed for the real Joss.

Finally, after two or three weeks he got promoted to the real patients' dining room. How great to be able to feed himself without help. This nice, bright space, maybe he could live here forever? Fake Joss said the house burned to the ground. No matter how nicely she treated him or what she said, he couldn't trust her.

Each day felt the same, except for the milestones of his physical and mental improvements, plus his girls' birthdays, Joss's birthday, and his own that helped him remember the name of the month. At least he thought he knew the right month.

He usually woke at dawn. Soon his favorite aide would come in and tell him to get out of bed. Phil resented the other staff who woke the patients too early. Their whiny voices sounded like they were talking to toddlers while they brushed the patients' teeth, then soaped up and rinsed their faces and hands. Some patients had to submit to being helped putting on their shoes or going to the bathroom. The humiliation of seeing other patients' humiliation reminded him of his own. He still needed help pulling up his pants.

The staff brought breakfast to all the patients' rooms. After eating, he wheeled himself to the gym. He used every machine the physical therapist told him to use. After the workout, he wheeled to the dining room for lunch, back to his room for a nap, followed by more work in the gym. After eating dinner in his room sitting in a chair, he had permission to crawl into his wonderful bed. By night his body ached all over, but he could tell he'd already built some muscle and would keep getting stronger.

The same workout every day, except when the therapist added more exercises. Even on weekends he went to the gym.

When did fake Joss lie to him last about the fire, this time saying only the upstairs rooms and hall sustained damage? But didn't the whole house burn up? Where did the real Joss go when she ran away?

Where would he go when he left this place? A doctor told him the staff would take care of it.

He wouldn't worry about all that yet.

Yesterday he used a walker for the first time. Granted, he shuffled like an old man, but he was making progress. He called it another milestone.

Trapped in his body, he hated looking in the mirror. But weren't all people trapped? He thought about inhabiting another body for a week to discover what that person hated or maybe loved about themselves. Kafka's cockroach saw the world from another viewpoint. Or did Kafka pick some other insect with multifaceted eyes? He couldn't recall because Kafka belonged to his depressed high school days when he might have been stoned or not bothering to listen in class.

Someday his memory would come back; without memories, who would he be? Someone stuck forever between the old Phil and the new one?

Had something bad happened between him and the real Joss? The doctor said those memories were probably gone forever. Had he phoned his girlfriend the night of the fire? Sirens sometimes blared inside his head. Had the real Joss set the house on fire? He couldn't believe that about Joss.

Chapter Nine: Terpe

TERPE AND HER MOTHER SPENT the morning wandering through stores at a suburban mall. Mom let her pick out sheets, a comforter, and two lamps for her bedroom. At lunchtime they headed for a restaurant. When Mom went to the restroom, Terpe felt lonely and frightened by so many people around her. She glanced at the crowd in search of someone interesting, a distraction from feeling nervous. She felt her sour expression coming back, her mouth falling easily into a pout.

All the booths were full. Standing exposed in the middle of the room, she picked the only empty table, which was smack in the middle of the room.

The waitress brought silverware, water, and two menus. They ordered their usual tuna salad sandwiches, side salads, and fries to split.

"Mom, when will Dad remember you? Until I saw him, I didn't believe it. I mean, I believed what you said, but when I watched him and heard him, he gave me the creeps. Sometimes I feel sorry for him and miss him. When I think about him not knowing who you are, I get suspicious. I never heard of someone not recognizing their wife or husband." She kicked the table leg. "It sounds made-up."

"Your father's brain injury caused memory loss. His tentative diagnosis is Capgras Syndrome."

Terpe twisted her napkin. "You told me about the Capgras thing, but you were too busy to explain what would happen. Daddy's reaction doesn't make any sense, even if he doesn't remember who you are. Why would you bother to visit this strange man if he's not your husband?"

"Excellent point. But your dad does recognize me. He just feels no emotional connection, so he concludes I'm an imposter. Nothing else makes sense to him."

"This whole thing doesn't make sense." Terpe drank the last of her water.

"His brain got injured and doesn't work as well as ours. His doctor recommend therapy with a Dr. Drummond, a psychologist with experience with this sort of thing. Once your father gets settled in the rehab center, the psychologist will start seeing him."

"I can't tell anybody at school about this. They already think I'm a freak."

"You *aren't* a freak. Don't exaggerate."

"If your name sounded nearly as weird as mine, you might understand."

"Terpe, you're smart and pretty. A little quiet, but you know plenty of girls are shy and quiet. You have to try harder. Stop pouting and smile. I bet you'll make plenty of friends."

Terpe wondered if Mom knew about Declan and Benjy. Inside she felt a sigh coming, but tried not to pucker her lips, a giveaway she had secret friends. She pulled another napkin out of the holder, shredded it, and made little paper balls until Mom changed the subject. She swung her leg under the table.

Mom said, "I told a detective we had a mysterious phone call. And told him again I didn't have a clue who'd want to burn down our house. He reminded me about the footprints at the base of some bushes and the rag reeking of gas. They suspected arson even before we received that strange call. They're interviewing your dad's colleagues."

"An accidental fire can't be arson, can it?"

"Not accidental. Someone set the fire. The upstairs roofing's made of some type of wood shingles, not slate. Sometimes you stay in la-la land with your pretend friends. You don't understand there are mean, sick people out in the real world. You have to stay in the real world."

"I'm in la-la land because I can't think of anyone doing this. The detectives looked around real fast and they left quickly. You're not stupid, you have a PhD, so you can't be a moron."

"It's not stupid to think someone hates us and wants to harm us. Stop living in fairy tales. Not all people are nice." Mom spit out the words. Her hands were shaking again.

"Like I don't know that? Most kids in my class aren't nice." For sure Mom had found out about Declan and Benjy. The creek felt safe, even in winter when some trees were bare. Still, she had to be more careful—Mom could be snooping, hiding in the bushes.

The waitress came with their food. They ate quickly, in silence.

Terpe patted her stomach. "Worry makes me hungry. Or maybe all the shopping gives me a bigger appetite."

"Worry burns energy," Mom said. "While I was waiting for my father to get out of surgery, six doctors were paged in a row. I decided there must have been a multiple car pileup. Someone I knew had died. Of course that didn't happen, but the mind goes to scary places when you're worried."

Mom signaled the waiter and said, "Two glasses of water and the check, please." She put on her mom face. "You don't drink enough water, Terpe. You should drink a few glasses every day. Water's important, it gives you energy." But Terpe was still worried about the fire. Had someone crept around their yard and set it? She fidgeted with energy, the worrying kind.

Chapter Ten: Adam and Joss

ADAM PULLED UP IN FRONT of a large house for his next job. He whistled at the sight of the sprawling two-story house on a wide lot. He could never make enough money to afford anything close to this house in this neighborhood of stately houses. A silver Volvo and a black BMW were parked in the driveway, but the front lawn was littered with leaves and fallen branches. Why would people who could afford to live in this neighborhood have such a messy lawn?

He parked on the street and headed up the walk. Before he could ring the doorbell, a woman with long, honey-colored hair opened the door. Almost his height, not thin, she had curves and a lovely mouth. He angled his head away. The contractor had told him all about the damaged second floor, but nothing 'bout this fine-looking woman.

"You're right on time," she said with a smile. "I'm Joss. Come on in. The electrical damage is on the second floor."

"I'm Adam Werther." As he followed her upstairs, his ears felt hot. The two rooms had been recently painted white with purple trim. The bathroom looked bare, without towels or toilet paper. With its clean, polished floors, the upstairs felt empty and calm. Yet the woman's hands trembled.

"Nice house. I suppose Fred told you the wiring might take a few days."

"That's fine. With extensive water and fire damage up here, the repairs have taken a while. Our guest bathroom is downstairs, in the hall by the front door if you need it."

"I'll have to go to the basement to check the system. Do I need a key?"

"No. The basement door's in the kitchen. I'll be in my room. It's on the first floor at the back of the house down the main hall."

Joss had tried to put her manuscript deadline out of her mind. With October closing in, her manuscript remained unfinished. While wandering through her worries, she had an image of the electrician upstairs. She called her editor, but he was out of his office. In brief terms she explained the situation to the editor's assistant and asked for a six-month extension. The response came as a maybe, but maybe not. The assistant would let Joss know the decision soon. Through gritted teeth, Joss explained her situation in more depth. The assistant repeated himself in a robotic voice.

Joss slammed down the phone. What a bastard. He probably had no money worries and a wife at home taking care of his kids.

She stared at the phone. Okay, if the number on the caller ID didn't show the hospital's number, or Terpe's school or Geline's day care, she wouldn't answer. She had to get the writing done.

Recently, she regularly spent less than half an hour visiting Phil. Let the physical therapists do what they were trained to do. When he first arrived at the rehab center, she occasionally fed him lunch. She found herself so irritated with his slow helplessness that she wanted to cram the spoon down his throat. Her irritation stoked her guilt for lack of compassion. Yet he treated her like a nurse's aide. Mostly he ignored her. When he fastened his eyes on her, he cocked his head like a bird studying another bird. Listening to her voice, trying to place it in memory? The doctors had not lied. He truly thought of her as an imposter.

An hour into writing, a soft knock at her open door startled her. She glanced over her shoulder at the electrician and stopped typing. "How's it going?"

"Pretty good. I'll be using the bathroom."

"Oh, fine. That's fine."

"You writing a book?"

"Right." She sighed, hoping he hadn't heard her sigh. Annoying, yet he looked nice; actually he was quite good-looking.

"What 'bout?"

"I don't discuss my writing until I've finished the original draft." Why would an electrician care?

"I don't know any writers. Maybe I'm being too curious?"

"It's okay, people ask." She turned back to her computer and said over her shoulder, "It's about mythology."

"Books take a long time to write."

"Obviously." She bit her lip.

"Mythology? Like those monsters that were alive, but aren't anymore?"

"Creatures of mythology weren't ever alive. The Greeks made them up, invented monsters to challenge their heroes' strength and courage. Sorry, I have to write."

"I'm starting community college soon," Adam said to the back of her head. "I graduated high school and began learning how to be an electrician in shop class. I apprenticed. Now I have my own business."

Joss didn't say anything.

"Well, you're busy." Adam backed out of the room.

Without any rugs upstairs, Adam's footsteps echoed back and forth through the empty rooms.

When her phone rang, she read the number on the caller ID, and read it again. The anonymous caller? She picked up the cell and said hello. Someone breathed close to the phone. She repeated the hello and the person hung up. Almost one o'clock on a Tuesday. She pulled a piece of paper with the phone number out of her pocket. She wrote down the identical phone number again, noting the time.

She wandered into the kitchen and fixed lunch. She didn't hear footsteps; maybe the electrician had left.

Adam strolled into the kitchen.

"I ate lunch in my truck, enjoying your tall trees and shady front yard. I'm a city boy who lives in a second-floor apartment. Trees outside my place are stunted and I got these bars across the living room windows messing up my view. But I got big trees out my bedroom window."

She took a bite of a roast beef sandwich. *Keep your sentences short.*

"My mother is missing," he said.

"What? She's what?" She put down her sandwich and took a sip of water.

"Two weeks ago I went over for our regular dinner, but she wasn't home. I figured she ran out to the grocery, you know how you discover you need something?"

He sighed and rubbed his hands together. "First, I looked around in case something happened. The back door, bolted. Nobody got inside. No broken windows."

He grew silent and laid his hand on his chest. "Finally, I found a note sitting on the TV. She left to go on vacation and would come back in a few months. She hired a man to run her shop. Told me not to worry."

"You called the police?"

"Nah. She'd hate me to make a fuss. The police wouldn't find her anyway. I bet she flew to Germany, to visit her brother, Bernard. As a kid, I asked about her family, she kept Bernard a secret. Then later she told me about him."

Joss didn't respond.

"Sorry I'm going on and on. I'm worried about her. I'll be finished in an hour or so."

"Your mother travels a lot?"

He shook his head. "Nope. But bad stuff happened to Mama. She married Waldo to get away from her family and come to America. I never told my friends this stuff."

Joss speared a piece of green pepper and held it like a cigarette, enjoying the crunch. She wished she could sit on her patio, read, drink coffee, and smoke as many cigarettes as she wanted without guilt. Yet, if she started smoking again, she might not be able to stop.

"Thanks for listening." His shoulders were slumped. "Almost finished. Probably an hour."

"Yes, you said. I'll give you a check when you're finished."

She ambled back to her desk to the sound of Adam's footsteps echoing through the upstairs rooms.

She dialed the detective's number, but he couldn't be reached. She left the anonymous caller information with another detective.

Only half an hour left before she had to pick up Terpe from school. Her hands rested on her keyboard. Adam's situation sounded bad, yet she gave him nothing, no comfort at all. At one time, she had considered herself compassionate, but another side of her had emerged. Compassion had become conditional. Drained of that energy, she'd turned uncaring and superficial.

Before he left, Adam suggested she install motion-sensor floodlights in the front and back of the property. She'd never considered floodlights. Perhaps they would have deterred an arsonist. She gave him a check for his work upstairs.

Two days later, Adam returned to install the lights. She sat at her desk, listening to his singing while he worked. Country songs drifted into her room and receded. Most songs weren't familiar. One could be Dolly Parton's "I Will Always Love You." And she felt sure she heard "Love Is Like a Butterfly." To her ear, Adam's voice had a high lonesome sound, a good quality for a country musician. She'd read that somewhere.

"Knock, knock. How's it going, Mrs. Montgomery?"

"Still at the computer. Call me Joss, and I'll call you Adam. Here's a check to cover the cost of lights and labor."

He grinned and nodded. "Just finished installing back and front lights."

He made himself look at her directly and added, "Your yard needs some cleanup. Fallen branches. Stuff like that. This coming Saturday I'll stop by and clean it up. You got a rake? I'll buy garbage bags."

"There's a rake in the shed. I don't bother with the yard with so much else to get done."

He grinned. "I'll come 'bout ten. Once in English class we read about griffins and Pegasus, that horse with wings? And those owls, Sticks?"

"The Strix. Yes, owls are interesting raptors. They swivel their heads, fly silently, and catch prey in the distance. The prey has no chance."

"I watched a PBS show." Adam nodded. "Them women monsters, like Gorgons or Medusa? Write 'bout them, or the guy who flew near the sun and drowned?"

"No, I haven't."

"Do you wonder if we're more than what we see? Can we change into another person, or an animal?"

She moved papers around on her desk and glanced at her watch. "Humans have multiple aspects, many selves, depending on changes around us, or inside us. If a person hurts his head, the person might change so much you won't recognize them." Phil. She hated him.

Adam frowned. "You okay? Want some water? Did I say something wrong?"

"It's not you. I'm fine."

He hurried down the hall, and she heard the front door close softly.

On Saturday morning, Joss sat on the patio and stared back through the glass doors into the messy living room. Since the fire, she and Terpe had rushed in and out, neglecting to put clothes, cups, and toys away. Saturday turned into catch-up time. In an hour, Adam would come to clean up the yard. The house looked and felt messier than usual, but it was a disarray worth the price for two writing days, five and a half hours a day, without interruptions. Except for Adam.

Her filthy kitchen stuck out. She didn't want to appear lazy with a dirty kitchen when Adam came, so she cut the daydreaming short and headed inside to scrub the counter, the table, and the refrigerator door. She washed a sink full of dirty dishes and dumped out the dead tulips sitting in greenish water on the dining room table, and scrubbed out the vase.

"Want me to do these?" Terpe stood at the kitchen door holding a pile of baby clothes.

"No, just put the dirty clothes in the laundry room for now. I'd rather you vacuum downstairs, please. After that you could call one of your friends to come over this afternoon."

"I'll think about it."

"Consider it, Terpe. You've been a great help. But I want you to have some fun, too."

Joss glanced out of the living room window. Adam held a plastic bag and was walking toward the backyard. She poured another cup of coffee and admired her clean kitchen. She walked onto the patio and watched him raking along the edge of the backyard. He moved to the other edge with grace, his motions deliberate. Maybe he felt her stare because he turned.

Caught, her heart skipped a beat. "Hey, Adam," she shouted.

He came toward her, dragging a half-full garbage bag.

"You don't need to clean up the backyard. That's not what we arranged."

"It's fine. I'm almost finished." He gathered a few more branches and stuck them into a bag. "Jus' gotta get to the area at the top of the hill and finish up around the patio."

When she sat in the lounge chair, she lurched, spilling coffee down her blouse. "How much do I owe you?" She patted at her pocket and looked at him.

"Nothing. I needed the exercise."

"I'm serious. How much?"

"No worries. Some sunshine and clean suburban air is good."

"You're sure? Really sure?"

"Yep, I'm sure."

"Phil, that's my husband, we used to live in Richmond. When he got tired of his commute, we moved out here. I didn't want to. I liked walking to the market and coffee shops. I walked Terpe to and from school. Our city had everything, except space for a garden, which is now an overgrown mess. But everything feels spacious out here."

"It's real nice."

"Coffee?"

"Let me finish up raking. I take it black."

Joss went inside, wet a dish towel, and patted at the coffee stain on her blouse. She made a fresh pot of coffee, glancing out the patio door at Adam working.

He came in the kitchen. "I'll wash up first."

She poured his coffee in a mug and refreshed hers. Terpe moved into the living room, dragging the vacuum. The roar of the machine coming on broke the silence.

He came back, sat, and picked up his cup. "Thanks. Hits the spot."

Not knowing what to say, she stared into her cup.

"The creatures we talked about? The guys on the football team called me Adam the Mammoth. I played center. A decent tackle. I read some guy's story online. While skiing cross-country, in the mountains, he found fresh crap from a huge mammal. Maybe mammoth scat? The mammoths on a TV show sure looked real. Could they still live in places like the Arctic? But more exciting—I jus' read in the newspaper that some guys at Harvard are trying to de-extinct mammoths. It said de-extincting animals will make healthier ecosystems."

"What makes you think mammoths are still alive?" Her voice rose with irritation.

"My mammoth dreams are different. I'm always on an island, and I know I'm having a dream. The animals, ice, and sky send me messages. I'm in recovery, you know, from alcoholism, so, maybe I have these dreams."

Joss said, "You have mammoth traits? Strong, resilient, and powerful?"

"Strong and powerful 'til sixth grade, when everything except football, got bad. But my island dreams started later, after the museum visit with Mama and Papa. One statue in the museum filled up a huge room. The dioramas made stuff look real. Papa and I had fun." His face closed, and his eyes went far away. "So, TV shows came after the museum."

"And something happened?"

"Yeah." He stopped.

"So?" Joss waited.

"I've saved around thirteen thousand five hundred dollars. If I don't drink, I make good money. Right when I planned to tell Mama I'd be going west, she went missing. I can't leave until she gets back. She's family. She's probably with her brother." He asked, "Where do your parents live?"

"You could call your mother. She has a cell phone?"

"She carries one but don't turn it on. So, your parents?"

"Daddy died a few years ago. Mother died the summer after my sophomore year in high school."

"You got sisters and brothers? I'm an only."

"My brother's a fishing guide in Sitka, Alaska."

"What a great job! I could fish, climb mountains, and ride sleds all day."

"When we were kids, Jackson stayed outdoors." She shook her head. "He's in his own time zone! A loose guy, getting places on time never meant much. He's usually late. At least he used to be."

"I hope he calls you. I feel sort of deserted. I go by Mama's apartment to take in the mail and water this ugly plant in her kitchen window. Some old rubber thing."

The roar of the vacuum abruptly stopped. Joss asked, "More coffee?"

"Got some work, I gotta go. Thanks, anyway."

When he left, she felt disappointed. She hated to admit to loneliness. Her watch read twelve thirty. *Finish cleaning the house, put one foot in front of the other.*

The next night at the mall, she and Terpe bought three pairs of shoes to replace the girl's ruined ones and picked up some groceries. Joss brought in the groceries, but Terpe didn't bring in her new shoes. Not typical. The child had run out of stamina. She had homework assignments, but how much she completed Joss couldn't tell. Lately, her daughter spent most of her time sprawled out on the sofa, listless, in front of the TV.

Joss still didn't ask about school in order to stay approachable for the important issue, talking about her father. Their best talks occurred at the coffee shop, offhandedly over a free hour or two. She told herself she should be monitoring her child's homework but couldn't bring herself to do it.

How much should she reveal about Phil? Was it time to prepare Terpe for his not coming home?

Terpe had no social life. Recently Joss dropped her off at the mall and picked her up two hours later. It pained her to see Terpe standing by herself while other groups of kids stood together laughing. Joss surmised she must not have a new friend after all. Terpe claimed Zoe had already been picked up. She claimed the movie was okay.

Joss told herself not to worry, that Terpe had always been a strange, aloof child who liked time alone. Before the fire, Joss and Phil had talked about this and decided their quirky child seemed fine. An introverted child born to introverted parents. Joss reasoned the stress of the fire and Phil's hospitalization had exaggerated her traits.

Twice in the past week, while taking the garbage to the cans by the driveway, Joss had heard her daughter's voice floating up from the hill. The last time, Joss had crept closer. Terpe was pacing along the creek bank, gesturing and talking into the air. Joss waited and listened, wondering if there could be another kid hiding behind a bush. But her child appeared to be alone.

The next day when Joss alluded to Terpe's imaginary friends, her daughter's expression stayed blank. She claimed not to understand before stomping out of the room. Joss caught her expression, though, which looked more afraid than angry. A typical response, trying to muster anger whenever her parents confronted her.

Imaginary friends had been a familiar way Terpe coped with stress. At five, six, and seven, she talked freely about them. Their names, identities, and abilities changed depending on the new adventure that ignited Terpe's imagination. She entertained Joss and Phil with their exploits. Even at seven, imaginary friends seemed okay. But what eight- or nine-year-old played with made-up people?

Everything about the fire had been frightening, enough to cause nightmares. Followed by Phil's rejection. What rejection could be worse than your father not recognizing your mother? Your father not recognizing you would be worse, Joss supposed. She didn't want to think of other ways parents rejected their children, refusing them food, beating them, locking them in basements and closets, or taping their mouths with duct tape.

What would her world—Terpe's and Geline's worlds, and Phil's—feel like in six months? After Geline came, Phil would still go with her and the kids to a Fourth of July parade, a Santa parade, a birthday party, and other big events, but he grew bored with the day-to-day caretaking of two children. He'd resisted taking the girls to parks and playgrounds by himself. If Joss begged, he sat on a bench reading a history book, glancing up when one of them screamed. When Joss challenged him about ignoring the kids, he said he didn't find children intellectually stimulating. She'd reminded him that a child could be kidnapped in the space of two or three heartbeats. Phil's eyebrows would go up, yet Terpe reported to Joss that Dad still didn't pay attention to her and Geline, adding that she'd taken over keeping an eye on her baby sister.

Joss believed children needed to play and interact with both parents, as child-rearing consisted of thousands of moments of connecting. Her pediatrician referred to this as the developmental dance. Her husband didn't dance well.

In six years Terpe would be in high school. Joss and Phil had only lived in this house a few years, yet she wanted to stay here, in this neighborhood full of trees, in this climate with discernable seasons. She wanted to keep the ritual of tending her flowers. When they withered, she wanted to gather them and bring them inside for arrangements. When she grew weary from writing, she surveyed the garden in late winter and thought about what needed to be pulled up and what needed planting.

When she imagined the new household six months down the road, she imagined herself with two daughters. Maybe a dog. Not Phil.

She recalled the terrible day Phil was to be moved from ICU. She'd made her last visit. She stood in his doorway and threw questions at him, the same question: Why would I visit if I weren't your wife? She repeated questions until he yelled at her to get out.

Like a caged zoo animal, rage poured out. She couldn't stop her mouth.

A nurse came to the door.

Joss turned. "I know I'm hateful. I'll stop. I should feel sorry, but I don't."

The nurse nodded.

"I'll take the things I brought for him." She dumped a CD player and CDs in a tote and slipped the cards Terpe had made for him into her purse.

She waved to the nurse and stomped to the elevator.

Driving home, she wondered how many couples survived affairs. When the betrayer arrived forty-five minutes late after a basketball game, the betrayed longed to believe the words, "I stopped for gas and had to wait in line to get the tires filled with air." But the betrayed person thought, *You liar, what blah blah bullshit.*

That night Joss dreamed about the word *philanderer*. The first syllable of the word echoed through images of the word scrolled in large, white letters floating in darkness. Her feet are stuck in mud. She can't run. Can't escape the shape and sound of that word floating above, echoing over and over. Phil comes after her, running, wielding a knife, demanding that she reveal where she was hiding his real wife. She stands against a classroom wall. Someone resembling Phil stands in front of a class. In a garbled voice, he tells each student to read a book and write a paper. All the students' skin turns red, and their long tongues flick in and out of their mouths. Suddenly the horde of kids makes hissing sounds and charges the professor, gouging out his eyes and ripping off his skin and snapping his bones into bits. They throw his bones into a raging fire. His screams for help woke her.

Chapter Eleven: Adam

IN ADAM'S DREAM, AN EMPTY rowboat rocks, barely visible in fog—its shape blurred, its blue paint abraded by waves. The boat sits halfway in the sea and halfway dug into cold sand. A voice whispers for him to meet the woman who is hidden some place on the island. He goes down on all fours, sniffing the air and listening to wind roaring through stubby pines. Rough sand scrapes his hands when he moves inland. He stops to rest, fixing his eyes on a spot across the water. How far did he row? But fog hides the other shore. Did he row across? He doesn't know.

Blowing sand stings his body. "Like how time travels," his dream voice growls, "like watching sand in the hourglass on a teacher's desk, you wait and wait for class to end."

Surrounded by saltwater and thirsty trees, he's scared. When he used to binge drink, he felt thirsty always. Fight Papa and fight the warrior with rotted teeth? Would he have to fight people to get anything? For the rest of his life?

Back in the boat, he rows. A huge hand comes up from the water and grabs the side of the boat.

His eyes flew open. Taking in his bedroom and gazing at the trees outside his window, he realized his island dreams were getting confusing, scarier. This was one he wouldn't write down.

Adam opened his mailbox and grabbed a letter with a German postmark. He took the stairs two at a time and dropped the wrinkled envelope on the kitchen table. Bad news? What if Mama won't come home? He pulled a can of Pepsi out of the refrigerator and took her letter to the living room.

Careful not to slice the nice stamp, he used a table knife to open the letter.

> *Dear Adam,*
>
> *By now, you've figured out I'm in Germany with Bernard. Felt afraid you wouldn't want me to visit Bernard. So, why I didn't tell you. I didn't want to fight about it.*
>
> *We're having a good reunion! Bernard's divorced. His two sons live with him. Your cousins are sixteen and nineteen.*
>
> *He's tired of fishing for a living and wants to come to America. He's waiting for a passport and visa. He wants to buy land to start a small orchard. Also buy a big house for all of us.*
>
> *He'll bring his girlfriend, but his sons say they won't leave Germany.*
>
> *If I can sell the butcher shop for a good price, I'll live with Bernard and his girlfriend. You will like living in the country, too.*
>
> *Not only just you and me any longer. Won't that be nice?*
>
> *I'll be home next month. Bernard's address is on the envelope.*
>
> *Love,*
>
> *Mama*
>
> *P. S. Even out in the country, people need electricians.*

Adam's hands shook like in his drinking days. Five dollars in his wallet, he grabbed his keys and went out for some air.

Live with at least two strangers in a farmhouse? What if Bernard turned out to be like Papa? No, if Mama liked Bernard, he wouldn't be mean. What if Adam did live with the other people, even his cousins might decide to come, and it made him forget his dreams? Voices from the next room might mess up his sleep. Sometimes dreams were all that kept Adam moving through a day. Now he'd met Joss. Still he felt scared.

In his truck he revved the engine, but couldn't think what he wanted. *Don't lie.* He wanted a drink. His favorite bar just a mile away.

The sign out front still looked faded and dingy. Three parked cars had AA slogans on their bumpers: ONE DAY AT A TIME and LIVE AND LET LIVE. Whoever sat inside the bar would have to pick up a new white chip to celebrate that they stopped drinking. While he wasn't drinking, he didn't come down this street. How many times had he staggered home from this bar? Why bother counting?

Just one drink to help him forget Germany. He used to ask Mama about their relatives when he was a kid whenever he opened a closet or a drawer, he hoped to find piles of paper with secrets written out by Mama, or by someone he didn't know. When he got bigger, Mama told him a few secrets about her parents and the most important secret: how much she missed her brother, Bernard.

Talking to one of his buddies might help his nervousness, but any friend would ask why Adam made such a big deal. People liked to meet relatives. People living together could be great. And a big house. His friends would tell him he could always leave if he didn't like his uncle and cousins.

The bar inside hadn't changed either, like he'd just sat on a stool the day before. The main room still wore throw-up green paint and had the wobbly tables. He held his glass and squeezed it, wondering how much strength it would take to break the glass. Would that stop him? The sudden release of pressure. The sting of the cut and blood was punishment. His double shot of bourbon went down fast.

At the other end of the bar, a pretty woman leaned back, revealing her neck. She had blonde curls, but too much makeup. Her perfume smelled dark and strong. He turned away, debating whether to have another shot before talking with her. No use for a woman, except when he felt like messing around. Once you went out with a woman a few times, she bossed you around and pushed you to make more money.

When Mama nagged Old Waldo, he'd nod, pretending to listen, but he acted like Mama had turned into a pile of dust he sometimes noticed in the corner. Papa was Adam's early lesson, showing what people were like under their smiles. One of the nasty people who enjoyed picking on someone smaller. Papa dirtied up Adam's view of people.

Adam downed another drink, this time just a single. It loosened up his body. *Drive around, finally go home, and get under the covers.* He'd have to pick up another white clip at AA. He asked for the tab and took out his checkbook.

The bartender, a scowling man with thin hair, leaned on the bar, his head close to Adam's. "I don't take checks. Cash only."

"Is Chuck around? He probably kept old receipts in the office that show you I always paid. I used to be a regular, but I moved."

The bartender wiped his trembling hands on his apron. Either the guy needed a drink or he had some disease. The bartender noticed him staring and laid his palms firmly against the apron.

"Chuck's been dead 'bout two years. I'm the manager. The new owner's in Florida."

Adam laid five ones on the bar. "Sorry to hear 'bout Chuck. A good guy, real fun to talk to. I'll go to the ATM and come right back." He got a glimpse of the apron and felt relieved not to see blood.

"You do that." The man chuckled. "I'll hold your check until you get back. Fill it out and sign it, leave the amount blank. If you don't come back, I'll fill in the amount."

Adam's stomach churned. He wrote the check and left the amount blank. He pushed it across the bar. The ATM wasn't far, but he already felt hammered and unsteady. Too many years without drinking. Three shots made him stone drunk.

The blonde moved to the stool near him. Adam fumbled, one leg swinging, searching for the floor. He stumbled off the stool, trying to appear steady on his feet. At the door he paused to peer at the parked cars. Enough problems without hooking up with a barfly. Better to date a woman with her feet on the ground than her face hanging in a glass of booze.

The truck tires scraped along the curb when he parked, but he made it okay. He staggered across a dark side street, following the ATM's light. Up close that light hurt his eyes. He leaned against it, fumbled for his wallet, and stuck a credit card in the slot. No cash. Certain he had money in his account, he shoved in his card again and entered his password again. No cash. He stared at the card and turned it this way and that. Something wrong with those numbers?

The answer floated near his brain. *Concentrate. The password, 7198? 9871?* He tried again and felt great when the machine made *thunk thunk* noises while his cash slid out.

Crossing the street, it dawned on him he'd forgotten to lock his truck, and that he hadn't once bothered to check for muggers. Stupid. In this neighborhood people locked their cars, even running ten-minute errands.

The last thing he did remember, he locked himself inside the truck and stared at his hands holding the steering wheel. Where should he go next?

Back on a sled, lying on his stomach. One push might be all he needs. Suddenly a push from behind. He plows through solid ice, pushing with his bare fists until the sled takes off downhill. A blur of green on both sides. He needs both hands to hold the sled, desperate not to fall. No gun, no provisions 'cept a jug he hopes holds water, or even better, some bourbon.

His sled probably his only way out. To fall off means death. Hot, stinking breath behind him. Gaining. A beast sinks its teeth into his ankle. He spins from the sled and smashes his face on the ice.

He woke abruptly, sweaty, his nose sticky with blood. It felt like ice took his nose halfway off. The truck keys lay on the floor. He leaned and grabbed the keys, and the sudden move made his head pound. Traffic passed by, but no one was walking along the sidewalk. Not yet. The clock read five. Sunday morning. He broke the speed limit on the way to his apartment. His nose still bleeding down his shirt.

At home, first thing, he pulled off his shirt and dropped it on the bedroom floor. He went into the kitchen for his hangover cure: two large glasses of water and four Tylenols. He made a pot of coffee. His first cup had to be black. He drank fast. He added milk to the second cup. He fell on the sofa, trying to remember why he got drunk after staying sober so long. Mama's letter. Two people might come to America, even four, if Bernard's boys changed their minds.

When he left town, he still wanted to head out west. Alone. But now there was Joss.

His nose still bleeding, but only a trickle. A cold washcloth helped. When the bleeding stopped, he threw it on the bathroom floor. In his bedroom he hunted for paper and a pencil. Before the sled dream went away, he sat on his bed and wrote about the island he'd seen from an icy hilltop. Shaped like an almond, the island was covered with ice, with a tall mountain range poking through ice. Guessing eighteen miles long and five miles wide. He couldn't wait until spring to explore the island. If spring ever came. A walk across the island would take two, maybe four days, depending on weather. He couldn't tell when one landscape kept sliding into the next.

Island creatures chased him in most dreams. Sometimes he couldn't see the animals, but he heard their panting and smelled their stench, reminding him of rotting crap. Four-legged beasts, horses with double faces, two big eyes on each side of their heads. Big brown teeth stained with blood. A strange-looking crone beat her horse with a whip. Did she want the horse, and Adam, dead? He had to find a way to make these dreams go longer so he could learn what to do.

Sometimes his dreams felt like no more than superhero movies. A real hero should fight off all beasts that attacked.

Go after what was important. Go after who he wanted. For darn sure he knew who she was. The woman who spoke Greek. He wanted to take her to bed, kiss her everywhere, and stay with her forever. They'd have a child together. He could have three children and Joss.

Chapter Twelve: Phil

AT THE REHAB CENTER, PHIL sat at his usual table in the dining room. While waiting for his tray, he tried to remember the familiar woman's name. One day she came in from the parking lot and walked into the dining room. She looked around but didn't see him. The first day he wondered if she were a stranger who'd come for free food, until he spotted her meal ticket. The aides were busy fetching the patients' trays. Almost all the patients sat in wheelchairs.

His girlfriend! With her lovely dark hair swinging against her shoulders, definitely her. Her eyes turned violet sometimes, unless she wore a blue blouse and then they turned blue. She knew how to use her mouth on him the way his wife wouldn't. Oh yes, Joss did know, how could he forget something that important? This woman wouldn't be his grad student, because students were too risky, too obvious on a college campus. Over the years colleagues had regularly emailed him gossip about their departmental scandals. Faculty sleeping with students seemed ubiquitous.

Did his girlfriend hear about the fire? It would have been in the newspapers. She'd never come to his house; maybe she didn't know where he lived. Anyway, his house had burned up.

Her name escaped him. But if he didn't try too hard, the name might arrive, like a surprise. He did love a surprise.

He didn't want to leave the dining room in case she came to his table. Another glass of milk could be an excuse to linger, so he asked the aide to bring him milk. Outside the window, the gray sky seemed to shift a little, like ideas plodding through his skull. He couldn't see her. Had she left the dining room? He decided to wait.

Patients left the dining room. An aide came to his table and pushed his wheelchair back to his room. His body ached for a nap.

In bed, he stared at the ceiling. A colleague's voice drifted into his head. Phones. He remembered a conversation with a colleague about phones. Phil said he wanted to put a basket by his classroom door for students to drop in their devices. But he never did it. The administration wanted donors and alums happy, and they wouldn't be happy if they couldn't text or call their baby darlings whenever they wished. If not a basket, Phil thought he could demand the students shut down their devices. He longed to say, "You'd like to be talking or texting or reading about some celebrity's latest calamity, but delay gratification. You're using your parents' money and your own, so learn something."

Phones. He no longer worried about them. Not many people he wanted to talk to anymore.

His big question would be where to live when he left this place. The sex felt good in his girlfriend's apartment, like teenagers getting away with something, but mostly she came to his office. She had a ritual: She came in and locked his office door and pulled off her shirt and bra right away. She walked across the small room to his closet where he kept two pillows, a sleeping bag, and two blankets. She tossed these on the floor, glancing at him to make sure he was still watching. He always watched. With a smile she sauntered over to him and slowly kissed him while unzipping his pants.

This affair hadn't been Phil's first. Best he could recall, most of them lasted one or two months. He thought they began soon before Geline's birth. When the baby came, it brought a ton of chores and left little time even for sleep. Why did they have another kid? His tired wife lost interest in sex; she drove him away, partly her fault he cheated more often. At least he thought it happened like that.

Mostly his memories made him sad. He cried when he got jumbled up and fuzzy. He rubbed his forehead to make memories go away, but they kept coming. Until he turned eleven or twelve, he'd been an obedient child. He discovered what his body could do, while going out to discover the world. The titillation of almost getting caught doing something bad was irresistible. At night, he sneaked out of his house and met guy friends in the alley. They drank beer and bragged about how they got girls. Sometimes girls came along, and a few of them even kissed each other. Phil always chose a girl right away, if he liked her. Or one of the fast girls picked him out right from the start. They'd talk a little, experiment with French kissing and rubbing up against each other. A few times they moved off into the bushes and did more.

Phil smoked pot in the school parking lot with older guys who had driver's licenses and cars. They'd squat beside any car to smoke, taking turns keeping watch for the assistant principal or one of his goody-goody students who monitored the parking lot. The few times he smoked, the pot hurt his lungs and made his head pound. He'd eventually stopped smoking, but he'd still hang out.

He practiced telling lies, trying them out on his parents first, before moving on to a few teachers. One big lie to his parents happened on the spur of the moment. He and some friends left school during lunch, drove to a vacant lot, and got drunk on the case of beer hidden in a cooler in the trunk of the guy's car. They told jokes and topped off the afternoon with a circle jerk behind some garbage cans.

Suddenly they noticed the sky getting dark. The guy who owned the car drove to a gas station, where they bought gum and washed their faces. Phil got home just as his mother started setting the table for dinner, a chore that belonged to Phil's list of tasks. He apologized for being late. He claimed the school bus had a flat tire, and the kids had to wait and wait with the bus. Phil didn't think his parents would buy it, but they did. Getting ready for bed that night, he laughed to himself, getting away with cutting school and all the rest. Who wanted to be grounded for the weekend with nothing to do except jerk off alone while thinking about some girl and listening to music?

Phil squirmed in his wheelchair whenever he had to meet with his psychologist, Dr. Drummond. The doc made him nervous with the questions. Phil wanted to rename him something amusing. Would the doctor even notice if he had a nickname? Doc Drumbeat. That sounded good to Phil. He didn't trust the man's calm demeanor when he suggested Joss might be his real wife. Every session, the doctor asked if he missed Joss. Phil always said yes. But Phil didn't miss their arguments: Joss's voice got shrill when she called him a liar. She stood in front of him, in a beautiful see-through nightgown, shouting at him. He wanted sex, but she pushed him away. She harped on and on about his work hours and kept asking why he went away to so many conferences. Who wants to be called a liar by his own wife?

He planned to ditch Doc Drumbeat when he left this rehab place. Not a single person to trust. Maybe Terpe? Yet he suspected his kid might be colluding with fake Joss.

Another thing about Doc Drumbeat, in every session he said that facts stayed facts. Phil knew this sentence wasn't a trick, but more like a strategy that had become a battering ram to pound him into conceding the imposter must be his wife. The doc kept asking why a fake Joss would bother to visit, bring him a quart of his favorite ice cream and books, and take away his dirty laundry and return it to him clean and folded.

Phil couldn't ever answer Doc D. with confidence, yet he speculated fake Joss had been collecting information in order to steal his money. The doc asked if his wife took money out of his pants pockets before doing his laundry. The remark made Phil laugh. He told the doc no, but he suspected fake Joss did little chores for him as part of the bigger plot to steal his money.

After talking about her stealing, Doc Drumbeat sat for a few minutes without saying anything. He slid to the edge of his chair and asked Phil if his parents were wealthy, if he owned property, if he had a lot of life insurance or had tucked away their money in foreign bank accounts.

Phil wanted to stand up and walk out. He felt so mad, his whole body shook. He wanted to hit the doctor, but trapped in his wheelchair, he squirmed as usual, wondering what to say and feeling stupid. He felt bad until he finally admitted he knew his parents pretended they had more money than they did. His mother worked as a checker in a grocery store, but she lied when she claimed to be the store manager who only helped out at the cash register. His father never went higher than manager of a hardware store, but in conversation he referred to "my other stores." Phil felt uncomfortable every time his father told that lie. There were no other stores.

When Phil revealed all that, Doc Drumbeat told him it sounded like his parents felt ashamed of their status and lack of education. They puffed themselves up to make themselves, and their son, proud.

Phil agreed with Doc D. He said he'd been young when he began to suspect his parents were faking about money. When he grew older, he couldn't figure out why they tried to buy him everything he wanted. By high school, he knew his friends didn't get everything they wanted.

Most of his parents' yelling fights were about money, yet they kept giving him expensive presents. At dinner between bites, Phil would casually mention the expensive clothes his friends wore: their high-dollar basketball and running shoes. Did they know some cool new computer games had come out? And he really needed a new road bike to keep up with his buddies.

For his fifteenth birthday, they bought him skis, boots, and ski clothes because he mentioned his friends were planning a weeklong ski trip. The presents were exciting, but while unwrapping the gifts, he suddenly felt guilty and had a sinking feeling. Why did he feel bad? He put on a happy face and thanked them. Stunned by the awful feeling, he lay awake most of the night and dragged his sadness into school after maybe three hours of sleep.

That afternoon he went to his mother's work and asked for all the receipts. She frowned, and he could tell she wanted to ask why, but she didn't. She opened her purse and gave him the receipts. He walked to the sporting goods store with the birthday packages, returned them for cash, and put the cash in an envelope.

He rode his bicycle to the hardware store, pulled his father aside, and gave him the envelope. "Please don't buy me any more expensive presents." He'd never forgotten his father's sunken expression, staring into the envelope while his face turned beet red.

Before his father could say anything, Phil grabbed him and held him tight. "I love you, Dad." His father gave him a little pat on the back.

Phil rode his bicycle straight to the park. Standing on a rock near the river bank, he tried to figure out why he acted so greedy, so rotten and selfish. He couldn't throw enough stones at the rushing water to stop feeling angry. His mother must be ashamed of him. That must be why she wanted him to dress well and fussed over his church clothes.

Phil stopped talking. The doctor said, keeping his focus on Phil, "That tells us about some of your family's values."

But Phil didn't tell the doc about wanting to jump off that rock into the river. His heart pounded. It felt now just like it had felt all those years before down at the river. Bad thoughts. By now he knew two ways, even though his plans were still fuzzy. He wondered if he could go through with either one.

Phil didn't tell the doc about his lies. How many during his affairs: he had to go out of town to proctor exams or to sit on some expert panel or attend a five-day conference. When he earned extra cash, he took his girlfriend to a motel on Saturday and Sunday nights, but when Joss asked where he'd spent the extra cash, he claimed he'd lent it to a faculty friend.

Yet he felt relieved that he'd told Doc Drumbeat as much as he had. He admitted his rank so far remained assistant professor at a college, not a university. And a mediocre salary.

Joss had big money. Her dad had bought her a new Volvo when she turned eighteen and paid her school bills. She'd earned a PhD without any debt. Money had been part of Joss's attraction. It hadn't felt like that when they started dating. But deep down, he knew he didn't allow himself to think about her money.

Maybe today the doc would reveal that the whole house had burned to the ground. Real Joss and the kids had already left town. The doc asked, "Phil, what does the fake Joss lack? What does the real Joss have?"

Phil held out his hands to show sincerity. "The person who came into my room felt phony. Something felt off-kilter. I saw it right away." His head dropped to his chest, and tears came. "Please understand, she's not my wife."

The doctor didn't say anything.

Phil growled, "You're confident you've met the real Joss? You're confident you would recognize the real Joss walking down the hall? If the two stood in front of you, side by side, could you tell the real Joss?"

Doc Drumbeat sighed. "That's enough for today."

Phil knew the doctor left because he didn't have an answer about Joss. And he hadn't noticed that Phil had renamed him Doc Drumbeat. He probably didn't care.

Back in his room, Phil struggled to pull himself out of the wheelchair and sit on his bed. Every day he practiced moving from his bed to his wheelchair and back again. A small sign of victory. Two weeks earlier, he'd needed help.

Once in bed, he wanted to take a nap before trying to read some historical book that fake Joss had brought him. Somehow, she'd found out what kind of books he liked.

His room phone rang and he answered.

Terpe's high-pitched voice. "Hi, Dad. I'm not having fun at school, but I might have a friend, Zoe. My grades are bad, and I hate school," she whined. "But the burned rooms upstairs are being fixed. You'll see when you get home."

"I'll be home soon."

"I hope so! I love you, Dad. I miss you every day."

"Oh, yeah, I love you, too. Bye."

When he got off the phone, he couldn't remember everything she'd said. Maybe he should sneak out and take a taxi to the house to confirm it had burned up. Terpe could be calling from anywhere. They'd loaded the car to drive away, while some movers loaded up a van with the furniture that didn't burn. Joss and the kids could have driven to Mexico or New Mexico. Joss liked to travel.

Wheeling down the halls, Phil recited the names of all the rehab center staff and patients to himself. He'd nod and say the person's name in a soft voice, if he could remember it. Around the staff, he didn't talk about his imposter wife. The staff acted impatient when he called his wife a fake. If he slipped up, the nurses reminded him he had more healing to do.

After he worked out in the gym, he wheeled to the dining room. Would the woman come? An empty table in the corner would be the best spot. He scribbled down his order and gave it to the aide to get his lunch.

The woman came through the door.

Ah! Vivienne. Her name was Vivienne.

At least the bandage had come off his head. His hair was still growing out. Almost positive he brushed his teeth after breakfast. No sense dwelling on his stained shirt. Who cared?

The aide brought his tray. He began with the chicken soup, one of his favorites.

Beautiful Vivienne stood by his table, touched his shoulder, and hurried to get in line for food. In a few minutes she came back with her tray.

"Phil. It's me, Vivienne."

"You've been here before?"

"Last week, but you didn't recognize me."

"I know who you are."

"I'm so sorry about the fire. I've wanted to visit but couldn't find out where they put you when you left the hospital. I knew your wife and daughter would be visiting. I don't want to run into them." Her charming, crooked grin. "I've missed you."

He felt his face turn red. He touched her hand. He tried to tell her not to worry because he wasn't married. The real Joss had left town. But he talked too slowly.

He smiled. "I'll show you my room. I have some news."

"I have to get back for a departmental meeting."

Busy with her yogurt, she didn't notice him staring. Bits of chicken floated in his bowl. He noticed his spoon pointed at the ceiling and put it on top of his napkin.

Would fake Joss burst through that door and make a scene? The real Joss had burned up, or moved to New Mexico or Mexico. Dr. Drummond must be waiting until Phil got stronger to tell him the truth about Joss.

Ideas came in and drifted away. He couldn't catch them, or if he caught them, he couldn't keep them straight. Mostly he'd stopped trying.

Vivienne finished her yogurt and selected bits of lettuce to nibble. She patted her mouth with a napkin. A picky eater, she worried about her weight, even though her body looked almost starved. Her flat chest and boyish hips were a shock each time he saw her nude. Not sexy. When they had sex, he pictured Joss, which turned him on. Vivienne didn't make a sound or talk until they lay side by side, finished and panting. He didn't much enjoy stroking her body, but he liked experimenting with different bodies. He met other available women, but Vivienne flirted with him the most, so he stayed with it. Her hair and her eyes were great.

Joss. He couldn't believe how lucky he'd been to find her. Smart, lively, curious, beautiful, and responsive in bed, as in most things. She had birthed two beautiful babies. Where had the real woman gone?

A good woman who loved him. Not like his bitch mother. Couldn't remember or understand why he'd started the affairs. He supposed he had a reason, but he couldn't figure it out. Something that kept haunting him with every woman he slept with. In bed with whoever, he imagined Joss. Her curvy body rosy and glowing and damp from the shower. She knelt on the bed and slowly climbed on top of him.

Chapter Thirteen: Joss

JOSS DIDN'T LIKE TO ADMIT to herself she felt attracted to Adam. She wouldn't introduce Adam to her friends. One of them would make some crude joke about the electric man, and gossip would start. People would say what a dreadful woman she'd turned into, taking up with a man while her husband lay injured, maybe dying, in the hospital.

Adam had broad shoulders and curly black hair, and his wide grin and dark eyes made him handsome. His only flaw was jumbled bottom teeth. She supposed his family couldn't afford to take him to an orthodontist. Sweet and eager for life, his talk about mammoths made him weird, but not scary weird, merely interesting. His belief appeared genuine and sounded like real concern about the survival of all animals.

An innocent, not like a smooth-talking guy at a cocktail party trying to shock her into going to bed with him. What kind of mind created such bizarre ideas in this apparently down-to-earth, practical guy? A partial answer lay in trusting himself. Adam believed his dreams paralleled reality, and in them he acted powerful and fearless. Something missing from his childhood. She could understand that.

She closed her eyes and thought over their conversations. Sometimes they were pure silliness. He also told her he'd stopped drinking. He appeared easygoing, the type who liked to go on adventures. Did he like backpacking and canoeing? Did he go to plays, foreign films, and documentaries? Probably not. Maybe vacations at the beach? She guessed his favorite movies were action adventures with lots of car wrecks and gun fights. She felt sure plays and films wouldn't interest him.

But would all their likes and dislikes matter? This wouldn't be long-term.

How many months since the house fire? It happened before Christmas, and now it was April. Last Saturday Adam had picked up dead branches and raked leaves in her yard. Winter debris. Over the past months, Phil's memory and ability to think hadn't improved. Even his sentences were jumbled. Dr. Drummond told her she shouldn't give up hope, even suggested she see a therapist for support. He'd given her three names and suggested she make an appointment with each one and have interviews before deciding who to work with.

She wouldn't go to a therapist. Support from friends and her anger kept her strong and helped her cope. Tears in a therapist's office wouldn't change her situation, or her temperament. Yet she knew her thinking needed to change. She needed to make decisions about her future and move forward, handling everything on her own with the help of a lawyer.

Ridiculous thoughts about Adam. She'd never cheated on boyfriends. She felt good about setting her standards high. She didn't lie. At least not often. With two kids, would she find time for an affair?

Still, her conversations with Adam had brought fun back into her life, and she'd laughed from her belly for the first time since months before the fire. When she sat with a friend over coffee, they didn't laugh or joke; their first question would be about how she was doing. Her signal to unload the latest misery.

Always they'd say something hopeful to encourage her. Even with her best friend, Dreama, they didn't stray far from what to do about Phil. Joss began to find the conversations repetitive, yet she couldn't concentrate on anything else for long.

The contractor hadn't told Adam anything about Phil, and Adam hadn't asked. Why would Adam be interested in a frazzled, harried housewife? Adam knocked her husband out of her head for a few hours. Not too big an age difference. She was thirty-nine, almost forty. He had recently turned thirty-two. An electrician with a high school degree dating a PhD? Maybe he used to be married, or had a girlfriend? The kind of man who'd cheat on her, like Phil? If they dated, she'd push him to get a college degree. They'd argue. He'd tell her not to push.

Phil complained she pushed him around, a tenacious woman carrying a boatload of strong opinions. In the next breath Phil confessed he liked smart, strong women. Joss knew that some men craved these traits for themselves, but she'd watched too many of her friends lose their way in marriages that trapped them in a game they'd forgotten how to play. But some of these little boys had figured out they didn't want too many smarts in the women they intended to marry, but some did marry these women. Often with regrets. Regrets probably fitted Phil.

Phil's childhood. Her own. What sort of effect did they have?

One summer morning when Joss had finished her sophomore year in high school, she came down to breakfast and found the maid, Sally, standing silent at the stove. She didn't turn and speak as usual. Abruptly she turned, her face screwed up from crying. "Your father left this morning. I came up the walk and saw him coming the other way, carrying two suitcases. His hair looked messy and his shirt all untucked. He set down his suitcases on the walk and hugged me. He said he hoped we'd meet up. He asked me to take good care of you kids.

"He picked up his suitcases, put them in the trunk, got in his car, and drove away fast."

Sally handed Joss a piece of paper. "This is from your father. This time he's going for good. I'm saying this because I feel it in my bones. I'm so sorry."

All that day, Joss wandered through the house as if she might find him sitting in an empty room, giving her a smile when she discovered him. She walked to the barn, thinking she heard his voice, maybe he came home and wanted to ride, so he'd saddled up a horse.

She felt alone inside the barn. While petting a horse, she remembered the slip of paper. She went back outside. Leaning against the fence by the barn, she read his condo phone number out loud to make it feel real. She read the note again as if it were a gift. Yet not knowing what to say about his leaving, she felt afraid to call him.

Two days later her father called. He came to the house and took her and her brother, Jackson, out to dinner. They ate lasagna and salads while Dad tried to explain why he'd left. He tried not to blame Mother. Yet they all knew the truth, or thought they did. Daddy reassured them that nothing else would change for us kids. We could live in the house with Mother and we could visit him whenever we wanted.

Daddy's fancy downtown condo was in a tall building with big views of the city. He gave her and Jacks each a key. The condo had three bedrooms, so everyone had a room where they could relax on weekends. Daddy wanted them to come anytime; they just had to call first.

They spent some weekends with him. Both she and her brother liked the arrangement, happy to see more of Daddy than when he lived at home. He showed them around the city, taking them to museums and grown-up plays. Their favorite thing was to buy sandwiches, little fruit pies, and old-fashioned celery drinks at the neighborhood deli. They'd put everything in a big basket and have a picnic in a nearby park. Jacks still went with Daddy to the horse races all summer long.

On the excursions to the city, Joss felt more grown-up. She and Jacks would ask Daddy questions about the plays over a snack in some restaurant. Drawn out by his serious expression, they asked serious questions about big topics, like how people learned to solve problems and how to forgive people when they were mean. Or how adults coped with people deserting them, or dying?

The three had fun together, yet as much as she and Jacks tried to cheer up Daddy, they couldn't fix his sad face when they went back to Mother's house.

At the beginning of summer, the weatherman warned of a hotter than normal summer. Joss groaned, as she hated to ride or swim if the temperature was too high. The pool water felt like a bathtub, so she swam in late evening. One morning in mid-June, Daddy and Jacks left for the racetrack, taking three of the horses. They'd be gone almost all summer. Joss stayed in her room, staring in her mirror and combing her hair. Moping.

Around ten she dressed and headed for the kitchen. When she walked past the master bedroom, her mother moaned. Not wanting to open the door to something scary, Joss dragged herself to the kitchen.

Sally stood by the stove, turning bacon. Joss asked her to check on her mother. Sally hurried down the hall and a few minutes later came back to the kitchen looking grim. She and Sally ate bacon and toast in silence. Two hours later a doctor came to the house and examined Mother. When he left, Sally drove Mother to the hospital. Joss refused to ride with them. Was her mother dying already? Still young, only forty-three, but she looked like hell. Skinny arms and legs and a big belly that made her look pregnant.

The next day, Sally pleaded with Joss to come with her to visit her mother. Joss immediately got a headache, but finally agreed. She didn't want to know if her mother had started to die.

The tubes in her mother's nose and arm scared her. She turned her head, but couldn't avoid what the light streaming through the window was showing. Her mother's yellowish, flaky skin and her thin arms inert on a white blanket scared Joss. Her mother lay still and appeared to be sleeping.

Joss darted into the hall to catch her breath. On the drive home, Sally told her things were bad. When Joss got home, she called her father and cried on the phone, pleading with him to come home. His calm voice soothed her for a few minutes. He said they'd leave the track right away, but as she knew, with the horse trailer, the drive would take three days. When her brother got on the line they cried together.

Daddy called every day from a pay phone. Luce and Polly called her, too, but Joss told Sally to tell them she was busy. Later Joss wondered how her friends found out about her mother: probably Sally had told them. Whatever, Joss didn't have the energy to ask.

A blue panel truck drove up to the house. Two men wearing gray uniforms hauled medical equipment into the master bedroom and unloaded it, set up a hospital bed, and brought in a big machine that made oxygen. They set the machine on a blanket chest near the bed. Sally carried in a small, gold-painted hall table with curved feet to hold a water pitcher, a glass, and medicine bottles.

The next day an ambulance brought Mother home from the hospital.

Except for meals and talking on the phone with Daddy and Jacks, Joss stayed in her room or swam in the pool on cooler evenings. Her whole body hurt, and she blamed it on the heat. Ridiculous since the whole house hummed with air-conditioning.

Mother lay in the strange mechanical bed, and the elegant master bedroom stank of sweat instead of Joy, her mother's favorite perfume. The scary room felt full with the noisy oxygen pump and the air conditioner running full blast. Despite the cold, Mother's thinning hair stuck to her forehead. When Joss came close to give her water, she heard her chest rattle.

In a hoarse voice, Mother suddenly said, "I wish I'd stayed around more for you kids."

Joss stood in silence. Her mother cried and fumbled with the sheets, leaning, struggling to reach the bedside table for a Kleenex, whimpering when she couldn't stretch far enough.

Joss watched and did not help her.

Mother did something she rarely did: she looked directly at Joss. In a whisper she said, "I'm so sorry."

Joss left the room before tears came.

Two days later, in the early morning, Sally knocked on Joss's bedroom door. Joss bolted up, and called, "Come in!"

Sally stood by Joss's bed. "I was sitting with your mother when the Lord took her, deep in the night. I waited until the birds were singing to tell you."

Joss slid out of bed and allowed her dear Sally to hug and comfort her. She showered and went downstairs. She and Sally sat in the kitchen, drinking coffee. Joss wandered to the window and laid her palm on a windowpane. Blistering hot. The window overlooked part of the swimming pool. Joss turned away so she wouldn't think about her mother swimming laps wearing her favorite black bathing suit, showing her slim body to no one, only sky.

A long, black car pulled up to the house. Sally ran to the front door, and Joss clutched her cup. She heard men's voices over the rattling of a gurney.

What did her mother look like dead? She poured their coffees into tall glasses and added ice cubes.

More rattling wheels bumping around corners. The front door closed, followed by clanking down the steps. Soon the black car drove off.

Sally sat again. "Thanks for the ice. It's a hot one, and it ain't even ten o'clock."

They sat in silence. Sally turned her head. "Listen, I think that's your daddy coming up the drive!"

Finally! Daddy and Jacks and the horses were home. While Daddy and Sally talked, she and Jacks unloaded the horses and took them to the barn. Daddy called the funeral home and made arrangements. No open casket, they all agreed. Mother had turned into a jaundiced skeleton. She would have hated for people to see her.

Sally fixed a late lunch or an early dinner. They were at the table when the blue panel truck returned. The same two men wearing gray took away the hospital bed and oxygen machine.

After Mother's funeral, Daddy moved back home. Joss watched him carry his suitcases into the bigger guest room.

The next morning, Joss asked Sally to show her how to bake a chocolate cake, Daddy's favorite. Sally showed her every step. Later she followed each step, watching over the cake like a baby kitten. It looked okay. She covered it to let it cool. But when it cooled, the runny fudge icing kept sliding down the sides of the cake, pooling in the plate and dripping onto the counter. Over and over Joss piled the icing back on the top with a large spoon. She stuck it in the refrigerator to help the icing to stay put. When she took it out, it looked messy, but with a decent amount of icing on top.

Before Sally left for the day, Joss asked her to take a week off.

"Now? But, Joss, I need to stay here. These are hard times."

"Yes, it's hard times. I know you loved Mother, and you took really great care of her. And I did nothing. But you have your own family that you don't see as much as you should. Now I'm sort of in charge of the house, so I can ask you to please take time for yourself. Mother never gave you hardly any time off. I'm telling Daddy to pay you more money, and you'll have a decent amount of time for yourself."

"Thank you, sweet thing. You sure now? You need me, you just call."

Joss hugged her. "Dear Sally, you know I'll call if I need you. Don't worry." She laughed. "The three of us will try to make it through dinner without you." She put her hand to Sally's cheek. "Now go and enjoy."

Joss felt like a grown-up while she boiled potatoes to make potato salad the way Sally had shown her months ago. Before slicing tomatoes, she put on water to boil to steep tea bags for iced tea. While she was frying hamburgers, the buns burned under the broiler. With the stove fan on high, she threw the buns in the trash. Not even the birds would eat them. She piled bread slices in a basket and set it on the table.

Jackson and Daddy came right to the table when she called them. They must have been in Daddy's room, laughing about what kind of cooking disaster they'd find.

Daddy looked surprised. "You sent Sally home and did all this yourself? Everything looks great!" His face got red, and she thought he might cry.

"Thank you, Daddy. Wait until you see dessert! Jacks, you'll love this potato salad. I used Sally's recipe, with those little pickles."

Joss glanced around the table as if she were making a decision that in fact she'd already made. She sat in her mother's chair.

Joss felt freer, more grown-up. The house felt different with Mother gone. Soon she walked by her parents' old bedroom and didn't give it a second look.

Daddy stayed downstairs, and he liked it that way. More relaxed, he laughed and joked. He rented a smaller office downtown, still working part-time as a racetrack design consultant when he wasn't traveling.

When school started in the fall, Joss felt relieved to have a diversion and a purpose after the summer. Daddy started driving her to school and picking her up. Around Christmas of his senior year, Jacks finally had enough money saved to buy an old Chevy, which he had painted bright red. After that, she got to ride to school with her big brother.

Joss liked school. She studied more and showed her grades to Daddy for the first time ever. But sometimes falling asleep or in study hall, she saw terrible images of her mother: staggering up the front steps, fumbling with her key, cursing, stumbling, and banging into a hall table and cursing some more.

One afternoon after school, Joss secreted herself in a cubicle on the library's second floor. She brought her biology textbook to cover what she intended to read. She skimmed one book at a time, shoving it back before pulling out another.

Footsteps close behind her. Heart pounding, she shoved her biology book over the larger text. But her book wouldn't stay put. Leaning both elbows on top of the books, she glanced up. Only some nerdy boy shuffling by. He took no notice of her.

When the third book started to repeat the basics, she closed it. She shoved the book back where it belonged, but later, running down the library steps, she was worried. Students were supposed to put the books on the cart. Only the library workers shelved. But she trusted herself; she'd always been careful with library books.

Now she had information and some understanding. More than she ever picked up in health class, though. She never asked the teacher questions. Her mother had been a drunk. Now she knew about addiction to drugs and alcohol. She read about depression and bipolar disorder. These problems occurred together and ran in families. Her family.

Chapter Fourteen: Phil

PHIL PUT ON A CLEAN T-SHIRT and checked himself in the mirror. He brushed his sparse hair with care, trying to convince himself it had already grown a lot. This T-shirt was still a favorite. Yesterday he came back from the gym and found his bed covered with folded clean clothes. Fake Joss had left him a note, which he threw in the trash without reading. Why bother reading a fake note? Where did she find his clothes? Had she broken into the half-burned house and rummaged through his closet and drawers? More likely she'd stolen his clothes before the fire and kept them in a storage unit as part of her bigger plan to drive him crazy so she could get the house, the insurance money, and his college pension.

And whatever other money there might be, but at this minute he couldn't think of any money besides his salary. Fake Joss would even have to pay off his student loans.

He reminded himself to forget about where his clothes came from. Clean clothes made him happy. In the dining room he sat alone at the corner table and watched the door. He finished the tomato soup just as Vivienne walked up with a tray.

Pointing to a chair, he said, "I'm glad you came."

She patted his hand. "Your color's better. Is that a new shirt?"

"Delivered yesterday. One of my favorites." He couldn't think how to explain the shirt's arrival. He picked up his tuna sandwich and opened it up to examine the amount of pickles and thin-sliced celery. The people here made tuna sandwiches like Joss. His favorite.

Vivienne ate yogurt and nibbled a cracker. Sun came through the window, and her black hair shone. He put his hand over hers. "When we finish, can you come to my room?"

"I suppose. I have a little time."

"Almost finished." He gobbled his sandwich and guzzled water to get the tuna taste out of his mouth because he wanted to kiss her. And maybe do more. He took her hand and leaned close to his beloved. Her lips felt soft and warm.

"Dad? Dad!"

He pulled back.

Terpe stood by the table, frowning.

He dropped his hands in his lap. "What are you doing here?"

"School let out early. I took the bus. Who's this?" She pointed at Vivienne, who looked down at her plate.

"Um. This is Vivienne. My department's administrator. She came to . . . Well . . . She came to bring me the latest news."

He turned to Vivienne. "My daughter, Terpe."

Terpe glared at Vivienne, who kept her eyes on Phil's face.

Vivienne grabbed her pocketbook as she jumped out of her chair. "I gotta get back to the office. Nice to meet you." She halfway glanced at Terpe and hurried out the door.

"Want some lunch?" Phil asked, pointing to the cafeteria line.

"Why were you holding hands and kissing that woman?"

"Oh, we're friends." His sinful hands shook, so he grabbed the bowl of syrupy fruit cocktail and ate a spoonful. Too slippery, it slid down his throat, making him gag.

"You're lying. You've been doing things with her. Is that why Mom made you sleep upstairs in the guest room? Now I get it."

The kid's red face made him nervous. The room spun. Where did the aide go? He searched for an eternity before he spotted an aide standing against the far wall and waved her to the table. "Hey, Louise, can you take me back to my room? I'm feeling dizzy."

The aide pulled his wheelchair from the table, turned it, and pushed him toward the door.

Terpe followed and said loudly to his back, "You're not sick, you're a puked-up coward!"

People turned and stared. He lowered his head and kept his voice low. "Okay, Louise, keep rolling."

Chapter Fifteen: Terpe

TERPE HURRIED OUT OF THE REHAB center and ran along
the empty sidewalk. Her watch read 12:50. If she walked fast,
she could make it back to school before the closing bell. Dad
kept pretending he didn't know Mom, so he could date this
person. *Hate him! Hate him! Hate him!*

For six blocks she kept up the pace before slowing. Almost
one o'clock. Hungry and thirsty, she sat on a grassy slope near
the curb, pulled off her backpack, and took out her lunch box.
She ate a peanut butter and banana sandwich and sipped from
a juice box.

The sound of a car slowing and stopping. A man sat at the
wheel, no one else in the car. She stared at the ground, waiting for
the car to drive away. Instead, the passenger window opened, and
a man's voice said, "Hey, you lost? I'll give you a ride. Hop in."

Terpe let the juice box fall to the ground and slid the lunch
box into her backpack. She stood and slipped on the pack.
Hunched over, she made herself as small as possible.

"Hey, it's okay," the man said in a fake nice voice. "I got kids.
I'm happy to give you a ride."

*Don't get in a car with a stranger. Scream. Run. Go to people.
Mom. Run.* Mom's and Dad's voices.

The car door opened, the man mumbling something under his breath, and though he said words, she heard monster noise. She took off into the trees, her legs thrashing through brambles, stumbling over tree roots but, no matter what, not stopping.

She darted behind a wide tree.

Listen for footsteps. Make your body stiff.

Her watch read 1:19.

Straight ahead where the trees thinned, she spotted a row of large brick houses, with ordinary back porches, lawns with kids' swings. She could make it to those before he got her. She inched around the tree. No one. No road sounds.

She took off to the nearest house and flattened herself against the wall. Her chest hurt as she edged along the bricks, easing herself around to the front of the house by a porch with columns. Scanning the street, she saw mailboxes in front of houses and parked cars.

She jumped at the sound of a door slamming, saw a woman turning to lock her front door and walk to her car. Oh, no, she looked like the mother of a boy in her class. Should she ask this woman for a ride to school? But the woman would ask Terpe why she was running around the neighborhood when she should be in school. She'd probably tattle to the principal. Nothing this woman could say would be good. But maybe this person wasn't even the boy's mother?

Terpe wiped her eyes with the back of her hand. She had fallen down a well into grown-up problems. Her armpits itched. She wanted water.

What to do? Run back through the woods? No, too scary. This road had traffic. Safer. This road connected with the side street by the rehab center.

It was 1:25.

She walked as fast as she could.

That man's fake voice stayed with her. Maybe someone would shoot him, like on TV.

How would their house feel without Dad? He didn't want to talk on the phone. The doctors were liars. Dad was pretending about fake Joss.

Her watch read 1:43. School wasn't too far now. Slip in a back door, try to avoid the hall monitors. Go straight to math class, act like she'd been in the bathroom. What about her backpack? Nobody wore a backpack to the bathroom during class time. If a hall monitor stopped her, she had to say something. Maybe say her dress got dirty, somebody threw up on her at recess, and she changed clothes. Everything would depend on which hall monitor caught her.

At 1:55 Terpe rounded the corner to school. Too early for the carpool line. The street running in front of the school was empty except for her mother's Volvo. She stood by the car. Right now, her mother would be in the principal's office; maybe the principal had already called the police, thinking she'd been kidnapped. Her classroom windows faced the front lawn and street; if the police showed up, kids in her class would watch her out the windows. Word would get around she skipped school a lot.

She hurried across the lawn. At the main office door, she stopped. Without knocking, she burst through the door and ran to the counter. A secretary glanced up from her paperwork, but Terpe kept moving toward the principal's door. Through the glass she could see her mother sitting in a chair. When she tapped on the glass, her mom turned, jumped up, and opened the door. "Oh, Terpe, thank goodness! We were about to call the police. Where in the world did you go? Why did you leave school?"

"I went to visit Dad," she whispered. "The place where he's staying isn't far from school."

Her mother hugged her. "Oh, sweetie, I'm so glad you're safe. I would've taken you to visit your dad. Why didn't you ask?"

"I wanted to see him for myself." Terpe turned to Miss Pollard, the principal. Younger than Mom, she wore a tight bun that made her face round and ugly. The principal appeared peaceful and nodded to students when she walked through the halls. But most kids whispered bad stories about her, and everyone warned new students to watch out. Miss Pollard knew how to make you feel terrible. She stared at you until you confessed, or made up a little lie so you could get out of her office. Only the biggest, meanest boys weren't scared to tell her really big lies.

Terpe closed her eyes, wondering if she would get a pile of demerits, which would mean every Saturday sitting in a room with other delinquents doing math problems and writing stupid sentences for the rest of the year. Or maybe a month's out-of-school suspension.

"Terpe." Miss Pollard cleared her throat. "What you did is inexcusable. Your mother, your homeroom teacher, and I have been concerned. Skipping school is dangerous, to say nothing of class instructions you've missed. Something could've happened to you. But your mother has explained about the fire at your house and your father's condition. I'm very sorry.

"I'll release you to your mother for today and the rest of the week. You will leave the school grounds immediately. You will not come to school until Monday. This should give you time to think about your actions.

"When you return, you will apologize to your homeroom teacher, in front of the class, so your classmates will feel included. Of course, you will also be expected to complete all missed class notes, assignments, and any tests you missed."

Terpe forced herself to look at the principal. "I won't do anything like this again. I'm sorry."

Her mother clutched her purse in one hand and shook Miss Pollard's hand. "Thank you for your kindness." Her mother nodded, and nodded some more.

Mom looked like a wreck. They didn't talk as they walked to the car.

Terpe forced herself not to look back at the classroom windows. Who was staring at her?

Her mother drove to their favorite coffee shop and ordered her usual latte.

Terpe's stomach growled, but she ordered a Coke, afraid to ask for more.

"Please explain. I don't understand why you didn't ask me to drive you." Mom scanned the room, probably waiting for them to call out her latte.

"Dad's faking he doesn't know you. I wanted him to tell me the truth when you weren't hovering."

"I don't hover."

Terpe laughed. "You hover all the time. You can't help it. I knew he wouldn't talk with you there, even if you stood by the door or were anywhere in the building."

"What did you find out?"

"I suppose you already know, or maybe not. I'll tell you. Dad was sitting in the dining room eating lunch with a lady. A grown-up, but younger than you. He got upset when he saw me."

"I'll bet he did."

"The lady left in a hurry. Dad said she worked in his department's office and they were discussing business. Holding hands and kissing? He called for some nurse to push his wheelchair back to his room. I almost ran after him, but I thought about it and came back to school.

"Her name's Vivienne. He's a liar. I hate him."

Mom's eyes went watery. "That's an awful way for you to find out. Before the fire, I knew he'd been dating someone. Your father and I argued. He denied it. But I know when he's lying."

"He's faking about you. That way he can keep his girlfriend and not think about you or me or Geline."

"The situation would be easier if that were true. He and I might be able to sort out this mess. I think he mostly wants me out of his life. But, remember the fire, those boards hit him hard, hard enough to knock him down. He made it down the stairs, but his brain isn't working well."

"But he won't talk to us. Like he doesn't know us."

"Terpe, the main thing is that you're safe. Once we get our drinks, we'll pick up Geline, go have a nice dinner, and after that take a nice hot bath. Just try to relax."

"I'm tired."

"Did you eat your lunch?"

"I finished some. I hurried and walked a long way."

"Your principal's a witch. It's stupid to keep you out of school for skipping. She should've just given you Saturday demerits. You'll be home all day Wednesday, Thursday, and Friday."

"I told you all the kids hate the principal. Now you see why."

Chapter Sixteen: Joss

THE KIDS WERE ASLEEP. Joss laid a book next to her on the bed. Desperate for more sleep, she refused to go to the doctor for sleeping pills. A few friends had taken them, and they felt groggy and dizzy. She needed all her wits and couldn't be spacey in the morning with two kids. It was a stupid idea.

When she dozed off, she found herself in an empty church filled with ringing chimes; she walked down aisle after aisle. The chimes rang and rang, growing louder until she woke. Palms down, she smacked the bed with both hands, irritated to find herself awake again already.

Her bedside lamp still lit the room. Suddenly the front door chimes rang. Who in the world? The chimes rang again. She lurched up and hurried to the door before the noise could wake up the children. The peephole didn't reveal anything; whoever was standing on the porch was too close to the door to be seen.

"Who is it?" she demanded. Glad she still had on clothes, trying to make her voice gruff. She should buy that tape of a barking dog she read about.

"Joss? It's Adam."

She repeated his name to herself, ran her hand through her tangled hair, and opened the door.

"Sorry. You were asleep?" He glanced at his watch.

"Not really. What are you doing way out here?"

"Just driving around. You crossed my mind. I wondered what you were doing."

"Reading. Come on in. Would you like coffee? I can't drink it this late, but I'll make you some. Maybe I'll have some decaf."

"Water's fine. With lots of ice."

The kitchen clock read 8:05, not late. She ignored the sink still full of dirty dishes and took two clean glasses out of the cabinet. She put their ice water on the kitchen table and sat. Adam drank his water, put down the glass, and drummed his fingers.

He laughed, a high-pitched, anxious sound. "So. Here I am."

She waited until he started again.

"I've been thinking about you. I should've called first. I'm being rude."

"Yes, sort of. It's always best to call." Alcohol. When she pinpointed the smell, her stomach tightened. He told her he'd stopped drinking; still, he didn't act drunk. What in hell could she be thinking, letting a man she barely knew into the house?

"From now on, I'll call first."

The jolt in her stomach didn't feel like fear. She waited.

On the edge of his chair, he stayed poised to say something. She supposed it was important.

He tapped his fingers on the table. "You're not like anyone else. Not any of the girls I knew in high school. You know, over the years, I've worked for my share of rich ladies, but you're not like them, either. Some were snooty—they just gave me orders and disappeared. Some flirted, but I didn't date them or have sex with them."

His words surprised, yet irritated her. So she wasn't the only lonely wife without a husband. He would not hurt her. Would she have the strength to make him leave?

"I thought about a special dream all day. You and I were sailing someplace, maybe on some ocean. I messed with the sails like I knew what to do on a sailboat. The sky turned dark. Lightning struck the water close by. We pulled the boat up on a beach. Weird that we could see where to pull the boat. We secured the boat right there and climbed back into it. We spent the night on a king-sized mattress. There were stars."

A pulse hammered at his wrist. He grinned like a shy teenager and looked away. "My buddy Fred, you know, the contractor, told me your husband's still sick? His car's in the same spot in the driveway."

"How perceptive." Her own voice sounded sarcastic, but she didn't care. "Yes. His recovery seems very slow."

"I want my dream to happen." Adam picked up her hand. "Do you?"

She pulled her hand away and drank water. "We didn't sleep on this boat?" She waited to feel scared, but she didn't feel fear.

His cheeks reddened. "We didn't sleep at all."

The two of them together? What a terrible idea. She had so much to do, she could barely keep up. And Phil? She and Phil would never be a couple again. Still, this attraction with Adam was moving fast. The two of them staying together for any length of time? Impossible.

She whispered, "No."

He took her chin in his hand. "You sure?" He moved closer. She didn't hesitate or back away. He pulled her off her chair and held her, stroking her hair. With Adam's hand cradling the back of her head, she felt Phil's hand on the same spot. While she rinsed dishes, Phil would hold her head, kiss the back of her neck, turn her to face him, and unbutton her blouse.

Adam led her to her bedroom. How did he know her bedroom's location? Oh, right, he'd stood at the door talking with her. He would leave if she asked. He wouldn't force her. At least she hoped he wouldn't try to force her. For sure, she'd hate him!

She felt calm, not thinking about anything while he undressed her, kissing her gently for a long time. He moved without haste. They lay together on her big bed. She stroked his cheek while he unbuttoned his shirt. She felt a jolt of happiness. His skin felt hot and soft, and she kept her hand on his chest before slowly moving it lower. She heard him gulp, and she smiled.

Later, as they lay close, she said, "We can't fall asleep. It's past midnight. The baby wakes up early, she'll wake up Terpe, and everything will be crazy busy until I get the girls fed and where they need to go. You have to leave now."

He stroked her stomach and moved his hand lower.

She laughed and grabbed his hand. "Oh, no, you don't. I mean it, it's almost one in the morning. You have to go."

"Okay, okay, lady." He kissed her and picked his clothes off the floor. He dressed slowly as if he were half-asleep. He looked pleased she was watching. She guessed he liked his own body.

She sighed, stood, grabbing her robe from the foot of her bed. He followed her down the hall, singing softly. Some Dolly Parton song again. At the door he touched her chin.

"I'll bring you and your children dinner tonight. Is that all right?"

"No. I stay busy with the kids around dinnertime. I've got an appointment. Maybe Friday?"

"But . . ."

"I said no. Slow down."

"Okay. I'll call you later."

"Don't call me lady ever again." She put her hand on his chest. "I'm not one of your housewives."

"You sure aren't." He laughed.

Joss fell into bed and slept instantly, until Geline's crying woke her at six. She stumbled into the baby's room, hoping she could get there before Terpe woke. But her older daughter lay in her sleeping bag with her eyes open.

"I'll get the baby, Mom. Go back to sleep. I'll wake you in half an hour."

Joss buzzed into the kitchen to make coffee. She hummed as she moved around the room. She waited for the remorse and the guilt, wondering when it would hit. Any minute, surely. For now she'd enjoy feeling untroubled and happy.

She stared into the refrigerator and wondered what to cook for dinner. Hours ago Adam had been in her bed. Their sex had been better than expected for a first time. His body felt good. She opened her eyes, still staring into the refrigerator. She closed the refrigerator door and drank coffee.

This thing with Terpe was another matter; Joss hurt just imagining what her girl must be feeling. Her image of her perfect father crumbling in a heap at her feet. Of course, from Joss's perspective, he hadn't ever been the great father Terpe imagined. He'd rarely played with her or shown interest in her hobbies, yet he would talk with her about literature. He didn't criticize her and rarely acted like a spoiled brat around her. More careful than caring, Joss judged. So Terpe had seen her father's competent, compassionate side. He'd saved the whining for his wife: his worries about his health, his irritation at colleagues in the department and no time to do his research. Of course, she'd told him not to accept a teaching position, but to seek a job in research. But he had brushed her off.

Events had sped up, and at any moment she felt her life might spin out of control. What would happen next? Dinner and nine hours sleep would help clear her mind. She hoped Adam would call early. To hell with the hospital expecting to be able to contact her any time of day or night. She'd talk to Adam, and turn off the landline and cell phone.

A quiet dinner meant Geline didn't throw Cheerios off her high chair while screeching in hilarity. Terpe fed her sister yogurt, which she didn't spit out. They watched Geline hold a banana, trying to cram it in her mouth and instead smashing it into her forehead. They all laughed as Geline waved her chubby hand, bits of banana clinging to it and flying to the floor.

Terpe took Geline to the bathroom and wiped off the banana. Over the squeak of the rocking chair, she sang to her sister. The baby got quiet, and Terpe put her into the crib and ran her own bath water.

Joss cleaned the kitchen to give herself something to do while waiting for the phone to ring. Could she keep a date with Adam on Friday? She'd like to see him again.

Would Terpe be too upset about her father and suspension, for Joss to leave her with neighbors? Terpe might start acting grumpy again if she had to spend yet another night next door. Joss predicted she'd regress, start hanging around the house sulking.

Joss was lying in bed in her nightgown, when he called.

She said, "Just getting ready to turn off my phones."

"Want me to call tomorrow?"

"It's okay. Had a good day?"

"I had three customers, but I've been moving real slow since you took over my mind." He laughed. "It's your fault."

"I'm flattered. We have to be careful not to make noise. I don't want the kids to hear us."

"Want to eat someplace nice, or casual? Whatever you want."

"Can you meet me for coffee in the morning? I'll take the baby to day care and meet you about nine? The coffee shop on Hamilton Boulevard?"

"You bet. It's a nice thing about being your own boss. Before we hang up, I have to say something. Remember when I told you I planned to start college? Until that minute, I hadn't even thought about college. I got worried you'd ask me about it, and then I'd have to think up a good lie. In high school, I did make good grades in math and shop."

"I barely remember you saying anything about college. I'm no good at conversation while I'm writing."

"I kept bothering you, interrupting."

"Yes, you bothered me. I hate interruptions. I didn't get a chance to tell you last night, but my daughter cut classes yesterday and got suspended. She went to the rehab center where Phil is staying."

"Your daughter's old enough to drive?"

"She's nine. She walked over a mile, each way."

"Is she all right? Are you?"

"I'm tired and confused about what to do. The principal suspended her for the rest of the week, so she's lucky it's only for three days."

"I can be there in half an hour."

"No. I'm tired. See you in the morning?"

"You bet. Sleep well."

Joss fell into restless sleep and didn't hear Geline fussing at six.

Terpe woke her mom at seven thirty and said, "Geline's back in her crib. I changed her diaper, and gave her a bottle. Any minute, she'll start screaming. I gotta get dressed."

Joss laughed. "Once Geline is up, she's up. Sorry I overslept, but I needed the sleep. Thanks for helping." She pulled on her daughter's hand until she sat on the bed. "Please don't worry about grown-up problems. No matter what happens with your dad, you'll be okay. What will you do with the rest of your days off?"

"Can you take me to the library? I need to find some good books. I'll hang out there this morning."

"The library? Good idea. It opens at nine." Take Geline to day care, backtrack to the library. She didn't want to bring Terpe to the coffee shop.

Adam was sitting in the back booth, a bagel with cream cheese and a cup of coffee in front of him.

"Sorry I'm late. I dropped Terpe at the library for three hours."

"You're okay?" He took her hand.

She glanced around the coffee shop to make sure she didn't recognize anyone. "I'm okay. I feel bad for Terpe. Her dad was eating lunch in the dining room with his girlfriend. He lied to her, then ignored her. He had an aide push his wheelchair out of the dining room."

"Protecting kids isn't easy," Adam said. "Mama tried to protect me. Around the house, she usually could, before things changed."

"What?"

"Let's talk about that stuff some other time. You got enough on your mind. Listen, I'd like to come over tonight and meet your kids. I could bring food and cook in your kitchen."

"No. I have a meeting with Phil's therapist. Our next-door neighbors will keep the girls and feed them dinner."

"I could drive you to the therapist."

"Not a good idea. I want to keep things separate. Maybe meet you back at my house? After I pick up the kids and get them in bed. Eight thirty? My daughter might be watching television. Making plans is complicated with kids."

"Why can't they stay the night?" He kissed her hand. "I want to kiss every part of you."

"They can't stay next door all the time." She jerked her hand away. "I'm embarrassed."

"You'll get used to it." He laughed.

"I don't want to take advantage of our neighbors. Let me think about it."

He nodded. "I gotta get to an appointment. Call you later." He stuffed the rest of the bagel in his mouth.

Phil wasn't in Dr. Drummond's office when Joss arrived. The doctor asked her to sit.

"Thanks for coming. I'm sorry to say your husband didn't want to come to this meeting. Let's you and I talk."

Joss took a deep breath. "You may have been told, my daughter came to this facility on Tuesday. She skipped school and walked over a mile each way. She recently turned nine. And what did she find? Her father making out in the public dining room."

"Well, Phil didn't explain it quite like that to me." Dr. Drummond moved back in his chair.

"There were plenty of witnesses in the dining room. My daughter does not lie. What kid could make up that scene? I'm not interested in Phil's version. And I'm furious none of your staff asked my daughter who she came with. Your staff just let a kid walk into the facility without her parents? When my daughter tried to talk to Phil, he got an aide to wheel him away. What a coward."

"Your husband has made progress in physical rehab. We're trying another medicine which might help to clear his thinking."

"Good. But at this point I don't care what you try."

"I understand."

"You don't understand! I'm done. Try another medicine on Phil. Or try them all. I don't care."

"Do you think there's more for us to discuss, the problems in your marriage?"

"Screw Phil. And no, that's all you and I have to discuss." She stood. "Thank you for your time. Good-bye."

She hurried out before he tried to persuade her to stay.

Sitting in the parking lot, she dialed Adam's number.

"Hey. You're finished already? Where are you?"

"In the parking lot."

"I'll come over to your place. Leaving now. Be there fast as I can."

"Yes." Yes.

Chapter Seventeen: Adam

ADAM DIDN'T SLOW HIS SPEED and made it to Joss's house in twenty minutes. Her car wasn't in the driveway. He checked his appointment book. At nine he wanted to be naked in bed with Joss, but that was impossible with kids. He hadn't dated anyone with children. The older kid would get in his way. With her father in the hospital, the kid needed extra attention. He understood. He didn't blame the kid—he knew about crappy fathers.

Joss pulled in the driveway. She waved to him when she got out of the car and went through the hedge to the house next door. A few minutes later, she crossed the lawn, holding the baby, the older one trailing behind. He came down the driveway and took the baby's tote bag from Joss. With a free hand she dug for her keys. The older girl glanced at him before turning away.

In the kitchen the girl asked, "You're the yard guy?"

"Yep. My name's Adam Werther. And your name's Terpe."

"What are you doing here?"

"I'm a friend of your mom's."

The girl glared at him, shook her head, and stomped down the hall. She wasn't as attractive as her mother. Her brown hair looked stringy and unwashed. She smirked.

Joss said, "Let me get the kids settled. Fix yourself water, Pepsi, or there's a carton of orange juice in the fridge."

He'd made a mistake coming here. He wanted to make their romance beautiful; he wanted her all to himself. Even though Joss had the people next door to help, and the kids were gone most of the day, her focus stayed on her kids. Maybe he could change his work schedule. What about weekends? *Think about that later.*

Finally, Joss's footsteps. She came into the room.

He stood and pulled her to him. "Good to see you." He stroked her hair.

"Me, too. Something to drink?"

"Water with ice is fine." No booze to calm down. He could do this. No more drinking, it took him nowhere. "You sounded mad on the phone. Things didn't go well?"

"Phil didn't show up. I'm on the verge of being done with the whole mess." She put the glass in front of him.

"Can I help?" He reached for her hand.

She pulled away. "How great of you to help. Just take me to bed, and all problems go away."

Her words hung in the air. His mind stumbled. He fought the urge to back out of the kitchen, get in his truck, and speed away. An image of a girl he dated in high school appeared. They'd both been sixteen. Once she'd made him really mad, some stupid argument he couldn't even remember. He'd walked away and never tried to understand what happened. Right quick he met anther pretty blonde girl at a party. But around that time everything stayed blurry. A time of heavy drinking, moving on to bourbon, with beer chasers. He thought he only remembered the blonde's first name. Sandra? Sandra somebody?

Joss said, "Adam, you haven't done anything. It's stupid to think we can keep this going. My life's full of problems."

"I'll try to help."

"Why? There are lots of women your age. You like to sing. Why not take up dance lessons or join a country band? There's always online dating."

"That's not what I want. You and I can make this happen."

"Why? And what will 'this' look like?"

"Why? First of all, there are lots of single girls in AA who want to party and don't talk about anything except clothes and money. I went out with three and heard scary stories about their friends burning and cutting themselves. While I felt bad for them, I moved on to some straight arrow girls. They're nicer, but I could tell by their questions they were hunting for a rich guy, or one who had a future and would be rich by thirty-five."

Joss said, "Your world sounds too small. You're young, you have time to explore."

He probably shouldn't say the next thing. "I'm not very ambitious. I don't have it in me to hurry around making money. You and I have fun talking. You have a big brain. We can teach each other stuff. I like to look at you. Can't that be enough for now?"

Where did that come from? He hadn't planned to say any of that. She didn't say anything, so he kept going. "What will this thing turn into? I haven't figured it out. We're moving fast."

"We both have other worries, and we're having fun," she said.

The kitchen clock ticked loudly and the refrigerator motor made a lot of noise. The ice in his glass was melting. He'd promised himself to go slow, but he ruined it. Or did he? The truth. At least he'd told the truth.

He pulled Joss from her chair. When he put his arms around her, she didn't resist; her body felt warm against his. "You're tired and I am, too. We don't have to figure out everything now. Let's go to bed."

She frowned. "Don't rush me. You're like some other guys. Just in it for the fucks."

Light leaked through the bedroom curtains. Joss was still sleeping and Adam wondered if he should wake her. When Geline cried, Joss probably woke on her own. Her older girl began jabbering to the baby. He rolled over, hoping to sleep longer before realizing his body felt wide awake. Joss's legs were twisted in the sheets and her hair all spread out. He rested his hand on her back.

A shriek from the baby roused Joss. She raised her head.

"I'll make coffee? Should I stay in the bedroom until the kids are gone?" He felt awkward, unsure what would be okay to do in her house.

Joss threw her legs over the side of the bed and slipped on a bathrobe. "Coffee's good. It's on the middle shelf. The big cabinet."

Adam washed, brushed his teeth, and dressed before he crept into the kitchen, wondering what to say to the kid. He busied himself making coffee. From down the hall, the children's voices sounded foreign.

As a kid, he'd lived in a silent apartment. During the day, he felt lost in that lack of noise. The roar of Mama's vacuum interrupted the quiet, and the hiss of the iron when she set it back on the ironing board, the water running and splashing over dishes, the opening and closing of cabinet doors.

Sometimes he and Mama took walks. She sang foreign songs. If he asked what the words meant, she shook her head and kept singing. He listened harder, trying to understand until he gave up and focused on the pleasing sound of her voice. When he was small and his Papa came home from work, the house might turn noisy for a while. He and Papa wrestled on the living room floor and played with Adam's train set or built stuff with blocks. When Adam grew older, Papa gradually stopped paying him attention. He never explained why; he and Mama fought more. After the fight, Papa walked away, into the bathroom and showered. Sometimes he'd leave the apartment.

When Papa wasn't home, the apartment would go quiet again. The silence made Adam afraid, made him wonder what would happen next. He suspected Mama felt afraid, too. Yet she'd never admit it.

Terpe came into the kitchen, squeezing Geline against her chest, the baby's legs dangling below her waist. The kid stood with her legs apart to keep her balance. He guessed the baby was too big for Terpe to carry. With a sigh, she plopped her sister in the high chair.

"Want some pancakes?" he asked. "Just tell me how you like them. Bacon's already in the pan."

She pulled milk and baby food out of the refrigerator and tied a bib around Geline's neck. She angled her chair so her back faced him. She talked to the baby, who babbled.

Of course the kid didn't want him here. He and Joss should have waited longer for him to sleep over. He felt sure he and Terpe would like each other, but not now. She stayed mad at her father, probably the whole world, and especially men hanging with her mother.

A mistake standing in the kitchen cooking pancakes. He should have stayed in Joss's room 'til the kids left? Had he acted any better than Terpe's father? Maybe the kid didn't know Joss was all done with her father. Still, Phil would always be her father.

Joss acted like she had separated from Phil. Last night in bed, well, she sure acted interested in him, not her husband. Adam told himself that he wouldn't push anyone, including himself. One Day at a Time, like they said in AA.

Adam tried to call Joss, but his phone acted all dead. He stopped by the bar where he recently had three shots. The bartender's eyes widened when Adam pulled cash from his wallet. He reached into the cash register and took out the blank check Adam had signed, just in case he didn't return. The bartender put the check on the bar.

With a smile Adam picked up his old check and slapped down the cash. He resisted gloating.

The bartender asked if Adam wanted a shot of bourbon. His mind on his cell phone, Adam shook his head. Walking out, he felt relieved he didn't want a drink. Today he didn't want a drink. Those sad, hopeless people at the bar hunched over their beers and whiskies and the people in the poorly lit booths had no appeal.

He drove to a phone store. The salesperson laughed and demonstrated how to charge his phone's battery with this new portable charger. Adam left the store feeling stupid. He plugged the phone into the new charger and drove to the next appointment. Around five thirty he finished the last job and hurried to his truck, eager to talk to Joss. If the neighbors could keep her children overnight, they could have a quiet dinner, maybe he'd cook for her or they'd go out. He was willing to pay for the meal, even an expensive one. Between jobs he went home and packed an overnight bag; he stopped by Mama's, brought in the mail, and watered her ugly plant.

Joss's car sat in the driveway. When he called her from his truck, he noticed several saved messages that he had ignored all day. "Surprise. I'm outside. Is it okay to come in?"

"It's fine. I just took the kids over to the neighbors for the night. I'll pick them up tomorrow, late morning."

"Let me check my messages. I'll be right in."

"I'm going to jump in the shower. I'll leave the front door open."

The same unfamiliar number came up four times. A man from Overseas Airlines asked if he was Adam Werther; if so, he should call the following number right away. Adam punched in the number. A woman answered.

"This is Adam Werther. Someone from Overseas Airlines called me."

"Mr. Werther? You're Adam Werther? Lydia Werther's next of kin?"

"That's me. I'm Adam, her son."

"Mr. Werther, I'm Margie Strother with Overseas Airlines. This morning's flight 435 from Berlin made an emergency landing in North Carolina, not far from the Virginia line. We don't have complete information yet. Please come to the airport as soon as you can."

He didn't know his mother had taken a plane home. It couldn't be her. Well, he supposed it could be.

"I'm coming right now. Where's your terminal? What's your name, again?"

Adam ran to Joss's front door, phone still in hand and hurried to her bedroom. In her underwear with a towel wrapped around her head, she opened her arms. He halted in the doorway. "The airline left four messages about Mama's plane. It had an emergency landing in North Carolina. The person on the phone wouldn't say anything except to get to the airport. Go to the Overseas Air desk, concourse three."

He couldn't breathe too good. "Come with me? I'm sorry, this isn't what I wanted. The plane landed somewhere in North Carolina. They won't say much over the phone. Oh, I already said that?"

"The kids are with the O'Tooles, so that's one less problem. Let me get dressed. Sit down and take a few deep breaths."

He went to the kitchen, got ice, and poured a glass of water. The grinding sound of the ice tumbling from the dispenser sounded like a plane cracking up when it hit the ground.

In the living room everything looked the same; everything appeared to be in its place. Nothing inside him felt the same.

Two, maybe three shots of bourbon would settle his nerves. But. And here came the but, even one drink would cause problems later. He hoped he wouldn't forget what he knew, because times were tough for Joss. He wanted to stay by her side. Times would probably get tougher for him, too.

"Want me to drive?" Joss jingled her keys.

"Great. We go to the main terminal. We find the Overseas Airlines desk, concourse three."

Joss's hair was wet from her shower. Without makeup and jewelry, she was still beautiful and elegant. Classical music played on the car radio.

When the news came on, Adam snapped off the radio.

"You don't know." Her voice was low-pitched. "Everything could turn out fine. We'll hope for the best."

They parked a long distance from the building. Adam felt glad to stretch his legs and move fast. At the Overseas Airlines desk, they were directed to a room crowded with family members of people on flight 435.

Joss grabbed Adam's hand as a tall man hurried past them to the podium. The man studied a piece of paper and read in a slow, deliberate voice: "Flight 435 made an emergency landing at a county airport in North Carolina. Most passengers left the plane with minor injuries. They have been treated and are on their way here, due to arrive in about half an hour, forty minutes."

The man stopped, took off his glasses, wiped them, and put them on again. "Now I'm going to read the names on this list. If I call your name, please remain for further information. If I don't call your name, Ms. Wilson will take you to the gate to wait for your relatives." He pointed to a woman in a blue uniform, with an Overseas Airlines logo on her breast pocket.

Adam coughed. "He's got the list of wounded and dead people."

Joss nodded and appeared to hold her breath. Maybe it looked that way because he held his. The man read on and on. Adam counted with each name. One, two, three, four, five, six, seven, eight. Then he lost track.

The man stopped abruptly.

Adam and Joss stood. His heart pounding, he held Joss close. They hurried to join the larger group.

"You okay?"

"This feels too familiar, the waiting and fearing," she said. "My body feels like I'm going to faint if I don't find out something critical to my life. While I waited and waited for my mother to die. Before she was actively dying, there were the drinking years leading up to it.

"I'm so glad you have good news." Joss hung her head.

"And I'm so sorry about the fire," Adam whispered. "And all that's happened to your family since the fire." He led her out of the group. She leaned against a wall. He leaned his arms against the wall on either side of her, protecting her for privacy. Her face was red, teary, and swollen.

He touched her hair, which smelled clean, a shampoo smell. He whispered, "So much we can't predict or control, but we fool ourselves. Folks in AA kept telling me that only I could control my drinking, unless I got locked up or ended up in the hospital. But sometimes I didn't feel in control. I'm scared my logical mind won't win my inside arguments."

She nodded, moved sideways, and pushed him away. "Let's catch up to the others."

They hurried to the lounge and took seats a short distance from the crowd.

"Don't think I could stomach coffee," she said. "But I'd sure like a Pepsi."

"I'll get you one."

"No, let's wait. Maybe we'll stop somewhere after your mother arrives."

They waited and soon three people appeared, walking side by side through the tunnel. Every face solemn. A young man in a business suit, red-faced, eyes puffy from crying, tugged at a little girl's hand. The child's other arm wore a cast in a sling. People came up the tunnel slowly, some with bandages on their heads and arms.

Adam sat without moving.

"There she is!" He jumped up and plunged into the crowd gathering at the tunnel's edge.

His mother raised both arms, her pocketbook that dangled from her elbow suddenly swinging in the air. She rushed to him. They hugged, and both laughed.

Chapter Eighteen: Joss

JOSS WAVED, WAITING FOR ADAM'S truck to pull away from her house, before stumbling down the walk to her front door. Finally, she was alone with her thoughts. Adam planned to drive Lydia home and spend the night at her apartment to make sure she felt okay. Joss appreciated Adam's kindness and concern for his mother, yet she hoped they weren't overly attached.

Drinking decaf coffee on the patio, she stretched out on her favorite chaise longue and compared Adam to Phil. Adam had more positive traits. What foolish thinking—she hadn't known Adam long. She'd spent years with Phil, had two children with Phil. The comparison wasn't remotely fair. She disliked how easily she fell into such comparisons. Her sloppy thinking. While planning for her new future, and the kids' futures, she had to make smart decisions.

At the airport, when Adam spotted his mother, he'd moved with deliberation through the people, apologizing, yet not stopping and pushing through at a steady pace. Maybe all his talk about mammoths caused her to see him walk like a strong, graceful animal moving toward something he wanted. Joss smiled at the thought.

His mother, Lydia, with flyaway gray hair and ruddy cheeks, what joy when she raised her hands the very nanosecond she spotted Adam, disregarding her pocketbook hanging off her elbow and swinging in the air. A sparkly woman. Joss liked her intelligent, alive face.

The sky had turned gray, and Joss wondered about rain. She stretched out her arms, still thinking about the chaotic day that had started at quarter to six with breakfast and taking care of the baby. She'd dropped Geline off at day care, grocery shopped, then driven back home, where she picked up dirty coffee cups and toys, did the dishes, changed the sheets, put two loads of laundry in, and put away clean clothes. She'd spooned up a quick bowl of soup for lunch, packed baby clothes and toys to go to the O'Tooles'. Terpe had already packed her suitcase, eager to spend the night with them. Joss then drove to Geline's day care center, picked her up, drove home, put the baby in her carriage, and pushed it across the yard and through the hedge.

She looked at the mail in her lap and finished her coffee. Enough about the day, why bother reviewing the day's events? To congratulate herself? No, to remind herself she could hold everything together and still enjoy some things. Even before the fire, Phil had been an energy drain. Often, she felt relieved when he left the house. But her life wasn't over. She hoped a new phase had already begun.

Adam's mother had talked most of the way from the airport. She sat in the front seat and talked with Joss, finally turning to Adam in the back seat. With her guttural German accent, her voice ranged from low to high, while she described the plane's abrupt noises, the fierce wobbling with a dropping feeling. All this happened while she was struggling with her seat belt.

Lydia said, "Everyone on the plane talked louder, until they were yelling. 'What's happening? What's happening?' A few people ran down the aisles, screaming. The flight attendants ran after them, ordering them to put on seat belts and stay calm. Calm? Ridiculous!

"I thought someone threw up, the back of the plane smelled like vomit. I got a quick happy feeling when someone said we weren't over the ocean. I never looked out my window. At least our bodies would be found on land, and Adam could visit me in the cemetery." She reached into her pocketbook, pulled out a handkerchief, and wiped her eyes.

"Oh, Mama. You're safe now."

Lydia said, "I couldn't stand the thought of rotting at the bottom of the ocean."

Joss said, "Ooh. I never thought about it before. Yes, it's gruesome." She said no more, not wanting to interrupt Lydia's story. Mostly Lydia repeated what she had already said. She seemed to Joss to be in shock.

At Joss's house, before getting into her son's truck, Lydia took Joss's hand. For a minute or so, she examined Joss's face, searching for something. Suddenly Lydia's questioning expression changed, and she burst into a genuine smile that brought out small wrinkles at the corner of her eyes. Words of gratitude tumbled out, as she thanked Joss for driving Adam to the airport and for her kindness to Adam. "My son, my beautiful son!"

Joss replied she'd enjoyed meeting her and was relieved she'd arrived home safely.

Adam's mother had been a sharp contrast to Phil's parents. During their marriage Phil had told his parents over and over that Joss was a good person, a good wife and mother. Finally, they admitted they were uncomfortable because of Joss's education and wealth. No wife should have as much education as her husband, and also more money.

Joss glanced at her lap, sighing at the pile of mail. But one citronella candle on the table wasn't enough light for reading. She flipped through the envelopes and stopped at an envelope with large dark print in the left corner. News from the rehab center wouldn't be good. She blew out the candle and went inside, tossing the mail onto the kitchen table.

Although ready to get into bed, she decided to read Dr. Drummond's letter. He requested her to meet with him and Phil next week to discuss discharge planning. She balled up the letter and threw it on the floor. Phil coming home? Impossible.

She didn't sleep well. For breakfast she stuck half a bagel in the toaster oven and spooned plain yogurt into a bowl. The newspaper lay on the table; she must have brought it inside. The headline in large type might be important, but she didn't bother to read it.

The yogurt bowl sat empty, and the bagel now a pile of crumbs. She looked around the kitchen as if searching for the person who had her breakfast since she had no memory of eating. She should dress, maybe pull weeds or maybe work on the book. When would Adam call? Lately she'd felt distracted and always surprised to see she'd already done a chore. She reminded herself about all she'd done the day before, and she remembered it all.

Chapter Nineteen: Terpe

TERPE SQUIRMED, TRYING TO RESIST banging her feet against the chair. Mrs. O'Toole's kitchen made her feel cozy and sometimes happy. The old-timey cuckoo clock still ticked on the wall, and the same yellow oilcloth covered the kitchen table. An old-fashioned kitchen, like the rest of their house, with old brown furniture they called antiques. These neighbors were the first people to have moved into the neighborhood, long ago.

Geline was already down for her morning nap. Terpe lingered over her cereal so long it turned into a bowl of blobs. She chewed the bacon into bits and waited for Mr. O'Toole to leave so she could talk.

When it felt safe, she blurted to Mrs. O'Toole, "Mom has a boyfriend. My father has a girlfriend. I want to make them stop."

"What, my dear?" Mrs. O'Toole turned from the sink and set a dirty plate back on the counter.

"You heard what I said. It's gross! It's gross, isn't it?"

This served Mom right. She should have told Mrs. O'Toole what was going on. Dad acted like an awful person, and a big liar, too. And a chicken. He'd left her alone in the dining room and got some woman in uniform to push his wheelchair away. Mom with the yard guy. She hated them both.

"Oh, my dear, you must be mistaken. I can't believe that!" Mrs. O'Toole glanced around the kitchen, everywhere but at her.

"I'm not! Dad held his girlfriend's hand and their mouths were glued together just like on TV. This guy who fixed our electricity and picked up branches in our yard spent the night at my house. If my parents get a divorce, what'll happen to me and Geline?"

"My dear, are you sure? It all sounds rather circumstantial. I'm sure your parents love each other. They've been married a long while."

"You don't know Dad. You only know me and Mom. You don't understand. When she visits him in the hospital, he won't talk to her. Because you're a grown-up, you think you know more than a kid. But you don't."

Terpe stormed out of the kitchen, ran upstairs, and threw her things in her small suitcase. Halfway through making the bed, she stopped. She jumped on the bed and swung her legs over the edge. Grown-ups didn't notice things; they pretended they knew everything because they were old. They repeated the same things.

She hummed two verses of the "Terpe Song" Dad had written for her. Only her. His voice was in her head while he sang it. "Terpe, Terpe, sweeter than a Slurpee. Terpe, Terpe, a lively turkey, running and running around the yard. Terpe, Terpe sometimes she's burpy, and sometimes she's jerky like a puppet dog dancing and running around the yard!"

While Dad sang, he jumped around the living room jerking his arms sort of like a puppet on strings. They laughed until their stomachs hurt.

Mom had stood in the doorway, a yellow blouse covering her big baby-stomach, her hair piled on top of her head. She laughed. "You silly things. Wash up, it's time for dinner."

Terpe hated Mom's big stomach. When the baby came, the three of them would stop having fun. At first she got excited and said she wanted a baby brother. As the firstborn, she had a right to stay smarter and more beautiful than a sister. When Mom said a sister would arrive in September, Terpe ran down to the creek. What if her new sister turned out prettier or nicer? Yep, she knew she could be sulky. Babies didn't sulk. They were cute and hogged all the attention.

She and Dad wouldn't sing any more songs. Ever.

The tester bed made leg swinging fun. Very high, which made it fun. Her mind sped up when she swung her legs, thinking about the Maypole Dance at school.

She finished making the bed and hurried downstairs, her suitcase bumping her knees. She wanted to say good-bye to Mr. O'Toole because he wouldn't know anything about her parents.

But Mrs. O'Toole stood in the hall, waiting to pounce.

"I'm going home. Mom will come for Geline soon. Bye."

"Dear, don't you want to talk some more about your parents?" Mrs. O'Toole twisted her hands. "The kitchen's cleaned up, we can talk."

"I won't talk anymore. You didn't believe me, so why bother?"

When she moved closer, she smelled Mrs. O'Toole's lavender, which reminded her of fairies.

"Dear, you caught me by surprise. I promise I'm not mad, I'm concerned about what you imagine."

"What I told you is a real surprise. A true surprise. Bye." Terpe's cheeks felt hot. She wanted to bolt. Instead she walked slowly, opened and shut the front door with care. Mrs. O'Toole might grab her and try to make her talk. No, she wouldn't do that, but Terpe was disappointed the old woman didn't try harder. She pushed through the hedge, snapping off twigs and stomping them into the ground. A mistake to think an old woman would be the right person to tell.

Terpe opened and shut her back door without making noise. The radio played in Mom's bedroom; she was probably writing on her computer.

Terpe stopped at her mother's door. "As you can see, I'm home." She tried to smile, but it felt like too much effort.

"How was your night next door?"

"Last night we watched a stupid TV show about some family. The kind of people who are always hugging and smiling. Mr. O'Toole made popcorn with cheese on top. That's all."

"That's all? Mr. O'Toole didn't sing to you and Geline? He's pretty good, you know."

"No. He didn't sing."

Chapter Twenty: Joss

Joss AND ADAM DISCUSSED THEIR dinner plans over the phone. He blurted out that he felt happy Terpe would be spending the night out. Joss said nothing, feeling irritated until she reminded herself he didn't have children, so to him they were a nuisance.

Joss hurried though the hedge next door, wanting to see Geline. The toddler held out her arms, calling, "Ma, Mama." Joss sat at the kitchen table and tried to quiet the squirming child in her lap.

"Do you have a minute, dear?" Mrs. O'Toole twisted a napkin. "At breakfast Terpe didn't eat much, which is unusual. And she had the jitters, also unusual. She said you were romantically involved with someone, and your husband too. She's worried about the family."

Joss's mind went blank. While her thoughts spun like a top, she kissed Geline on the top of her head. "Phil and I were having problems before the fire. His injuries, including the head injuries, have made the situation worse. I'm sorry Terpe bothered you with family problems. Kids hate change, and I don't blame her. Adam's just a friend who is doing work around the house. The fire did more damage than is apparent from the outside. The upstairs hasn't been livable."

She held on to Geline and put on a wide-eyed innocent look, but she knew her answer wouldn't satisfy Mrs. O'Toole.

Her neighbor took a step back and leaned against the counter. "I told her I thought you and Phil had a good marriage. When I told her she must be mistaken, she got mad." Mrs. O'Toole stared down at Joss, her brows knitted. She wanted more.

Joss flicked her hand. "You know how kids mix up what they hear. They don't have the whole story. I'm sorry she bothered you. Things will settle down."

Joss stood and shifted Geline onto her hip. "I better get going. I've got to run some errands."

"I'll get the diaper bag." Mrs. O'Toole left the room.

Joss waited by the back door. The woman hurried back with Geline's bag.

Joss opened the door. "Thanks again for keeping the girls. I'm sorry about Terpe. Don't worry, she'll get over being mad."

Mrs. O'Toole's expression went from a frown to a fake smile.

Joss took the short path and pushed through the hedge. Her hands shook. What if Terpe had ruined the connection she had with these kind neighbors? The couple was wonderful with the kids, and the girls usually liked going over there. She could find other sitters, but neighbors had the advantage of convenience.

Until the fire and the chaos, Joss had enjoyed her children. Now their needs and demands were draining what little energy she had. How in the world could she work? She had to finish the manuscript on deadline. She could support the girls on her book advance, for maybe a year. She could supplement the income by tutoring grad students who had to have a second language to earn their PhD. But only a few students would select Greek. Her heart beat faster when she told herself she must write another book, as soon as she finished this one. But her books took time to research and write. She worked slowly and meticulously. When she felt calmer, she had to figure out more about the money.

Just last night, she told herself she'd do fine as a single parent. Which was the truth? Maybe both scenarios would turn out to be accurate: some of the time she'd do well as a single parent; sometimes she'd be grumpy and tired. Like she'd felt and acted since the fire, yet without Phil she'd stay calmer.

Adam distracted her from her problems with Phil and all the planning she had to do for the future. If she could get away with it, she'd lie about her relationship with him. It wasn't Mrs. O'Toole's business or anybody else's. Damn Terpe's big mouth.

Right on time, Adam knocked on her door. When she answered, he held out a yellow rose in green tissue paper. "For you," he said, blushing like a teenager when he handed it to her.

"How sweet. Thank you. I'll put it in water."

A pan covered with tinfoil sat on the doormat by his feet. He picked up the pan and they went to the kitchen.

"It smells like lasagna. The garlic smells delicious. You made this?"

"Yep, mostly. I bought the noodles, mixed ingredients, and stuffed them. Mama's a great cook and taught me tricks."

While they ate, she focused on the rose in a bud vase. When had Phil last given her roses, or any flowers? Maybe on her birthday a few years earlier? She couldn't remember.

Geline smeared food all over the high chair tray and her face.

"I'm letting her practice feeding herself," Joss said.

Adam laughed. "Looks like she needs a whole lot of practice."

After dinner, Joss wiped food off Geline and bounced her on her knee. Adam asked to hold Geline, but he picked her up at such an awkward angle, Geline twisted away and maneuvered to the floor.

"You're not familiar with babies, or children?" Joss said.

"Not really. There are kids in my neighborhood. I see them playing on the sidewalk, but I don't have any cousins in this country."

"Once Geline gets used to you, she'll follow you like a puppy. She's ready to go from creeping to walking. Every time I notice something dangerous, I stick it on a top shelf. I get on my hands and knees to survey everything: books on low shelves, anything on tables, light sockets, poisons."

"I guess you can't leave her in the crib. She climbed right off my lap, so she'll climb out of that?"

"Yes, she will. She's at that insatiably curious stage. Most of what they pick up goes in their mouths. Of course, parents want curious kids, it means they're smart."

"You mentioned a letter from the hospital?"

Her voice changed. "Yes. The doctor wants to meet with me and Phil to develop a discharge plan. Not looking forward to the meeting, but it is one step closer to being done with the whole mess. Well, not for Phil, but for me."

Adam poured a glass of water and added ice too fast, and when he jammed the overflow into the glass, two cubes spilled onto the floor. He picked up one and kicked the other under the table.

Joss picked up the cube and threw it in the sink. "Don't leave ice cubes on the floor! She could choke."

"Oh, sorry. You just talked about it, but it didn't connect."

She felt her face and neck flush. "Maybe you weren't listening."

"Yes. I'm listening. I said I'm sorry." He gulped down water. "I'm afraid your husband will come back to you. All this is happening fast."

"The past five months, almost six, hasn't felt fast for Phil and this family! The fire happened before Christmas. Phil will never live here again. He's delusional. Even if he claimed to recognize me, I don't want him here. How would I know if he were telling the truth? We're finished." She crossed her arms. "And that's that."

Geline screamed. Joss picked her up and the baby quieted. "She's tired. I'll put her in the crib. Back in a few minutes."

When Joss returned, he didn't look at her, but stared at the table. She carried on the conversation without asking what was wrong.

"I'll schedule the appointment for Monday or Tuesday. I want to get the social workers to find Phil a place long-term when he's finished at the rehab center. How's your mother doing?"

"Happy to be alive, but guilty that fifty people didn't make it. This morning she said, 'Go visit Joss. I have work to do, and my neighbors want to hear about my adventure.' Sometimes Mama's generous, but I hate that she keeps secrets, like flying off to Germany. And she can be a nag."

Joss took a Pepsi out of the refrigerator. "I tried not to nag Phil, even when he betrayed me. I noticed attractive men, but didn't play around. Maybe, if I didn't have kids. I don't know."

"Mama's scared I won't marry. She wants grandkids. I had a few romances, but none lasted more than a year, so I can't brag about being faithful for years. I'm getting used to the idea of an uncle and two cousins in Germany. Whoever they are, I don't want to live with them on a farm. Since I met you, I don't want to go out west, either."

She frowned. "This worry about your uncle seems over-blown. Most people would be happy to meet an uncle and maybe cousins, especially having a small family like you do. I'd be happy to discover I had more family I'd never met."

"But I'm not that easygoing. I don't like big changes." He gulped water. "I've thought about it. Maybe because Papa changed so fast when I was little, going from a nice person to a mean person. Starting when I turned twelve, I had to work in his butcher shop every Saturday. He kicked me, tripped me, and hit my back with a broom handle. Twice he punched me in the face."

"That's awful. Didn't your mom notice the bruises?"

"I'm a good liar. I told her boxes fell on me. Clothes hid most bruises. After a year, I told her. She went nuts on Papa. Whatever she said, he didn't bother me after that, but I still worked there on Saturdays."

"I bet she cut him off. Withholding sex is one of the few weapons some women have. No sex could do it."

"When I turned sixteen, I told Papa I was too busy with sports and school and wouldn't work at the shop. I said, 'I quit.' I surprised myself how tough I sounded."

"And?"

"I'd grown four or five inches, lifted weights, and played football. I looked down on him. I kept hoping he'd come after me, itching to beat the crap out of him. But the coward left the apartment whenever I tried to pick a fight. Very satisfying I could make him leave."

"Your father drank?"

"Nah. Waldo's father was the drunk. Grandpa beat Waldo. Mama made Papa give up alcohol. Maybe she used the no-sex threat then, too. Waldo just turned fifty-four when he died."

"No child deserves to be hit." She took his face in her hands and kissed him. They kept kissing. She slid her hand into his lap. They walked down the hall to her bedroom.

Adam washed the breakfast dishes while she dressed herself and Geline. After she took Geline next door, Joss went to her computer and printed out some pages. Adam wandered in with two cups of coffee.

"Writing this early?" He put her cup next to the computer.

"My second cup! Thanks." She sipped coffee. "Here's something I wrote a few years ago. Want to hear it?"

Adam settled in the chair, placing his coffee cup on his knee. "Okay."

She read:

My friends Luce and Polly were spending the night at my house. It's August, before ninth grade. We hung out at the pool and walked over to the barn to visit Thistle and Plenty. We fed them apples, petted and talked to them. They were lonesome because Daddy and Jackson took the other three on the circuit.

Sally made supper. We ate at the kitchen table. Polly kept cutting her eyes at Sally, as if she'd never seen a black person eat at a table. I kicked Polly under the table and gave her the finger. Later we went up to the sleeping porch and lay on the cots. The summer porch felt like a treetop swing, I pretended it swayed in the breeze. Screened in, but still we slapped mosquitoes.

We talked about sex. None of us had done more than kissing.

Smoke! I smelled smoke.

The sky near the barn flared orange. Dry grasses around the barn and the house were catching fire. I couldn't see the back of the barn, but I knew a grass fire would spread. Everything in a barn is flammable. The barn wasn't far from the house.

We ran downstairs. I almost yanked the phone off the wall calling the fire department. I grabbed Sally's hand, with Luce and Polly running behind, I yelled, "The pool, the pool!" We darted where the grass hadn't caught fire. Polly peed on herself. Her pediatrician said something didn't work in her bladder. I let her in the pool anyway.

Thistle and Plenty were braying.

"I'm getting the horses out!" I'd gotten halfway out the pool when Sally grabbed my nightgown and pulled me back.

"Don't touch me!" I jerked away. Two fire trucks came up the driveway. I raced to the truck and yelled,

"Horses first. Get the horses in the barn!" I ran toward the barn but a fireman grabbed me.

"Hey, kid, back in the pool! Go!"

"Thistle! Plenty!" I yelled at the man's shadow through smoke.

I obeyed. My nightgown stuck to my legs, running back to the pool.

Sally yelled, "Come on, precious girl."

We coughed and ducked and propped our arms on the side of the pool. The firemen aimed the hoses at the ground around the house. I kept yelling, "The barn! The barn!" Thistle and Plenty, their terrible shrieking. At last the firemen hosed down the barn, but too much smoke to see anything.

No sounds from the barn. When the smoke cleared, the barn looked wet and the doors were open.

I couldn't go down to the barn.

Sally took my hand. "I'm so sorry. I know how much you loved them." Luce and Polly were clinging to each other. The warm breeze gave me goose bumps.

Sally talked to the firemen.

Of course, Mother wasn't home, so I offered to drive her home, but she just shook her head. "You don't have a driver's license. Don't want you to get in no trouble."

"I don't care. The AC is on. I'll get some towels." We dried off. I ran downstairs. Sally talking on the kitchen phone. I gave her two towels. She hung up and said she had a ride. She waited on the front porch.

I yelled to Polly and Luce to get back in bed. I'd come up in a few minutes.

I sat on the staircase. At eleven o'clock, Mother's footsteps on the gravel driveway. The key in the door. The tapping of high heels in the hall. Whiskey and cigarette smells.

"You're late. The barn burned down. Thistle and Plenty died."

Mother said, "Oh, my God! How terrible. You look okay, so that's good." She glanced around the foyer. "I'm glad it didn't get to the house. I'll go check the insurance. That barn cost big money."

I went upstairs and lay on my cot. My friends were asleep.

Joss took a gulp of coffee. "That's it."

Adam stared at the floor. Finally, he said, "Your horses died, and last Christmas your house almost burned up? What caused the barn fire?"

Joss thought, *I did.* But she didn't say it. If she'd been outside, she would've spotted the fire when it started. She could have put it out with the hose.

Losing the horses became a marker, a date more important than her own birthday. Events either happened before, or after, the barn fire. Her mind darted to the following August when her mother died at forty-three.

Joss quickly turned from that memory. "Later the fire department said a cigarette smoldering in the barn had caused the fire. Our groom smoked, but never anywhere near the barn if he was smoking. Horses were his life. A group of neighborhood kids used to sneak into our yard hoping our pool gate would be open so they could swim. I'd seen those kids smoking. I'm guessing they ducked into the barn to pet the horses. One of them, or all of them, were smoking. Maybe they heard someone coming and left in a hurry."

"Your family's rich," Adam said. "Horses, a big house, and a pool. Even without photos I can imagine your life."

"No. You can't. Lots of possessions don't mean happiness. When my brother, Jackson, started fourth grade, and I started first grade, my parents began disappearing. Off in different directions. By high school, Mother rarely stayed home. Occasionally she breezed in for dinner, sat at the table, and talked with us kids for a few minutes. But she didn't eat with us. She had cocktails and ate dinners with friends.

"Daddy traveled the race circuit, hobnobbing with horse owners and doing whatever those men did at the track. And he had an office in the city and traveled. I never knew what business and stopped asking because he wouldn't talk about it."

Adam asked, "Something illegal?"

"I imagined different things. A playful person, he made fun of business like it didn't matter. The summer my older brother turned thirteen, Daddy started taking him to the races for the whole summer. Daddy never let me come. He said racetracks were no place for girls. I rode much better than my brother. Daddy knew I adored horses, but no matter how much I pleaded, he wouldn't relent. When Daddy was home, we rode together. Mostly I rode with the groom or by myself, even though I was forbidden to ride alone, for safety reasons. Nothing bad ever happened when I rode alone. Of course.

"My brother and I fought. He pestered me to play games. Usually I wouldn't, and sometimes just to be mean, I ignored him. He pulled the heads off my dolls, cut up my party dresses, and hung them back on the hangers. I opened my closet and found tatters hanging there. Once he built a bonfire out by the pool and burned my fashion magazines and some favorite books.

"Sally always played peacemaker. She said someday we'd be sorry we acted so hateful. She said we'd grow to understand that we weren't really mad at each other. Jacks and I sort of got her meaning. As we got older we understood completely."

"You were lucky," Adam said. "I always wanted someone to play with. I can still feel the silence in that apartment when I go visit Mama. Like the quiet is inside the walls. It's kinda creepy."

"If Mother and Daddy went out, Sally set the kitchen table and the three of us ate dinner together. Sometimes she got me and my brother laughing. We wouldn't fight for a few days. If one or both parents happened to be home, Sally ate alone in the kitchen. I hated that!"

Adam said, "Mama said that was the way it had always been in the South."

"So, you think it's a good custom because it has always been that way? A good Southern custom?"

"Well." Adam stopped. "Uh. I dunno, I guess the South will keep its ways."

"You think customs, even if they're evil, shouldn't be changed? The South has some gracious customs, but this hatred is terrible. Inhuman, an awful way to treat any person. We will fix it."

Adam didn't answer. His head hung down.

Joss took a breath, trying not to be irritable, wanting to finish talking about her brother. "Jacks drifted away. He had summers with Daddy and of course school, sports, and girls.

"One day mother complained to me about Sally taking over her role. I remember yelling at her, "She's trying to fill the hole you leave." Mother slapped me so hard I fell against the refrigerator. But I laughed in her face, stuck out my tongue, and said her slap didn't hurt. She left the room. I didn't speak to her for three or four days.

"Sally never married or had children. Jacks and I were basically her children."

Adam tried to pull her close.

She moved away and told him to go home. He left quietly. Later she understood she wasn't completely mad at him, just blowing off steam at her dead mother. She wondered if she'd ever forgive her mother. While getting ready for bed, Joss thought about events after her mother died. How her best friends, Polly and Luce, drifted away. Probably their parents thought her family completely unstable, first a fire killing the horses, followed by her mother dying young.

The three friends still ate lunch together at school, but they didn't call or ask Joss to do anything with them. Joss recalled being too hurt to ask why they'd deserted her. She kept hoping one of them would have the courage to tell her why. The truth, not an excuse. Did they think her too weak for the truth? Now weekends felt empty and aimless. She couldn't wait to grow up, to leave home for college and begin a different, wonderful life.

Chapter Twenty-One: Terpe

TERPE FELT HAPPY HER MOM let her sleep over at Zoe's house on Saturday night. They sat on her bed in their pajamas, listening to music and talking. Terpe took a deep breath before blurting out about her dad being in the hospital and rehab. She told her what the principal said about the class apology.

Zoe yawned. "Let me tell you, an apology's no big deal. The principal's a bitch. Still, you got off light. Both my older sister and brother used to skip school. They got suspended all the time! They're doing fine now."

She reached over and took Terpe by the shoulders. "An apology will only last a few minutes. You'll see. We'll laugh about the bitch at recess!"

Terpe laughed and clutched her stomach.

Zoe didn't say anything about Terpe's father being in the hospital, so Terpe didn't bring it up again. She felt relieved by what her friend said about the suspension and apology. They went downstairs, ate bowlfuls of chocolate ice cream, and watched some stupid sitcom on TV.

On Sunday evening, Terpe practiced her speech over and over in front of her bedroom mirror, but Monday morning she woke with her stomach in knots. She didn't eat breakfast, but her mother didn't notice.

On the school bus, she tried to think about something else, but her thoughts kept racing. When she walked to the front of the class, of course, she tried to stop her knees from trembling. With her eyes fixed on the teacher, she supposed she appeared sincere. Her speech probably lasted about two minutes. She walked slowly back to her desk and fell into her seat, with no idea of what she'd said. The teacher nodded, so she must have done okay.

The rest of the day, she felt a surge of energy, unusual because Mondays were naturally awful. Today she smiled at everyone in the hall between classes. During history class she considered letting her hair grow so she could curl it, like Zoe's. When she grew older, she intended to buy blonde hair dye, even though she couldn't imagine herself as a blonde. What about her dark eyebrows? Would she have to dye them, too?

Mom said she could invite her friend to sleep over next Saturday night for a celebration, now that her room looked good. Zoe could help Terpe decorate because her room should look much more grown-up. Maybe Mom would take them to the mall to buy posters.

A few days later, Terpe rode home on the school bus instead of with Mom. When she jumped off the bus, she galloped home, making happy horse whinny sounds on her way. Her hair flew loose like the mane of her imaginary horse. At last year's Maypole Dance, the girls had galloped around, their skirts like balloons twirling to the record music, their shoes zooming over the grass. When the dance ended, the younger girls handed out blocks of pink, brown, and white ice cream. Filled with sounds, she made up a song to the beat of the dance. The Maypole Dance meant school would be over for the year.

Last spring Mom watched, but she wouldn't come this year. Too busy and upset. Terpe didn't even remind her the dance would be coming up soon. Since the fire, Mom sometimes moved like molasses while talking to herself like a crazy person.

Sometimes memories fell on Terpe like a truck, reminding her why she didn't deserve happiness. Mom should punish her for not remembering Dad had been sleeping in the den the night of the fire, in the room right next to hers. She should have woken him first. If the fire had come into her room first, she'd be in the hospital. Now she and Geline might not have a father.

The first thing Terpe noticed when she got home was that Yard Guy's truck wasn't parked in front of the house. She found Mom in the kitchen chopping carrots and celery for a stew. She poured a glass of milk and grabbed an orange from the crisper.

"You look sad, Mom."

"I talked with the doctor about where Dad would live. His physical rehab has progressed, and the doctor told me he could leave that place."

"You've already told me all that. Are you getting forgetful?"

Mom used her patient voice. "Sweetie, if your father came here, he might get scared and run away. Or try to hurt me or you and your sister. The medicine hasn't helped much. The doctor also said some people with Capgras believe imposters are tricking them, and, well, they can get violent."

"Don't forget about his girlfriend. Still, I want him to come home."

Mom made a hissing noise. "I haven't forgotten. I don't want to talk about her."

"I want him to come home."

"You're not listening to what I said. He could get violent! He is never coming home."

Terpe turned away. "Mom, I did hear you. But I just never thought about Dad running away or getting violent. I don't want him to come if he's scary." She faced her mother. "Because I couldn't have Zoe or anyone over."

"It's hard to think about."

With a pouty mouth and a loud sigh, Terpe left the room.

Chapter Twenty-Two: Joss

Joss called Dr. Drummond at eight-thirty Monday morning. He answered his own phone and scheduled her for eleven o'clock that day. Driving in heavy traffic, her confidence ebbed. She looked at herself in the rearview mirror. She hadn't even combed her hair. She growled and forced herself not to pound the steering wheel and curse every time someone cut her off in traffic. Instead, she shouted louder than the radio's music. No backing down. Under no circumstances could Phil move back into her house.

She ran a comb through her knotty hair, combing until it looked normal. In Dr. Drummond's office, her hands felt sweaty. She wished she had on gloves. Phil sat slouched in a chair, a walker next to him. She picked a straight-backed chair as far away from Phil as possible, arranging herself so that Dr. Drummond sat between them.

The doctor turned to her. "We're here to make plans for your husband's discharge. Your husband and I have been talking about that in our recent sessions. You've been giving the situation some thought?"

"Of course." She clenched her fists, trying to appear composed. She focused on Dr. Drummond and watched Phil out of the corner of her eye. "I can't imagine him coming home, for several reasons, as I explained to you last week. Even before the fire, Phil had been having an affair. My daughter walked in on Phil, right here in the dining room, and saw him holding hands with this woman, even kissing her. In my daughter's words they were 'glued together.' This incident occurred in a public place with a roomful of people watching."

She stopped, debating whether to reveal the next thing. Could they hear her heart pounding?

She pointed at Phil. "The fire department detectives and I have been talking. In a few days I should know whether his girlfriend caused the fire at our house."

Phil wobbled to his feet. "What? Are you out of your god-damn mind? You think Vivienne started the fire?" He raised his arm and lost his balance. Close to falling, he sank into his chair.

She felt a surge of sadness at his frailty. His sad mouth made her turn away.

Her voice sounded loud in her ears. "The detectives are sure it was arson and are interrogating suspects. This woman Vivienne works in the history department's office, and her office and Phil's are close together. How convenient.

"Also, he recognizes his girlfriend, unlike me." Joss waited for her remark to get a rise out of Phil, or for him to deny the affair. He stared at the wall.

"I'm mad as hell. How convenient to call me an imposter. He has already left me out of his life. While I know about his head injury, still, I do wonder about this whole imposter thing. Why would he even consider living in an imposter's house?

"I plan to file for divorce. Probably sell the house and move. We have good insurance, so paying for long-term care should be okay. At least for a while. His parents should help out, too."

Phil lifted his shoulders. "Why should I care what you do?"

"See, there it is! That's how he acts toward me." She felt tears coming and looked away from them both.

When she turned back, Dr. Drummond had shut his eyes and didn't speak for a couple of minutes, which felt like an hour to Joss.

The doctor said, "All right, I'll proceed with finding a place where your husband can live. I'm thinking of a beautiful facility called The Ivy. I'll suggest this as a good option to his social worker."

Joss stood. "A social worker will find him something?"

"Yes, she'll be calling you for input. Thank you for coming."

She shook Dr. Drummond's hand. "I appreciate your helping Phil. I hope you'll be able to find a medicine that works."

Phil mumbled, "I don't need more pills." His expression was blank, only his body was in the room. His arms rested on his thighs, his hands hung loose between his legs, and his lips had no color. Sad and lost, a reflection of how she felt.

All the way home, she cried and found herself sitting in her own driveway. The house looked huge, empty, and haunted. She pulled back out of the driveway and drove to the coffee shop. As she stood in line, her phone rang. Adam's number came up. She let the call go to voice mail. The people in front of her ordered sandwiches. After ordering a latte, she hesitated. No appetite, but still, she should eat, so she wouldn't be grumpy with the children. Peering into the glass case, she picked a plate of cheeses, tomatoes, celery sticks, and crackers. She peeled off the Saran Wrap and ate, hoping she could keep the food down.

Still avoiding her empty house, she busied herself with errands and later parked her car in the front of the pickup line at Terpe's school. She avoided looking at the building, not wanting to see pain on her daughter's face when she came running down the sidewalk. Terpe's apology had probably been a disaster. No, Joss swallowed hard, for sure it had been a disaster.

Terpe opened the car door, laughing. "Guess what?" She slid across the seat. "'Apology Monday,' went great! I gave my speech, and the teacher kept nodding. Of course, she didn't smile. I talked so fast later I couldn't remember anything I said! Some of the girls congratulated me after class. One girl told me I got off easy. Everybody hates the principal.

"I think you and I tricked Miss Pollard good. You were really nice, and I guess she didn't expect that. She's probably used to nasty parents.

"Anyway, Zoe and three other girls sat with me at lunch."

"Sweetie, close the door. Cars are backing up." Joss's tears stung her eyes. "I'm so proud of you. How brave you were. And no, you didn't get off easy. Miss Pollard owed you a lot of consideration."

"Mom, you have the worst problems. And Dad, too. Is he any better?"

"I had an appointment this morning with Dr. Drummond and your father. They'll find him a place to live."

"Are you happy?" Terpe squirmed in the seat.

"No. I'm not happy. But there's no other way."

"I hope Dad gets well."

"Let's get Geline. Maybe the three of us will sing songs in the car."

"That yard guy won't be coming over tonight, will he?"

"Adam's not a teenaged yard guy, he's only a few years younger than I am. He was nice to rake our yard. He's an electrician and owns a business. He lives in an apartment in the city."

"I don't like him."

"You don't have to. But be polite. He hasn't done anything to you except try to be kind."

"Whatever. Whatever." Terpe displayed her obvious fake smiles. One of her favored ways to express anger.

"You're learning more smart-mouth from your new friend, Zoe? Don't. I won't tolerate it."

Terpe didn't respond.

"I don't expect Adam will come over tonight."

Terpe didn't respond.

Joss knew she wouldn't be polite. If she were in Terpe's place, she'd feel the same way. Still, she wouldn't give up Adam to please her daughter. She had to keep reminding her to be polite because it would take her a long way in life, especially since she was prone to turn quiet with that sulky, pouty mouth. This attitude would follow her through life, unless she made an effort to talk about why she felt mad.

Joss sighed at yet another thing she couldn't fix. She hurried up the steps of the day care center, thinking the thing with Adam could fall apart any time. For now, they enjoyed each other, and she got a break from the rest of her life. Back at the car with Geline, she found Terpe singing with the radio. Joss joined her. Geline screamed and babbled, swinging her arms.

At home Terpe chopped vegetables. Joss stabbed the baking potatoes, making holes so they wouldn't explode in the microwave. She sliced meatloaf while Terpe set the table in the dining room instead of the kitchen where they usually ate. She lugged Geline's high chair to the dining room table. They took turns feeding the baby.

Terpe even offered to tell her what had happened the day she ran away from the rehab center.

Joss sighed. "Not tonight. I'm happy your apology went well. You were a brave girl! Maybe tomorrow we'll go to the coffee shop after I pick you up from school. Maybe that's a good time to tell me."

Later Joss passed through the dining room and saw Terpe reading a textbook, papers spread out on the dining room table. At least she appeared to be studying.

"Almost time for lights out."

Joss got ready for bed. Adam had called twice more, but she didn't pick up. At eight forty-five she went to the dining room. "Time for bed. You'll be dragging if you don't get to bed now."

Terpe slammed the book shut. "Just finished a test review."

"Good. Sweetie, please, no reading tonight." She laid her hand gently on Terpe's head. Terpe didn't respond.

Joss set her cell phone by her bed, checked to make sure she'd turned it off, and switched off the landline.

In the morning, Joss turned on the landline while she made coffee. Back at her place on the patio, she wrote down her mental list. First, make an appointment with a lawyer to go over her medical power of attorney, her power of attorney, her will, the divorce, and the sale of the house. Make an appointment with her broker. Find a real estate agent. Too much, yet she had to make a start.

Geline cried, and a few minutes later Terpe's alarm clock went off.

Robot-like, Joss went into the kitchen and opened the refrigerator. She gazed at the contents, but nothing registered. She closed the door and opened it again, trying to focus on food, on breakfast.

After a meager meal, she dressed, monitoring Terpe dressing the baby. Terpe ran for the school bus, and Joss dropped off Geline at day care.

At the coffee shop, she chose a small table in the back. She took out her address book to call the lawyer that Dreama had recommended. The second she turned on her cell, it rang.

"Mrs. Montgomery, Jim Thompson. I'm with the fire department. Thank you for the information on Mr. Montgomery's girlfriend. We've interviewed her and expect more developments soon. Your husband's memory loss means he isn't reliable. Unless you think he might remember something, we won't interview him."

Her stomach hurt. "Don't bother with Phil. He's still very confused from the head injury. If the girlfriend's housemate sent any letters to Phil, they would have been delivered to Phil at the college. I suggest checking with his department if you haven't already. From the first, I suspected arson, so I went through

Phil's emails on his home computer, but I found nothing unusual. We live in a safe neighborhood. But her boyfriend could have a motive to burn up our house."

"You have your husband's computer password?"

"Sure, it's 27OldPoemsZ. And he has my password. Until the past year or so, we didn't have secrets. Or, at least I thought we didn't. He could have another account I don't know about."

"We're on it. Thanks for the information."

"Thanks for calling." She hung up, feeling rattled. Sick to her stomach, she rushed to the restroom.

Phil kept making her life miserable. Arson, she'd known it all along. But would this saga ever end? A few weeks earlier, at the rehab center, she and Phil's parents had accidentally converged from opposite halls. They stumbled through small talk about the weather. Joss claimed she had to run errands and would come back later. She wished them a good visit with Phil. His parents smiled, maybe the only time they ever meant it.

Joss told herself she felt glad to give them time, actually hoping they'd enjoy their visit with Phil, but by the time she reached her car, she was trembling with anger. She jammed her key in the ignition and sped out of the parking lot, almost sideswiping a car coming in the other direction.

Chapter Twenty-Three: *Phil*

PHIL PRESSED HIS HANDS AGAINST his forehead to make the pictures disappear, but the one of his mother's face—from one Sunday morning when he was about eight—moved closer.

That morning her mouth looked dark and evil, covered with purple-black lipstick. Her eyebrows were smudged black. An old-fashioned fox fur curled around her neck; her beige wool suit showed off her figure. She always showed off, but did his father even notice? A lot of the time his father left the room, even when he was sitting right there. Phil watched his father glance around as if searching for something, a puzzled expression on his face. Was he bewildered, wondering who these other two people were?

Phil's mother shrieked at him. "Wear a tie!" Her voice closed in. "Don't dare look away from me, son. Put on the goddamn tie. Hurry, we'll be late." Before he could nod yes, her hand flew at him. "Don't embarrass us." His cheek burned with her slap.

From the back seat of the car, Phil studied his father's profile. His father was humming to himself in a soft voice, and his hands appeared loose and relaxed on the steering wheel. Phil tried to imitate his father's tranquility by loosening his fists and humming a little bit. But his heart kept beating fast, and he stopped humming and made fists again. At eight, he started to worry after watching a man in a TV movie have a heart attack and die.

His mother turned, reached across her seat to the back, and swung her hand at him. When Phil ducked, she frowned. "Your tie's still crooked. Straighten your goddamn tie. Don't you use mirrors?"

They walked up the church steps. Beautiful organ music rolled down through the open front doors. Once inside, the glow of candles and the smell of incense welcomed him. At first.

But Phil hated Sundays and church, and hated being trapped in the middle of the pew with a parent on each side. Once they settled in the pew, he wiggled, trying to lean away from his mother, but where to go? During prayers, he prayed for his mother's fur to come alive and choke her. He imagined laughing when her eyes popped out of her head, and all the blood poured out of her eye sockets. He wouldn't try to help. He would watch her bleed to death.

His thoughts and the pictures in his mind made his stomach hurt. The bacon, orange juice, and eggs rumbled, fell down into his bowels. He doubled over, wishing he hadn't eaten breakfast because he should have known this would happen.

Stomach problems happened a lot. Mother slapped him and yelled a lot.

No escape until Communion, when people would be moving around. As soon as Communion music began, he stood. He ignored his mother's tug on his sleeve and hurried to the bathroom. After he finished on the toilet, he didn't want to leave the safe room. No incense would cover his stench.

Phil opened his eyes to stop the pictures.

He laid his hands on his chest to soothe his heart. Dr. Drummond told him he must learn ways to calm himself. Doc D. said if he practiced, he could change his sad and bad thoughts into happier ones. *Think. Okay, here comes a good thought*: The

Ivy looked like a much nicer place to live, much better than the hospital or the rehab center. Except for the nurses' station, the building didn't feel like a hospital. Smaller and quieter, almost like a large house. He had his own room and didn't have to deal with a dull roommate. He could walk around the courtyard safe inside the high, ivy-covered serpentine brick walls. The courtyard reminded him of old courtyards in London.

The first day at The Ivy, Phil planned to cheek two pills to see if he could get away with being sneaky. Women always told him he had a charming smile. The proof came when a nurse walked into his room. She handed him a pleated cup, looked down, and fiddled with a button on her sweater. She should be watching him swallow pills. After a few more seconds, she left. Her medicine cart rattled down the hall. He smiled.

How many pills would they give him every day? Not important. He would decide. It would be fun to make up a pill game. For two days he took the red and blue ones, then switched to three white ones and back to red and blue. The ones he saved he put into an empty toilet paper roll and stuffed both ends with toilet paper to keep the pills safe. He hid the roll in his underwear drawer.

Like that big day when he gave his birthday present money back to his father, his mind sped up with thoughts. He saw himself riding his bike to the river, staring at the fast-moving water and wondering why he had turned into a terrible son. How would it feel to jump in the river, bash himself on the rocks, and make everything go away? He still felt the same way about himself. Still that selfish, greedy boy.

The Ivy wasn't near the river he used to visit as a kid. He didn't have the energy to go far, the fault of all the pills they forced him to take. Thank goodness he had the sense to only take half of them each day.

What if he got lost searching for the river? Someone would catch him and put him in jail forever. They'd call his parents.

Would they call his parents? They were so old and sad now, they couldn't help him anymore. Suddenly he felt happy about his mother growing old, maybe even dead. He and his dad might get along then and talk a lot more without her around.

Instead of the river, he had all these pills. He'd always kept an escape hatch in mind.

Doc D. came to see him once a week. The man was okay, even though he asked confusing questions and wrote everything in a notebook. Why did the doc take notes? Maybe the guy had to spy on him? Last week when the doc asked for his full name, Phil began to wonder what that question meant. Of course he knew his first name, but couldn't remember his middle or last name, no matter how hard he tried. After a few minutes of trying, he remembered his last name. An obvious reason to forget such a name, because of all the letters. His memory was okay because he could remember his hamster's name, from fourth grade. Sir Teddy Hamster. The doc laughed when he heard the hamster's name.

The next time Doc D. came, he brought three heavy books. He wanted Phil to have something better to read than the detective paperbacks in the lounge. Surprised, Phil thanked him. He really meant it. Later while leafing through the books with thick pages, he discovered that under their fancy covers was just boring, slow writing. Pedantic. Decorative books that he didn't plan to read. His intellect was still way above that drivel.

Phil stacked the books on his nightstand. They reminded him he remained a respected and admired professor.

The next day he chose the thickest book, took it into the bathroom, and closed the door. With a nail and a pair of child's scissors he'd stolen from the craft room, he went to work. Using the nail, he gently poked at the paper, making a circle wide enough for a lot of pills. He used the scissors to finish the cut. He did the first five pages, careful to leave the borders intact. Between Doc D. appointments, crafts, group therapy, and exercise, he slipped the trash into his pocket and walked around the courtyard at a slow pace, waiting until no one was around. A tall hedge camouflaged the trash cans. He sneaked behind the hedge and dropped the paper into a can.

Once the hole in the book looked deep enough, he dumped the pills from the toilet paper roll into it. He put the book on the nightstand between the other two books. Every day he dropped in two or three more pills. His rainbow of pills made him feel giddy.

Could this be June? Or July? The days felt much warmer, and even the nights felt muggy when he went outside. One of the nurses told him the date, again. Already? He must be sleeping away the time. The fire happened around some holiday, he felt pretty sure it was Christmas. For months he'd wheeled and finally shuffled along on shiny linoleum floors, and for months he'd slept in steel beds and talked with strangers. Sometimes when he walked away from someone, he couldn't remember a word of what the person had said, or even what he might have said. Or had he talked at all?

His academic work must be piling up. Who had taken over his classes? He hoped his colleagues were okay. Had the department suffered from budget cuts? He did miss eating lunch with some of them.

A colleague did visit him last week, or maybe the week before. Yes, they'd sat on a bench in the courtyard under the trees, grateful for shade. The bright sun made patches on the lawn. He couldn't remember the guy's name, but knew his office was down the hall from his own. Phil thought he taught ancient history. They'd had a few laughs. Back inside he saw black spots at first. He needed to find his sunglasses right away. Maybe they were in one of his dresser drawers.

The courtyard was the nicest area at The Ivy. At one time this place had been a mansion. He liked some features: five or six stained-glass windows and mullion windows were everywhere.

A chandelier hung in the entrance hall, and another hung in the huge group therapy room. The therapy room chandelier looked silly, out of place with metal desks, posters with cheerful slogans, and folding chairs arranged in a circle, sometimes two circles. These beautiful touches helped him forget his captivity, sometimes.

Did he miss his students? Hell no. Not true, he missed a few. Joss was right—he should have been a full-time researcher. He detested slackers, ordinary students who turned into whiners before the end of the semester. Always begging for extra time to finish papers, wanting to do something easy for extra credit. The two or maybe three geniuses, the attentive, sharp students who met deadlines without complaint, who took on extra projects. Those students he liked. Even if they acted weird, as some very bright kids tended to do, the weird factor didn't matter. Actually, he kind of liked weird stuff; the behavior amused him.

What about the den in his burned-up house? He missed it, except for the lumpy sofa. Joss had bought him a colorful oriental rug for his birthday, after workers finished the addition. She'd put two comfortable chairs in the room, and he added shelves for his biographies, eighteenth-century poetry, and history books. Where he'd been sleeping when the house burned down.

Do not think about that den. Do not think about that house.

Somehow Terpe found The Ivy. She visited every night before he fell asleep. She sat cross-legged on the windowsill, calling to him, grinning and whispering, asking him to talk and sing songs with her. He sat up in bed, turned on the light, and studied the double windows covered with blinds and pale curtains. The blinds and curtains did not move, but she'd moved to another part of the room. Her song came and went, came and went, and sometimes she floated near the ceiling, just staring down at him for a long time and refusing to talk. She disappeared. No longer in the room. He could not find her, not even her whiny voice.

Despite crawling under the bed in search of the crying baby, he couldn't find his other daughter either. She should be lying in her comfortable crib, but a crib could not fit under his bed. His bed sat too close to the floor.

Joss floated through the window and crawled into bed with him. She stroked his head that always hurt now. This would be the only time his weird headache went away. Even if he took all the pills he should take, his headache remained. At least sometimes he took every pill; anyway, he might have that day.

His head on his soft pillow, he pulled up the covers over his eyes. Only the light in the hallway stayed on all night. He must not think about Joss and his daughters. Joss had sold the house and moved to Mexico? Or New Mexico? She liked one of those places.

This afternoon in group therapy, he'd tried to figure out where Joss went, so he could answer some guy's question about where his wife lived now. Just last night she'd crawled in bed with him. Did she drive back from New Mexico just to visit? He hoped she'd moved back to town, but where?

Joss got in the way of his thinking because suddenly outside the group therapy room, standing in the lobby—Vivienne. No kiss hello in the lobby. They went to his room because she said she wanted privacy. He could have visits in his room because, right, because he had good behavior.

On the edge of his bed, he leaned forward and waited for something to happen. She sat in the chair and crossed her legs. He waited, but he didn't know why he couldn't say anything, couldn't even open his mouth. She uncrossed her legs, told him the man she lived with wasn't a roommate. All along he'd been her lover, too. She liked sleeping with both of them. But her boyfriend did bad deeds. He got locked up, even though she said he wasn't guilty.

She said she'll stick, stick, stick with her boyfriend. Even if he stayed in jail, she'd visit him. Her voice sounded far away.

Phil watched her mouth move. Suddenly she made a sound like a hissing snake when she said "stick, stick, stick" by him.

He tried to reach for her hand. He needed to do something important. Yes, he had to tell her he loved her. But he couldn't reach her from his chair. Standing, he moved to her. He smelled her summery perfume, making his heart race.

She jumped out of the chair. "Stop it!" Her hands, tiny hands, pushed against his chest. "Phil, Phil, Phil," she said in a sad voice before turning away.

What had gone wrong? He clutched the door handle to keep from falling.

She turned to the door and walked by him. Down the hall, her heels clicked on the linoleum until the sound finished. Another lover? When did she have time for another man? They'd spent nights together for? Oh, he couldn't remember, but he guessed they'd had sex for months. Why would her lover boy land in jail?

Too late. Vivienne won't come back.

Group therapy the next day ended with voices calling him away from thinking about Vivienne. He stood to leave the room but got distracted in conversation with a new resident. The poor guy was still sitting in a wheelchair just like he'd been. He did remember the wheelchair.

While walking down the hall, Phil pretended to appear normal, and sometimes he smiled when he passed a staff person. He no longer needed any help getting back to his room; the familiar halls led him back to his room with its remarkable view of the courtyard.

But this could not be his house. Not home.

As if a knife had cut hunks out of his body, he knew his insides were bleeding. His life, probably all lives, when you got to the bottom, ended cruelly.

People in his life. Ghosts. Imposters.

Back in his room, he thought about what Doc D. had told him. He had to take a nap when he felt confused. Rest his brain.

He laughed because when he peered across his room, his brain already knew what to do. His brain lay on a pillow on the bed. His whole head with lots of hair like when he was a young man and full of energy. The brain just lay there with its eyes closed. Dead? The hair could be thick with blood. He couldn't really see. The head probably fell asleep.

Make the total body disappear.

His plastic water glass sat on the edge of the bathroom sink. The water had to be very cold, so the pills wouldn't stick in his throat. Halfway through swallowing, he ran more water. He kept going until he finished all of them. The pills tasted awful. Bitter.

He leaned over the toilet, stuck his middle finger down his throat, as far as it would go. Nothing came back up.

In the middle of his bedroom, he felt unsure. A note, a proper note, in case they ever found Joss.

The room wobbled. Doc D. would say he needed a nap. Later he would find some paper and a pencil. Yesterday, he put a pencil on top of the dresser. There must be one sitting on the dresser. His room turned blurry. He staggered to his bed. Sleep.

Chapter Twenty-Four: Joss

JOSS STARED AT THE DREGS of coffee in her cup and glanced at the coffee shop wall. Why paint gory bodies in an unframed canvas? Paintings not even hanging on nails, but scotch-taped right to the wall. She supposed these paintings were intended to make some sort of statement. To her it looked sloppy. She turned away, summoned a waitress, and ordered another latte.

She glanced at a morning paper that someone had left on the table. On the front page, near the bottom in medium print, she read: "Former Volunteer Fireman Arrested for Arson."

"Otis Jordan, 29, of 12 N. 15th Street has been arrested and charged with arson. The police report stated he confessed to setting fire to a house at 4784 Elm Street. The police had cooperation from his housemate and former girlfriend. Mr. Jordan is due in court July 7. Bond has been set at $500,000."

This Jordan guy, he's the one. 4784 Elm was her address. Joss's heart pounded.

The fellow behind the counter called her name, and she picked up her latte. Back at her table, she tried to fill in some details. Vivienne had probably admitted to a year-long affair with Phil, told police the guy was never a roommate, rather a boyfriend she kept around for rent and groceries and sex. Maybe this guy claimed he couldn't remember where he was the night of the fire. Later he claimed he'd been out drinking with friends. The police got a warrant. Joss figured they'd find gas cans. For a former volunteer fireman, setting a fire would be easy.

What kind of woman lived with a boyfriend for rent money and slept with him as well as a married man? Maybe a lot of women did this; she didn't know. For Vivienne, Phil's purpose must have been the prestige of sleeping with a college professor, bragging rights with her friends.

How many families had Vivienne ruined? Yet the woman filled in only half the picture, the easier half to condemn. Phil had probably pursued her. Joss felt almost positive of that. No, not positive. To be fair, she condemned both Vivienne and Phil.

Joss wouldn't directly retaliate against the beautiful Vivienne who'd implicated her own boyfriend. Joss imagined various scenarios: Maybe Vivienne had told the guy about Phil, or the lover suspected an affair and followed them to a motel. The guy probably learned more by slyly questioning Vivienne and following Phil home from campus to discover where he lived. The boyfriend studied their house, planning the fire.

Vivienne would be scared of her young, muscled, tough lover. He probably carried a knife and a gun, yes, both. Maybe this guy threatened Vivienne, made her swear to stop seeing Phil; but she kept on with Phil because his office was nearby. Or had Vivienne and her boyfriend been in cahoots all along? What for? To kill Phil's whole family?

Joss had created a film about how it went: Vivienne would slip into Phil's office and lock the door. They'd take off their clothes; they had an hour, maybe more. They loved sneaking around, touching each other when they passed in the halls, she standing in his office doorway asking bogus questions and leaning over to display her breasts.

Joss told herself to stop thinking about this, but she couldn't.

After some months, Vivienne realized no matter what Phil whispered or yelled during sex, he wouldn't leave his wife. That could be when Vivienne confessed everything to the boyfriend. She'd probably lied and said that Phil forced her to have sex. Pulling her boyfriend close, she suggested he retaliate and said she knew where Phil slept in his house. Phil had probably told Vivienne his wife banished him to the upstairs den. Stupid move.

Joss felt no guilt in gloating; rather, it would be her revenge. She might call Dreama and tell her about Vivienne and the arsonist-lover. She missed talking with friends, and their comfort had helped, initially. But events were moving so fast she had little time for anyone, except her children.

At her first meeting with the lawyer, Joss told her that her parents had been divorced before they both died. After they separated, Joss had hoped they'd reunite, but they couldn't ever find their way back. "Their divorce turned bitter and hateful, yet they still loved each other."

Her lawyer asked, "Their way back?"

"Yes, they said too many horrid things to each other. Too much pain."

Her lawyer nodded.

Early this morning Joss had left another message for the lawyer: time to start divorce proceedings and rewrite her will; copies should be distributed to her and her brother. Trusts for the children. Her brother would get her estate, except for a small amount to charity.

Now the most important part would be talking with Jacks about taking custody of the girls, if she died, until they were twenty-one. He'd take her place as cotrustee of their trusts until they each turned thirty-five. He could take the kids to Alaska; they wouldn't have Phil or their grandparents in their lives again.

Focusing on the grim possibility, however hypothetical, that she wouldn't see her children reach adulthood made Joss squirm. But she had to plan.

Her cell phone remained off. She finished her second latte and drove without haste to Terpe's school and parked at the front of the pickup line. A dazed feeling of unreality and dread about the future rose up as she stared at nothing through the windshield.

Abruptly she recalled this must be Terpe's last week before summer vacation. What would Terpe do all summer? Joss hadn't made any plans, in truth hardly thought about it. Terpe opened the car door, jumped in, and slammed the door. In a breathy voice, she said she'd been invited by a friend of Zoe's to a sleepover.

She'd been admitted to the clique. Zoe the lifesaver.

Joss's wave of relief told her how long and how much her daughter's isolation had worried her. Having more than one friend was quite an accomplishment for her shy daughter. More friends to play with over the summer.

After dinner, Joss put Geline in her crib while Terpe half-heartedly scrubbed the dishes. Terpe turned off the water when Joss came in the kitchen and leaned with her back against the sink. She took a deep breath and looked at her mom. "I want to tell you what happened that day when I left the rehab center."

Terpe didn't wait for permission. "Right after Dad left the dining room, I left. While I was eating lunch sitting by the road, a man stopped his car. He wanted me to get in his car."

Joss's mind closed down. She put her hand over her heart and watched her daughter.

Terpe's voice rose. "Did you hear what I said? I was in a hurry to make it back before the bell rang. I got really hungry and sat down and ate a sandwich. A man drove up and said he would be glad to give me a ride. When he got out of the car and started walking toward me, I ran through these woods to some houses. A big neighborhood. A woman locked her front door and went to her car, but I didn't ask for a ride because I recognized her. I didn't want to talk to her. Her son goes to my school."

"Slow down. Say again. Did you know the man in the car?"

"Of course I didn't know him! He wanted to stick his thing in me, beat me up, and maybe kill me. He had a pretend-nice voice."

"How do you know all this stuff?" How did a nine-year-old know all this? Joss stared at her daughter, her stomach heaving at the words *thing* and *kill*.

"I watch TV, and everything's on the internet."

Joss jumped up and hugged Terpe. "Now you see why your dad and I told you never to go off by yourself. You're too young to be walking alone past our neighborhood boundary. You acted smart, and you got lucky. Very lucky! You could've called me. I will always come for you."

"I got upset seeing Dad kissing that lady."

The room spun. Joss sat. "Did you get that man's license plate? What kind of car? What did he look like?"

"A big white car. Pretty old, fifty or fifty-nine. I might not recognize him, but I could recognize his voice if I heard it."

Joss poured a glass of water and tried to use the ice maker. The glass cracked in her hand, ice and glass shards flushed all over the floor. The side of her hand was bleeding.

"Mom, you pushed too hard. I'll clean it up," Terpe chided. She wet a dish towel and handed it to her mother. "Wrap this around your hand."

But Joss's hand was leaking blood through the dish towel. Terpe carefully swept up the glass and ice and dumped it in the garbage.

The kitchen suddenly felt far away. Joss's ears rang, and everything turned yellowish. She stood, hugged the wall, made it to her bedroom, and fell on the bed.

Terpe whispered at the door, "Are you all right? I shouldn't have told you. You should put a Band-Aid on your hand."

"Telling me, that's the best thing to do. Now I'm sorry I didn't let you tell me right after it happened. I'm just tired. Do your homework, and when you finish, it's straight to bed. Love you."

"Love you, too." Terpe stood there. She wouldn't leave.

"What?"

"Nothing." Terpe walked down the hall.

The hall light filled her room with shadows. Please, sleep, Joss needed sleep. She closed her eyes. Had she turned off both phones? She reached over, took the landline off the hook, and turned off her cell. She felt like a punching bag with all the stuffing knocked out.

With a start she woke. The clock read two o'clock. She trudged down the hall and upstairs, checking on the children. She wandered through the house, turning off lights. In her room, she slid between the blankets and covered part of her head with the comforter.

Joss sat at her desk, working. She heard Terpe's footsteps at her door. "Oh, I didn't hear you come in."

"The O'Tooles' got boring. Geline's having her nap. Can you take me to Zoe's now?"

"Sure, but first I should talk to Zoe's mother."

"Her mother already said fine."

"Let me finish writing this paragraph. Get your things ready."

"Mom, I'm waiting."

The kitchen phone rang, and Joss answered. Her editor's assistant said they moved the deadline forward one month, which meant November. She thanked the assistant, grabbed her car keys, and hurried to the front door.

"Who was that on the phone?"

"Just something about my book." She went down the walk with Terpe close behind.

Terpe fastened her seat belt. "I don't really care. I'm tired of this house and tired of everything about Dad."

Joss suspected Terpe had grown tired of her and all the work around the house. Joss didn't blame her daughter. When would they get their lives back? She had to keep working at it. *Talk with the lawyer, make the decisions, and talk with Jacks.*

Chapter Twenty-Five: Adam

ADAM SMELLED HIS OWN SWEAT and wanted a shower and some food. He would be wiring this damn house all day. He grabbed his plastic water jug and took a few gulps. Where had his dreams gone? They'd disappeared once he began sleeping with Joss. Maybe he didn't need his special dreams anymore. But if stuff didn't work out with Joss, would they come back? Some old-timers in AA said drinking dreams were normal, but he never had any. His mind stayed a mystery to him. How did people figure out their minds? High school sure didn't help with those sorts of questions.

Another break for water. The job dragged on for another hour or so in the heat. Most of the afternoon was now shot to hell. Toolbox in hand, he headed to his truck and stowed the toolbox behind the front seat. He let the passenger's door stay open for some breeze. Two banana and peanut butter sandwiches, with salty potato chips, were all he'd packed. He felt halfway hungry when he finished eating.

Joss's phone rang and rang. He listened to her sweet voice on the message, but she didn't pick up. No worries. He'd call later. He liked to think about hearing her voice. Maybe her silence didn't have to do with him. Something could be wrong with her husband or one of her children.

First thing when he got home, he showered and threw his filthy stuff in the hamper. At least Mama had taught him housekeeping, and now he kept his apartment in better shape.

He tried calling Joss a few more times; when she didn't answer, he grabbed a hunk of cheese and a box of crackers and took them to the living room to watch a little TV. Later, back in his own bed, he tossed, woke, and fell back asleep.

At dawn, light filtered through trees and threw patterns on his bed and floor. He used the toilet and fell back into bed. A ringing phone woke him, and he stumbled, bumping off a doorframe, chasing the sound. The phone sat on a black table. Its loud dial tone kept buzzing, and through the buzz, Papa's voice rose: "Fool, she don't love you. She's out of your league." A chorus chanted in jagged voices: "Hey, buddy, you could use a drink. A drink, buddy, drink, buddy, drink, drink, drink."

Adam woke, propped up the pillows, and rested against the headboard of his rumpled bed. His dead father couldn't hurt him. What gave him the courage to go after Joss? His island dreams helped. At least he kept telling himself they had. Still, he never felt as desperate as Mama must've been when she married Waldo.

With Joss some of his worries didn't feel as big. All the stuff from his past had been fading. Once Joss had told him she liked to hear him sing. Even though he didn't have a great singing voice, he'd been singing more when he rode alone in the truck. Thinking about what she said, he could feel himself blushing all over again.

When Mama finally said more about her big brother, Bernard, her face lit up, and her hands flew all over the place while she talked. Usually she told Adam stuff all at once: when they were still kids, Bernard would slip into the house when he should be chopping wood or hauling brush. How he took over her heavy chores whenever he could without her father catching him. She told Adam about the times they walked to the village where they visited stores, but only looked because they had no money of their own. Their last stop, their real destination, was the dock. She and Bernard bargained with the fishermen before pulling out her father's money to buy fresh fish.

Adam asked, "You and Bernard were twins?"

"We thought of it that way."

"What?"

"We're about a year apart. Bernard's the oldest, but his father left our mother before he came into the world. His father never come back. But my father didn't care that Bernard wasn't his own. He only wanted Bernard for free labor."

Bernard's name sounded kingly. He asked Mama about kings' names and fidgeted, trying to think up more questions to keep her talking.

She said she didn't know about kings' names. She moved to the sink. "After these dishes, I have more ironing."

"Where did your family live? Where does your brother live now?"

"Adam, not when I'm busy. I'll tell you more, later."

It hurt to think how he kept trying to piece together information, to understand the family. The many secrets she wouldn't reveal made a wall between them.

Chapter Twenty-Six: Joss

TERPE'S SILHOUETTE HOVERED IN JOSS'S bedroom doorway. "I called Zoe, and the line kept beeping. Call Dr. Howard right now. Here's his number."

While Joss dialed, she said, "Terpe, turn on the coffeepot. Get dressed."

Dr. Howard answered on the first ring. "I'm sorry to say I have bad news. Your husband is back in ICU. You should come right away."

"What happened?" She tried to keep her voice from betraying hope.

"We're piecing it together. One of the evening staff found him when he didn't come to dinner. It appears he took a lot of pills."

"On my way." She dialed Mrs. O'Toole's number.

"Hello there, this is short notice, but there's an emergency. May I bring the girls over?"

"My dear, let me come over there. The girls won't be disrupted."

"Thank you, thank you." Joss glanced around her room, trying to think what she needed. Clothes first, her pocketbook with car keys. She threw on jeans and a T-shirt and ran a comb through her hair. Ran to the kitchen and poured coffee in her portable mug.

"Mrs. O'Toole's coming over to stay." She laid her hand on Terpe's head. "Zoe can't come over. I'll call you as soon as I can."

"Can I come with you?"

"No. I'll call you."

"Please let me come, I'm scared."

"Let me check on things. If everything's okay, I'll come get you. Is that good?"

"No. I want to come right now!"

"No. You. May. Not. Come." What if Phil had done more than pills, cut his wrists, or looked horrible?

"I'll get dressed and wait for you to call. I'll tell Zoe no."

Joss kissed her cheek. "I love you, sweetie."

Terpe's head hung. "Yeah, love you, too."

When the doorbell rang, Joss yanked open the door, and a thin stream of coffee spilled down her shirt. She ran past Mrs. O'Toole. She drove as fast as she dared, crossing the parking lot. Halfway into a parking space, her car jolted.

"Shit!" She jumped out. Her right front tire had scraped into a huge black SUV. She backed out, drove to a bigger space, and parked. She scribbled a note with her name and cell phone number and stuck it on the windshield. Yep, she'd dented the damn thing, but the damage looked minimal. She hoped the owner wouldn't call. Just one more damn thing.

The lobby felt blurred. She paced as she waited for one of the elevators, then hurried into an empty car and mashed her palm against the button.

Even though Phil lay in a different room, ICU looked and felt the same. From the doorway she tried to gauge his condition. He was pale, but otherwise she didn't see any change. The nurse touched her arm, and they walked to the nurses' station.

"We've made him comfortable. His organs are shutting down, the machines are doing the work. We were waiting for you."

"His parents?" Joss asked. "They should be here."

"They came very early this morning. They're in the cafeteria, having breakfast."

Both of her phones had been off last night.

Joss moved a chair close to his bed and took his hand. "Phil, I don't know if you can hear me. This is the real Joss. I wish we could go back two years and spend time talking like we used to do. I don't know how everything got so awful between us. I'll miss you and I love you."

He didn't stir. Hearing, she'd read, left the dying person last. Joss hoped he could hear her. But . . . but she'd hoped for so much that never happened. She wouldn't delude herself about the power of her words now.

She stood slowly, afraid the room would spin and throw her to the floor. His room had the same bed and polished floor, the same medical computer in the corner, the same beeping. Yet none of her flowers, none of the cards Terpe made for him, and no CD player with his favorite music that she'd brought and set on a table in his other room. Remembering these details felt good, glad she could still remember scenes from a few months earlier.

Call Terpe. What to tell her? The child needed somebody with her, but that wasn't a good task for Mrs. O'Toole. Did she have time to drive home, pick Terpe up, and bring her back? First, she'd wait for Phil's parents to return from the cafeteria. She had medical power of attorney, but they would want to be with him.

Oh, please let her daughter be resilient enough to endure this loss. Even with Zoe and her other newfound friends, Terpe might regress to the make-believe ones. If she did, Joss promised herself she'd find professional help for her.

Joss recalled their conversation after one of her sleepovers. Terpe told Joss how much fun it was hanging out with Zoe's big family. Joss sensed her holding back, maybe wanting to ask for a better family, including a healthy father, but too kind to say it.

She hoped her brother, Jacks, would come to the funeral, but a flight from Alaska would be long, and he was probably busy. Since they both left home years ago, they'd moved in different directions. She tried to get used to missing her dear brother. Did he miss her? She didn't know.

When they were kids, her big brother helped her survive bad situations and told her she had to toughen up to survive. By the time she reached fifteen, she'd grown proud of her endurance. When she and Jacks fought, they yelled insults, and sometimes threw pencils or notebooks designed not to hit, only to scare. Sometimes they kicked each other's bedroom doors.

Joss acted like the hurt didn't matter. She practiced closing her lips into a tight line: no smile, no frown, only a blank stare. Stoicism became her armor, and she hoped only she could sense where the cracks were and where the armor might leak air.

Lately she'd begun having recurring images of the recent fire: she stood in front of her house, watching the flames. But the images must be a conjuring. That night she'd stayed busy rescuing Phil, rolling him in a rug and dragging him across the hall to the front door. She would not have seen the house burning from the outside.

The two fires, the recent one and the one all those years ago, felt the same. Panic at the smoke rising to the sleeping porch, panic at the smoke moving through her current house. Her own crazy-voice in her ears: calling for Sally, for Luce and Polly, and later, for Phil, Terpe, and Geline. If only Daddy and Jackson had been home, the three of them could have saved the horses.

Fires took away almost everything.

Joss looked up as Phil's father shuffled into the hospital room. The old man's fingers twitched while he whispered that he'd just made arrangements with a funeral home. A hearse was waiting on standby for the call. Phil's mother crept in the room all hunched over, slipped past her husband, and halfway collapsed into the chair next to Joss. Joss touched Mrs. Mont-gomery's hand but got no response. Joss wondered why she kept trying with this woman. Even here at Phil's deathbed, the woman probably held on to stupid hope.

Phil's mother's expression stayed frozen. A cold vibration moved through Joss's chest and stomach; probably she feared the woman would collapse by her son's bed.

Abruptly the old woman stood and crept out the door. Her husband followed. The woman's voice rose into a whiny complaint somewhere down the hall. Joss figured Phil's mother could be whining about Terpe's absence or about a million other things. Nothing ever suited Phil's mother.

Joss didn't want to drive home for Terpe. She needed to be here in this room until the end. Maybe Dreama, her closest friend, could bring Terpe, but Dreama's office was way out in the suburbs, so it would take her forever to pick up Terpe and bring her to the hospital. Joss knew Dreama would be glad to do it, and the thought comforted her.

Joss went into the hall and pulled out her cell phone. Adam answered on the first ring. She asked if he could bring Terpe to the hospital immediately.

He said, "Of course. On my way."

Sweet, reliable Adam.

Dr. Howard stood by Phil's door. "I put in a call to Dr. Drummond. Unfortunately, he's in London at a conference. He's very sorry about your husband and sends his condolences."

"Thank you."

"You're waiting for family?" Dr. Howard's voice, low-pitched, well-modulated, stayed steady. Familiar with this scenario, he probably dealt with it every day. "This has been a long struggle. I'm sorry we couldn't do more for him."

"Yes, a long struggle. I'm waiting for our daughter. I've asked a friend to bring her, they're coming now." She walked past the doctor and sat by Phil's bed. Her eyes stayed focused on his face.

Chapter Twenty-Seven: Terpe

TERPE PICKED OUT A RED COTTON dress and sandals. She bathed and gave her damp hair a few whacks with a brush while pacing in circles around the living room, checking out the window for Mom's Volvo. She should be home, or she should have called by now.

The blue truck drove up in front of the house and parked.

Oh no, Yard Guy. What should she say? Tell the truth about Dad? He'd find out, if he didn't already know. She wanted him to go away.

She let Mrs. O'Toole answer the door.

Yard Guy still stood on the porch when she came near the door. Mrs. O'Toole blocked the doorway because she'd probably figured out his identity.

"It is okay, Mrs. O'Toole, Mom and I know Adam."

Mrs. O'Toole huffed and walked away.

"What do you want?" Without thought, Terpe put her hands on her hips.

Yard Guy frowned. "You've talked to your mom?"

"About Dad being back in the hospital? I'm waiting for her to pick me up."

"Your mom asked me to bring you to the hospital."

"No way." Her face felt hot. She wanted to throw something at him—a planter from the patio, maybe a kitchen chair.

"Call her." He looked directly at her.

In a loud voice she commanded, "Stay right here." She pointed at the porch. "I'm calling her right now."

Terpe grabbed the kitchen phone. Mom breathing funny, crying, when she answered.

"Did you ask Adam to bring me?"

"Yes. I need to stay at the hospital. We'll talk when you get here. I'm with your grandparents." Mom hung up.

Terpe put on a sweater and told Mrs. O'Toole good-bye.

"Does your mother know?" Mrs. O'Toole asked.

"She asked Adam to bring me. Things with Dad are really bad. Thanks for helping." Her anger at Mrs. O'Toole over not believing her about her parents felt childish now, and also embarrassing. With a sigh the anger loosened its hold, and for a few seconds Terpe felt relieved, or maybe happy. Strange how a nice feeling crept in right in the middle of her big worry about Dad.

"I'm glad to help, dear." Mrs. O'Toole moved closer and Terpe allowed herself to be hugged.

"Okay, let's roll," Yard Guy said, dashing to the truck. She cut across the yard to catch up. He opened the passenger door and she jumped in the truck. He closed her door and ran around to the driver's side.

She rolled down the window and leaned out as far as she could. The breeze felt warm, and she tried to think about summer, but her thoughts were racing. They rode in tense silence. Near the hospital, he said in a soft voice, "No matter what happens, remember you're going to be okay."

She rolled up the window, then turned to him, inching a bit closer.

Not many sounds in the ICU. Some low voices, and of course those machines. They hurried down the hall. When she saw her grandparents, she turned her head. She hated them, and suddenly felt sorry for them, from a distance.

"Where's Mom?" She sped up.

A hand rested on her shoulder. Expecting her mother, she whipped around. Yard Guy.

He whispered, "No matter what happens, please remember you're going to be okay."

She didn't know what to say.

Mom came out of the nurses' station. "Terpe. Come with me to your father's room." She followed Mom and they stood at the door.

Mom said, "The machine is breathing for him because he is dying and can't breathe on his own. A doctor examined him. His parents are here, you and I are here. If you have anything to say, say it now. If not, that's okay. The nurse is going to take him off life support."

"Dying? No way! He looks okay, see, his chest is moving. He's okay! See!"

Mom put her hand on her shoulder and drew her close. "The machine makes his chest move. He can't breathe without the machine. I'm so sorry. I'm so sorry."

The nurse moved toward the machine. Mom raised her hand and the nurse stood still.

Mom leaned close to Terpe. "Want to say anything to your dad before the nurse turns off the machine?"

"I don't know. Can I think about it?" She focused on her dad's chest, fighting back tears by swallowing over and over.

"Terpe, come on. The nurse will turn off the machine when I tell her. Say it now."

Mom counted to one hundred. Terpe put her hands over her face and said nothing.

Mom waved at the nurse, who moved to the machine.

Terpe tried to say something; her stomach hurt and she couldn't think of anything to say. He looked young. Around

Christmas they were going to build a tree house. He would have said yes as soon as she asked. They would have had so much fun, making mistakes, laughing and fixing the mistakes until the tree house became sturdy. He'd test out the flooring before he'd let her climb up the ladder.

She listened to the nurse moving closer to Dad's bed. The machine stopped. She uncovered her face. That tube still stuck out of his mouth. His chest moved only a little and stopped. The room got strange. Empty and suddenly quiet.

Through the quiet, the room slanted like the Tilt-A-Whirl at the fair. She grabbed the bed, held on until she could walk, and then rushed out of the room. Gasping, she halted. Her dress felt sticky, with awful snot all down her front. She grabbed for the person following her. Yard Guy.

She gagged. "Bathroom?"

"I saw one when we came in." He hurried ahead of her and then pointed. "There."

She pushed up the toilet seat, leaned over, and waited to throw up. Nothing happened. She squeezed her stomach. Nothing. She washed her face and hands and dried off with paper towels. Then she tried to wipe the spots off her dress.

Yard Guy stood outside the door. "Feel better?"

She shrugged.

"Your mom said they're going to a room where she and your grandparents can talk." He led the way. Mom walked with her grandparents, and she and Yard Guy followed close behind.

In the small room, everyone stood around. Mom announced they were short one chair. Yard Guy left and came back with another one. The chairs made sort of a circle in the too bright, crowded room.

Her grandparents sat side by side. She sat between her mom and Yard Guy.

In her watery, creepy voice, Grandmother declared the doctors were right to let him go.

Mom nodded.

The first time Mom and her grandmother had agreed on anything. Terpe felt surprised.

Grandmother said they wanted to hold the funeral service in their church. Mom's voice sounded angry when she announced the service would be held at the funeral home, followed by a short service at the cemetery. Afterward everyone could come back to their house because their house was much larger.

Grandmother made a face like someone had thrown a dead fish at her and shook her head.

The grown-up arguing floated to the ceiling, and Terpe caught only a few words. She sneaked a glance at Yard Guy, wondering if he felt stupid. If she were him, she'd want to be invisible. He should leave the hospital right now, as fast as possible. Yard Guy didn't know or really care about her father, and he looked relaxed until she noticed his shuffling feet. Could he be upset? With Dad gone, life would go easier for him. That thought made her feel more hateful toward the damn Yard Guy.

Yard Guy caught her looking at him and gave her a quick smile.

She didn't smile back.

Chapter Twenty-Eight: Joss

JOSS TRIED TO CONCENTRATE ON the funeral plans Phil's mother kept describing over and over. Scattered, afraid of forgetting, Joss repeated the woman's words like an awful piece of music stuck in her head, an earworm.

Why hadn't she brought a notebook and pen? *Stop.* What always stayed at the bottom of her purse, besides her car keys? A notebook and pen were always in the tangle at the bottom of her purse.

Phil's father took over from his exhausted wife. He droned on about the importance of having Phil's funeral at their church, followed by the burial in the family plot, followed by the reception at their house.

Joss's agitation grew. She held the image of Phil's face, remembering how he had described his Sundays and how he'd grown to detest everything about church except the beautiful music. His mother harped on his clothes and would slap him if he didn't look perfect. He'd told Joss he felt suffocated sitting between his parents in the pew. Even worse were the long weekend afternoons and evenings at home. Not allowed to go out with friends, he worked on regular and extra assignments to keep his 4.0. He wanted to try to win a university scholarship in a state far from home.

Joss rearranged her body in the plastic chair. She felt an urge to cover the coffee stain on her shirt, but didn't want to let go of Terpe's hand. Her child's pale face and sweaty hand broke her, cramping her gut the way it did when she'd worried about Terpe just before Geline arrived. Joss hadn't realized how fragile her marriage had become until she told Phil she was pregnant. His face showed alarm. He asked how it happened. She held back a sarcastic remark about where babies come from, but he wouldn't have enjoyed the humor. She reminded him birth control pills still didn't work one hundred percent.

Joss forced herself back into the cramped room. She interrupted Phil's father and talked over him. "Enough, you've said that twice already. If you all want to plan the funeral, burial, and reception, go ahead. Since you're in charge, you can pay for all of it, too.

"I've had enough. Come on, Terpe." She stood, and Terpe and Adam followed her out the door.

Streetlights winked on as Joss pulled into her driveway. The porch light revealed a shape on the front porch, which turned out to be flowers in a large vase. Who in the world knew Phil had died and sent flowers so quickly? Adam unlocked the front door so she could carry the vase.

Mrs. O'Toole came into the hall. "Oh, I thought I heard someone outside, but Geline was still jabbering away in that screechy little voice. I just put her down for the night."

"Dad died," Terpe blurted. "They're taking him to the funeral home. We stopped for hamburgers."

"Oh, my dear. I'm so sorry." Mrs. O'Toole opened her arms and her glance included everyone. "Shall I make coffee?"

"No thanks." Joss set the vase on a table and glanced at the card: "Sissy, leaving for the airport now. Alaska Airlines out of Sitka. Flight 493. See you Sunday night. Love, Jacks."

"Uncle Jackson will arrive tomorrow night," Terpe said, her voice almost a shout.

"I emailed him early, very early, this morning," Joss mumbled. "I didn't expect to hear from him this fast. I have to lie down. Thank you, thank you, Mrs. O'Toole."

"My dear, you let me know what I can do. I'll let myself out the back way."

Adam followed Joss to her bedroom door. "How can I help? Want me to leave?"

Her thoughts stopped when she saw him, a handsome, rugged man so different from Phil. Her mind drifted, then ground to a stop. Stuck in first gear. "I'll lie down for a while. Can you stay with Terpe?"

"Sure. Maybe we'll watch some TV." His grin appeared false, yet she didn't have the energy to reassure him. "Fine." She couldn't keep her eyes open.

Once Adam left the doorway, her thoughts picked up. Snippets of conversations with Phil. His voice alive and strong, as if he were beside her in bed. How could her brain, or any brain, reproduce a dead person's voice? She'd always enjoyed how she picked up information quickly, but hearing Phil's voice felt like a curse. If she kept hearing him, she wouldn't be able to function.

She slowed her breath and tried a relaxation exercise until jumbled pictures floated through a growing darkness. Phil's laugh came from his dorm room. They were wrapped around each other in his narrow bed. His pillows smelled musty and she murmured to him that he had to do his laundry. He laughed and whispered that he learned a new poem for her. He mumbled a name.

"What? I can hardly hear you." She felt frantic to hear his words.

He put his mouth to her ear, and his voice felt wet and real. "It's called 'August White Sky.'" In a slow voice, he quoted:

I can see you, you, you,
I can see you, you, you,
Saying that someone has died
Saying that someone has died.
White sky. White sky.
Saying that someone has died.

His voice trailed off.

"Phil, dammit, don't stop. There's more."

"Between us, Joss, there's always more." His eyes closed as if he were sleeping.

"You left out part of the poem?" She gripped his shoulder until he rolled over, halfway on top of her. She clutched his head close and ran her fingers through his thick hair, settled his head on her chest, breathed in his familiar smell. "Tell me, tell me. Phil, talk to me. Please."

Chapter Twenty-Nine: Adam

ADAM HAD NO IDEA WHAT to say to the kid lying curled on the sofa. He sat at the other end and stared at the fireplace. His face felt hot, so he counted to ten slowly. At least the baby was asleep. He didn't think he could manage both of them.

The girl moved her legs.

"Hi. I thought you were asleep. Want me to make a fire?"

"Why?" Terpe asked. "It's June." A pillow muffled her small voice.

"True. But fires feel nice. Cowboys, people on hikes, in some places people roast hot dogs and s'mores on the beach all year long. President Nixon had a fire in his office every day. I read that somewhere."

"Okay." She didn't move.

Newspaper, kindling, and dry logs were stacked by the fireplace. He opened the damper and arranged the logs and kindling. He felt her watching him. The dry logs caught quickly, surely the easiest fire he'd ever built. The kid had made it clear she could barely tolerate him, and she hadn't been relieved when her father died, like he'd felt when Papa died. He tried to imagine how she felt, but only felt numb about Papa.

Yes, he'd felt nothing except relief when Papa died. An image from long ago. Sitting in Papa's lap when he was maybe three or four. Papa held a blue toy truck, explaining stuff about fire trucks, tow trucks, and garbage trucks. His thick finger touched every part, talking slowly, naming the parts and saying what they did. Every time he moved his head, Adam could smell his aftershave. Adam always asked for more, wanting explanations about his other toys or to hear a story. The image came, unbidden. It hurt his chest, and he had to gulp air to breathe.

Adam still didn't look at Terpe. He spoke to the fireplace. "When my father died, I didn't feel sad because we didn't get along. Mama and I had a funeral for him, of course. But you and your father, well, you're upset because you loved your papa."

The kid jumped up and left the room.

What a dummy. He should have kept his mouth shut.

Something heavy banged against the counter and Adam hurried to the kitchen.

The girl picked up a cast-iron frying pan with both hands and put it on a burner. "I'm making popcorn. Want some?"

"You're gonna use a frying pan?"

"That's how we make it."

"Mostly I eat popcorn at the movies."

"Mom wouldn't like microwave popcorn. She does popcorn old-fashioned. Me, too." Terpe poured oil and popcorn in the pan, covered the pan and turned up the heat. Her forehead wrinkled in concentration. After a minute or two, she shook the pan slowly and leaned close to listen.

Popping sounds grew louder, faster. The noise got to him a little. It must remind him of something long ago.

She shook the pan back and forth, finally turning down the heat. Her laugh brought him back to the kitchen. He supposed little girls would laugh, cry, and laugh again within a minute.

"It's all popped." She poured the popcorn into a large bowl. "Here, take the bowl. I'll get drinks."

They sat on the sofa with the bowl sitting on a pillow between them, and a soda on each end table.

"You like checkers?" he asked.

"No."

"I bet you know how to play gin rummy?"

"I hate games."

He ate two handfuls of popcorn and drank his Pepsi. "You made good popcorn. What do you like to do?"

She gulped her drink. "I draw in the back of my notebook when the teachers get boring, which is usually every day. I play with my friends at recess. Sometimes I play down by the creek. That's it."

"Sounds like some good stuff. I grew up in the city. We played ball in the park. I skateboarded until I grew too tall and clumsy. Of course being big helped with football and basketball. You're lucky to have a creek behind your house."

"Yeah."

"You have a bike?"

"In the shed. But I stopped riding."

"Why?"

"I'm too busy helping with Geline and doing house chores with Mom."

"Stuff will change again, I suppose." He tried to look sincere. Louder, he said, "Stuff will probably get better." He rose to tend to the logs, taking time to rearrange them and poke at the embers.

"Dad and I were going to build a tree house. Anyway, he would've built it with me, but I never had the chance to ask him because of the fire. He stayed and stayed in the hospital. Everything in my family sucks."

"Yep, sometimes everything sucks." He looked over at her.

She didn't answer or look at him.

"Aren't you excited about your uncle coming?"

"Yes. He's fun, but we hardly see him. Jackson and Mom talk on the phone and email each other. Dad's funeral will happen on Monday, so says my bossy grandmother."

"Monday, at two o'clock."

"You're coming?"

"If your mom wants me to."

"You should not come. Do not come. You didn't know my dad. You are not family."

Her cold voice and words hit him like adult words. His stomach felt like she kicked him. He stood to leave before he said something he'd regret. "Thanks for the popcorn."

She pulled one of the pillows over her head.

He walked out the front door and headed to his truck. He stuck the key in the ignition and revved the engine. Should he drive away and leave this whole mess? He took a few swigs of the Pepsi, which made him want a cold beer.

Joss's neighborhood wasn't familiar, but he could find a bar, no problem. He felt bad leaving Terpe. Joss would be disappointed in him. He felt sorry for the kid, but what a brat. *Slow down and think about this.* He turned off the engine and kept the radio playing.

Mama had warned him, right after Joss drove them from the airport. She said he'd taken on too much. Joss's brother would be coming for the funeral. He sure wouldn't like anyone messing with his sister, trying to replace Phil. Adam hadn't known Joss long enough for them to feel like a couple. Her brother would ask why she thought an electrician with a high school degree would be interesting in the least.

More than the kid's kick in the butt, he felt jealous of her. To be sad about a father's death. He wanted to feel sad.

A sappy love song came on the radio, and he saw himself with a broom, sweeping the wooden floor at the butcher shop. This song had been playing on the radio the time Papa punched his upper arm hard with his knuckles. Adam's arm had stayed bruised for days. At school, every time he picked up an armload of books, the pain reminded him.

Adam switched off the song. A tap on the passenger window. He reached over and opened the door for Joss.

"I stayed with her awhile," Adam said, "even though she didn't want me there."

"Any man who isn't her father or uncle would make her mad right now. Come inside. I can't stay out here and leave Geline."

In the kitchen, he sat in his usual chair while she made coffee.

"Did you get some sleep?" He tried to keep the worry out of his voice.

"About forty minutes. A nap always helps. Thanks for trying with Terpe. Just now she wouldn't talk except to say she felt tired and had to go to bed."

"I won't come to the funeral. Terpe's right, I didn't know your husband. You'll be fine."

"Sometimes Terpe will speak her mind. Yes, I'll be okay. Jackson's flying in. Mostly I'm dreading the tedious sermon and the social niceties. I suppose some of Phil's colleagues will come. I'll be relieved when it's over."

On the drive back to the city, Adam calculated how much money he had in his account. His last statement had shown a bit more than $21,000. More than enough to move out west. He only needed some of it now; first thing Monday morning he'd visit the bank. He let the classical guitar music on the radio calm him. Not his favorite sound, yet sometimes that sort of music soothed him. After the song finished, he switched the station and sang along to some of Ralph Stanley's "high lonesome sounds."

He drove home and called his old high school buddy. Freddie picked up on the second ring. "Hey, Adam. How's it goin'?"

"Pretty good. Is that crying? Sounds sort of like a cat? You guys went and had your baby already?"

Freddie laughed. "Yeah, our girl arrived three weeks ago. I tell you, she's a pain in the middle of the night, but also the best thing ever. Besides my beautiful Darlene, of course."

Adam heard Darlene's high-pitched laugh.

"Yep, she's a prize," Adam laughed. "Way better than that hot black-haired girl you dated awhile? The girl we met at that loft party with all those weird, arty people? We called her Morticia. Her hair all stiff with black dye and that pale face. Those long silver earrings. You two lasted, what, maybe a month?"

"No, man, you were the one calling her Morticia. She went to our high school, and you were hot to date her. You were always interested in the weird girls. The way different ones."

"I liked her that much? I don't remember. But I'll think about it, and meanwhile I'll take your word for it." Adam laughed.

"I forgot all about her," Freddie said. "Listen, I got a whole different thing going now."

"I know, man. Just kidding." Adam's neck felt hot. What a jerk, he couldn't keep his mouth shut.

"So, you got a girlfriend?" Freddie asked.

"Maybe."

"Bring her over sometime."

"When I get back from my trip. Good to catch up. Great about the baby."

Morticia in our high school, yeah, Adam remembered, sometimes he did hang around with that sad Morticia. They were in the same freshman English class. She had a nice smile, but didn't smile often. She made better grades than he did. Most mornings she smoked dope with him and the guys in the parking lot. They all complained about their parents; they swore they wouldn't end up like the people they hated most. His senior year, the sad girl got pregnant by some sleazy dropout. She dropped out to have the baby, like her own mother had done. Adam never called Morticia to say good-bye and wish her luck. He didn't want to know her anymore. She frightened him.

Adam made Cs in English, history, and chemistry, As and Bs in math and shop. The clean smell of lumber, the ragged sound of drills biting into wood reminded him of wild animals howling, and he loved working with his hands and enjoyed every class. He dated a few girls but mostly hung around with three guy friends, one of them, Freddie. These days the three were employed and married. None of them had turned into drunks or druggies, except him. They'd left him behind, but he'd catch up.

He drove home thinking about Joss but didn't call her. Joss's kid had worn him out, and he wanted to sleep.

In the morning before he showered, he made the call he'd been putting off.

"Hey, Joss, how's it going?"

Joss sighed. "Terpe and I are getting ready to leave for the funeral home. Since Phil's parents are having the funeral and burial at their church, I gave them money for food so they could have the reception at their house. It mattered more to Phil's mother than it did to me. What are you doing?"

"Nothing much. An old friend and his wife just had a baby."

"Want to ride with us to the airport this evening? We're not leaving until seven fifteen, unless Jackson's flight is delayed."

"I can't go."

"Why not?"

"I'll be packing."

"What?"

"Remember, I told you I'd been thinking about moving out west? Yes, I did talk about it. Don't worry, this will be a short trip. I'm not moving anywhere."

"Why now? Adam, why now?" Her voice screeched, and he held out the phone.

"Sometimes a guy has to get away and think about stuff. You'll be busy with your brother and the funeral. I'll call you every day."

"How long?"

"I don't know. Two, maybe three or four weeks?"

"Great timing, jerk." She hung up.

His hands shook. He had to keep moving. A shower and breakfast helped.

Make a quick visit to Mama, you have to tell her you're leaving.

He found his old parking space out back of Mama's apartment. Upstairs he followed her into her tidy kitchen. She poured two cups of tea, sat, and put her elbows squarely on the kitchen table, fixing her eyes on him. The harsh kitchen light made the bags under her eyes darker than usual. He sipped the tea, which he didn't like, but Mama preferred it to coffee. He sure didn't want to argue, yet waited for what he suspected she'd say.

"I'm happy you're taking a vacation," she said. "And I'm happy you earned the money for your trip. That must feel good. Son, I liked Joss when I met her. I think you know that. She's pretty and nice, except . . . except, the woman's rich, with lots of education and two youngsters.

"Your father and I had problems, but at least we had the same background. We wouldn't have lasted, or even met, if Waldo had been a rich bully instead of a poor one."

"Yeah." He began bumping his fist on the table.

"I did love Waldo. We were young, poor, without good sense. When you were born, your father had been truly happy. When you were helping in the shop, he told customers you were a good boy and a big help. But by high school you had more schooling. He only finished the equivalent of eighth grade. Ashamed, but he'd never admit it."

"I never knew he was proud of me or only finished eighth grade." Adam sighed. "He never said anything like that to me."

"Sorry I never told you. I didn't keep it from you on purpose. Or maybe I did a long time ago. Maybe I thought it would upset you. I don't remember."

"You damn well should be sorry. You and your secrets! You know I hated you for that. Papa was bad, but you made it worse.

Now I find out you didn't tell me things Papa said and how he felt ashamed of his poor schooling."

Her hand trembled when she picked up her cup. She sipped her tea and frowned. "Son, people are complicated. Who can understand other peoples' motives? Even our own?"

"You're lucky I keep trying to forgive you. And stop lecturing me about Joss. I plan to get off around noon tomorrow, and I have lots to do before I leave."

He rose from the table with a jerk, knocking over his cup. He watched the tea soak into the tablecloth, turned, and strode down the hall.

She followed. "Please call. I'm sorry to harp on you and Joss. I just want what's best for you, that's all."

At the door he gave her a quick hug. "I'll call from the road."

She didn't answer and shut the door.

That night on the dream island, Adam rides the red horse across the snow, feeling happy. Suddenly from behind, arms grip his waist so hard it hurts. Joss's perfume and beautiful hands. The horse lunges, and she slides off. He stops the horse to search for her, but she has disappeared.

Monday morning, he woke excited about his trip; he wouldn't let the dream bother him. He showered and packed. Weather could be changeable in the mountains, so he packed jeans, T-shirts, work shirts, and two wool sweaters. His heavy jacket, fur-lined hat, gloves, and old hiking boots. His bowie knife and Swiss Army knife, the phone charger, and shaving kit went into pockets. He left space in his duffle for souvenirs for Joss, Terpe, and Mama. He unplugged appliances, except for the refrigerator, in case of storms.

After going to the bank, he drove to a large bookstore and flipped through books on mythology. He looked at Jewish, Norse, and Japanese myth books, and finally he picked the book about the hero with a thousand faces because he liked the title. Once he had seen some writer named Campbell talk about myths on PBS. In case the myth book got boring, he also bought two thrillers.

On the road he reminded himself to keep a clear head, but he came back to the phone call with Joss and acting like a dumb coward. He didn't belong at Joss's husband's funeral with creepy cemetery stuff and standing around with strangers. Even that nine-year-old girl could see that.

He turned up the radio and hummed along with a tune he didn't recognize. Soon he'd lose reception on this station anyway. The song helped to block out thinking. On the road, running away.

Terpe was right. Sometimes everything sucks.

Chapter Thirty: Joss

JOSS STARED AT THE KITCHEN WALL, waiting for the gurgling of perking coffee to stop. The kitchen phone rang. She didn't move. Without checking the caller ID, she guessed who it could be. She waited six rings before picking up.

Phil's mother squawked into the phone, reminding Joss to schedule a viewing for Sunday evening.

Joss barely hesitated. "I'll be leaving for the funeral home soon. Sorry, there won't be a viewing or visitation. There's not enough time to publicize it. Plus, I don't want it, and your son wouldn't want it either. Since I gave you money for the reception, I get to choose the schedule."

She hung up, feeling only a little guilty, not enough to call back and make nice. How could she hate that woman any more than she already did?

Phil's parents must have had a challenging time convincing their minister to officiate at the funeral and burial. The sin of suicide would prohibit a church service and burial in the church-yard. Joss assumed his parents had lied and told the minister Phil's death had been an accident with his prescriptions.

Joss knew his death wasn't an accident, the notion never entered her mind. Even with brain damage, he'd be too smart to kill himself by accident. He'd told her more than once that he'd considered suicide a few times as a teenager. Of course The Ivy would try to spin his death as accidental, too. Suicides weren't good for business.

She understood how Phil's mind worked. He'd conned the nurses and hoarded meds in some secret, clever place he had fun devising. He'd waited, calculating the amount until the hoard seemed big enough. He probably added a few extra pills to make sure they would do the trick.

At the funeral home, Joss hoped she was making the best decisions while talking with the nice bald man. She'd arranged her parents' funerals and felt confident buzzing through the list of services. The man marked each choice and nodded. She told Terpe to speak up if she had an opinion. Terpe sat, hands folded, a scowling statue.

Joss couldn't wait to leave the dark, thick-carpeted building with maudlin music playing in the background. They hurried to the car. They had to get clothes for Phil. Why did clothes matter if the casket were closed? His obituary with funeral notice would be published in the Sunday paper and the Monday morning paper. The service would be held Monday at two in the afternoon, at the Montgomerys' church.

At home Joss snatched Phil's black suit and a white shirt off the hangers, pulled a red-striped tie off the rack, and grabbed underwear out of his dresser. She threw everything on the bed, not bothering with shoes, which wouldn't be needed.

Terpe put her hands on her hips. "They're in a heap, they'll get all wrinkled!"

"It's okay. People overcome with grief act weird sometimes. There's a lot going through my mind at once. But not all the time." Joss jammed everything in a garbage bag.

Terpe let out a loud sigh.

Joss threw the bag over her shoulder. "Okay, back to the funeral home."

Terpe didn't move from her spot.

"Come on! We have to get back to the funeral home. We told that nice man we'd come back. After we'll have a quick lunch. I have to pick up Geline from Mrs. O'Toole's by two. Ready?"

"Ready." Head down, Terpe led the way to the car.

On the drive home, Joss's cell phone rang and went to voice mail. In the kitchen she checked the message. The owner of the SUV she'd hit in the parking lot had left a message. He sounded pleasant enough. She put down the phone. Oh shit, one more thing. She'd call back tomorrow.

Later she checked with the airlines; so far Jackson's plane was still on schedule. With Geline buckled in the car seat and Terpe up front, they drove off exactly when Joss had planned to leave. Feeling organized and in charge of this small thing gave her a feeling of relief.

"What do you think he'll be like?" Terpe stared out her window.

"He sounds the same when we talk on the phone. You know we talk about once a month. And email sometimes. So, he's the same, even though he hasn't been here in over three years. You were little, I'm surprised you remember him."

"Almost six, that's not real little. He threw me in the air and tickled me until I got the hiccups. We played hide-and-seek. I always won, because he was too tall to fit in the good hiding places."

"You and I have talked about his visits quite a bit. A good way for memories to stick in your head."

"I'll know him when I see him, you wait, you'll see." She rolled down the window and hung her head out.

Tourists and businesspeople jammed the airport. Terpe insisted on pushing Geline's stroller, but after a few minutes Joss pried her hands off the handle. "It's my turn. See that board with the numbers? You know his flight number, so, which gate?"

"Number ten!"

They went to an enormous waiting room. Terpe paced, peered out the large windows, her arms outstretched and tilting like a bird while she watched planes land. She moved toward the tunnel. "People are coming. The tunnel's super long."

Before Joss could gather her purse and stroller, Terpe stood at the rope. After what felt like a long thirty minutes, but was probably less than five, Jackson's head appeared above the crowd.

Joss waved and he hurried to her. He pulled off his backpack, dropped it, and hugged her.

Terpe crept up beside him and tugged on his jacket.

"Who's tearing off my jacket? Someone's stealing my jacket. Who's that?" He turned, "Ah, it's a jacket thief. They're haunting every airport these days! No, maybe this one isn't a thief. Could this be Terpe? Nooooo, this girl is way too tall, way too grown-up! She can't be Terpe!"

He grabbed her in a hug and spun her around. Terpe beamed. When he set her down, he took hold of her hand and peered in the stroller. "And here's the little brown-eyed beauty. Sissy, your children are the best thing Phil ever gave you."

Joss frowned. "Not now, Jackson. We'll talk later."

Jackson promised to cook pancakes for breakfast if Terpe would agree to go to bed without a fuss.

He came downstairs and set a fifth of scotch on the kitchen table.

"Oh, I didn't know you drank. Polluting your temple these days?"

"Ha. You remembered that old wrestling team pledge. I still don't drink much, but I bought this so we could celebrate my visit."

He poured an inch of scotch and added ice. Joss shook her head and filled a glass with water.

She sat at one end of the sofa and he sat on the other. "Smells like you just had a fire. You all having cold weather this late in the season?"

"Nope, it hasn't been cold. Adam built one yesterday afternoon. He hung out with Terpe while I napped. He tried to entertain her, but he's not used to kids. He didn't know what to do or say."

"This Adam, he's a keeper?"

"We haven't been seeing each other for long. I thought he was a good guy until he called this morning to tell me he would be leaving town, because he always wanted to take a trip. He leaves tomorrow, running because he's in over his head. Terpe doesn't like him. She's back to her sulky, smartass behavior. Plus the baby and me to deal with. I'm the needy widow."

"The hell you are." Jacks laughed. "You're not a clinger-whiner. You have a PhD, a book out, and you're working on another. You've got contacts. When you want a boyfriend, you'll find one."

"Just being sarcastic about needy. I don't plan to look for another boyfriend. This whole thing has been nothing but a nightmare. Well, Adam and I did have some fun, too."

"This whole thing? You mean the fire and Phil?"

"Yes, but I've told you that Phil and I were unraveling even before this past December. The new baby broke our last threads. When I told Terpe she'd have a baby sister, she stormed down to the creek, that's where she summons her magical, made-up friends. She argued with Phil, refused to wash dishes or laundry, refused to clean her pigsty of a room, refused to help take out the garbage. Phil tried to reassure her that he'd still play with her, but she wouldn't listen. Maybe her confidence in her dad had always been shaky? I don't know."

"Kids eavesdrop and watch and figure things out. You and I sure did." Jackson's voice sounded loud and firm.

"Enough about my troubles. Tell me how you are."

"I told you I added another room to the cabin. I like it, now it's over eighteen hundred square feet. I took that job opportunity I told you about. A nature interpreter on a tourist ferry. I give talks about the water, animals, the Inuit people, that sort of thing. Tourists ask tons of questions, so I'm always doing research. My schedule's tight in warmer months.

"You'd love Alaska. The ratio of men to women is in your favor. Course a lot of those guys are total misfits." He laughed. "Way worse creeps than me."

"You are not a misfit or a creep."

"I use my biology degree, but it's different. I still don't know a tenth of what a native Alaskan does."

"Remember how many books lay around the house growing up? Strange Mother and Daddy had so many, but they didn't read. Mother read beauty and fashion magazines. You and I were more scholarly than our parents."

"I know what Dad liked to read." He snorted the way he used to do when he got angry.

"What?"

"Porn. I found his collection in the wine cellar. I must have been about eight." He gulped the scotch and set the empty glass on the table. "When the weather's bad, I do business. Over the years I've met a lot of tourists and developed some friendships."

"Wait! Daddy into porn? If anything, I imagined girlfriends."

"Really, Joss. Would you expect him to tell you? He wanted to keep you sheltered. You are the lucky one."

"Oh, real lucky. Watching the barn burn down, killing Thistle and Plenty. Watching Mother die. Yes, a big pile of luck. Tell me about this business of yours."

"My clients aren't only tourists. I met a few nice folks at the tracks and they kept in touch." He ran his hand through his hair, a gesture Joss remembered from childhood.

"What sort of people?" She watched his face, aware of crossing her arms over her belly.

"Businessmen, mostly. In the winter when I have time, I study the market. Give them tips. Daddy taught me to play the market."

"I don't understand."

"Don't worry. It's legitimate." He stretched out his long legs.

"What went on at the tracks?"

"Such a long time ago."

"You know, I never got over Daddy refusing to let me come. And when you got home, you bragged about how rich the people were, getting their pictures in magazines and on TV. You alluded to other wild events. You acted like a turd. No, you turned into a turd."

He nodded. "I promised Daddy I wouldn't tell you."

"He's gone."

Jacks picked up his glass, looked, and saw it was empty. "Prostitutes. For my thirteenth birthday present, Daddy bought me a hooker. Of course we gambled on horses, too. Things like that."

"Prostitutes?" She kept her expression calm, squeezed each finger, one by one.

He watched her hands. "Well, you asked."

"It never occurred to me you all would be doing that. Yet, I don't know why I'm shocked."

"Yep, a beautiful girl named Ellie was my first. Daddy's birthday present. She claimed she had to put herself through college, so I figured it must be Ivy League because she charged top dollar. Daddy called her Top Dollar. Night after night, he'd give me a wad of cash. I thought Ellie treated me special because we were dating. For nine or ten days, I went to her hotel room every night. But one night I didn't bring enough money. Well, she cursed me and told me to leave. I stood in the hall outside her door, about to cry. Lonely and humiliated, just a kid who'd made a fool of himself. I never told Daddy she kicked me out. Luckily we moved on to another track a day or so later."

"What on earth could he be thinking?" Her voice trembled.

"He believed a gentleman should learn to hold his liquor and learn how to handle a woman in bed. A woman wants her man to know what to do. Mother felt like that about holding your liquor. How old were we when she offered us cocktails? Fourteen? Fifteen?"

"If you'd told me Daddy was having a long-term affair, I could understand. Why didn't he divorce Mother?"

"Sissy, have you forgotten? Mother had the big money, going back three generations. Maybe he really loved her, too. I don't know. You'd be amazed how many married men use prostitutes. Girlfriends come with messy demands, with prostitutes all you need is cash." His voice came out loud, rough. "And where did Mother go, and what did she do while Sally almost lived with us, taking care of us?"

Joss arched her back to stretch her tired shoulders. "Oh, God. I don't want to speculate. As a kid, I spent a lot of time wondering why she always smelled like whiskey and her clothes looked messy when she came home. It hurts to remember her that way. I don't want to hear all the answers about their marriage. I'm tired. It's late, and you must be tired, too."

He leaned toward her, took her arm, and held it gently. "Listen, telling you all that. My bad timing. I should've waited, at least until after the funeral. Or better, I should've lied."

"You don't need to lie to me," she said. "Not ever again! You know, you're my Jacks. Remember when I used to call you that? You were my favorite person. Still are. We got past our fighting. I hated that we went off to college in different directions. I'm going to call you Jacks again."

"We've been good about staying in touch," he said. "I've kept your letters from those summers while I was traveling with Dad. And now our phone calls and emails. But I just couldn't make myself tell you what was going on with Dad. Probably afraid you'd tattle to Mother. You remember how worldly and powerful we thought he was? How we admired him? But by college I couldn't wait to escape him. When I got older, he scared the crap out of me when we were at the track."

Jacks let go of her arm. He leaned back on the sofa and stared at the ceiling. "I can't stand horses and don't ride because they remind me of those summers. But one day I finally got it.

If not the racetrack, he would've had some other obsession, another reason to get away from Mother. Stupid, it took me so long to figure it out. Later he got worse, with more and more prostitutes, as well as gambling. He talked too fast and acted like some sort of king."

He leaned back and shut his eyes.

"But you were going on thirteen when that started. What Daddy did? Despicable. I'm glad you're here. I hope you'll stay a while." She stood slowly, then took his hand and kissed it. "My dear Jacks. I'm exhausted."

"I'm gonna sit here for a few minutes. See you in the morning." His voice was sad.

She walked around the house, checked door locks, and turned off lights. She left on the light by the stairs for her brother.

Before sleep she smiled, recalling Jacks's wrestling and tennis matches. He always asked her to come and watch and she went to them all. He didn't act puffed up like some of the other boys. Easy to spot on the court, tall with red hair; his easy laugh carried across the courts and drew attention. Girls told her they loved her brother's soft Southern accent. Yet he ignored their admiration most of the time.

Joss felt content, even happy, with him in the house.

In the morning, she sat on the patio with iced coffee, thinking about Adam bolting out of town. Unreliable after all. Jacks often lost track of time and arrived late. Yet he always showed up. Daddy had acted reliably, at times. He came home faithfully at the end of each race circuit. He took her and Jacks to the movies, and afterward they'd go for burgers or something fancy. The three of them watched their favorite TV shows and waged popcorn-throwing battles. Some days they rode horses together.

Occasionally her parents would swim in the pool and go to their club and cocktail parties. But one morning Daddy didn't come to breakfast. In her matter-of-fact tone, Mother would say he'd left early on a business trip. She never looked sad or weepy, never explained further. She'd revert to her charities and bridge clubs. And in late afternoon, all dressed up, she'd leave for cocktail parties. Most nights she stayed out late and slept late the next day.

Joss always saw and felt the distance between her parents. They had nasty fights when she and Jacks were out of the house, or they merely passed each other without speaking or turned and walked away. Over time the distance widened.

Did she and Phil act like her parents? When they dated and through the early years, their attention stayed fixed on each other. He forgave her faults, like she forgave his, except when he came down with bronchitis and turned into a grumpy child.

Phil plunged into affairs. The first time, she refused to believe the evidence when she found it on his desk in the den. An unknown phone number and the name "Alice" written in his handwriting. It sat in the center of the dusty green blotter. Hotel receipts from his supposed conferences spaced over several weeks, but none matched the supposed conference dates. She dialed Alice's number. A woman answered in a breathy voice, "Phil?"

Joss hung up. She bought nightgowns, a red one, a pale green one, and a sexy black one. She reminded herself to kiss him when he came home, even when he was late. She brought a fat candle and matches and set them on the dresser. The first night she rolled close to him in bed. She couldn't see his face, but when she stroked his body, he responded. Most nights they had sex. Even when she felt exhausted, she made an effort.

Sometimes the candle's flame cast shadows across the bed. She pretended they were romantic.

Alice wasn't worth mentioning. Maybe until a couple weeks later when Phil called and claimed he couldn't come home for dinner because of an emergency faculty meeting. "Don't hold my dinner, the meeting could run late."

That night she lay in bed, eyes on the clock until the numbers blurred. Images of him naked, on top of a blonde woman

232 | Other Fires

with perfect skin and a perfect body. A few minutes before midnight, his footsteps crept down the hall. What kind of faculty meeting lasted until midnight? She rolled over to her side of the bed, hugging her pillow tight. If only Alice had been his first, but she wasn't. All of this sounded like a big cliché until she remembered it described her and Phil.

Taking a gulp of ice-cold coffee, she resolved that right after Phil's funeral, when she took a short break from writing the book, she'd force herself to read her old journals. She wouldn't avoid any details. Why hadn't she confronted her parents about leaving her and Jacks with Sally most of the time? Why hadn't she asked them where they went and what they did? Part of her still didn't want to know.

Another part she knew and wanted to fix. Sally deserved better. Mother had worked and worked Sally, taking advantage of Sally's deep kindness. Joss had felt angry with her mother and sorry for Sally, who never had enough time off. She deserved whole weekends, a monthlong vacation, and holidays off. Yet Joss couldn't remember Sally once complaining. One thing Joss had done right. After Mother died, she'd told her father that Sally should receive regular time off for vacations and holidays and days off whenever she asked for them. Dad had to give her a raise now and keep up regular raises. He had agreed.

Maybe Phil's doctor had given her good advice. Maybe Joss did need therapy. Could she tell the truth without help? Too late to tell Mother, unless she talked to a stone at the cemetery. Maybe she'd have to do that.

If she didn't have Terpe and Geline, she might move to a cabin in the woods, take walks, and write books about herbs and Greek literature. Maybe become a witch, dress in black with a gray shawl, a lone woman striding over heather-covered moors and mourning by the fire in her hut. She'd walk to the sea, long hair blowing wildly in the wind. These images dredged up from old romances and movies and teenage fantasies set her to laughing, which surprised her with fresh tears. This moping might work in a bad romance novel, or in a movie if it had those great period costumes and lonesome mansions, but she suspected those lives weren't quite her sort. She'd be bored to death quickly.

Chapter Thirty-One: Terpe

UNCLE JACKSON MADE BREAKFAST FOR Terpe. Besides bacon, he made blueberry pancakes and stewed apples with lots of cinnamon. Terpe ate three pancakes as big as her plate. She felt full, but she ate the bacon and apples anyway. Once she and her uncle were really full, he said they should walk around the neighborhood to settle their breakfast. Terpe guessed this settling thing could be a grown-up idea. She didn't always understand grown-ups, but she'd walk miles with Uncle Jackson.

Her fixed-up bedroom looked cool. Her uncle liked sleeping in the den next to her room and said he didn't mind the lumpy pullout bed. She stopped worrying about fires. Probably Mom planned to slip out to buy a nicer bed and toss the pullout in the garbage. All part of a plot to get Jacks to stay longer.

From her bedroom window, Terpe could see down the hill, almost as far as the creek. Sometimes she missed playing with her imaginary friends. Yet so much had happened since last Christmas that her friends had come to feel less real. At times when she felt babyish and small, she thought about them. But feeling little again never lasted nowadays.

She and Mom stayed too busy for Terpe to pretend to be a little kid any longer. She discovered that her mother's problems had somehow become more of her problems, too. One problem that had gotten worse as Dad moved in and out of ICU was the phone ringing with people asking how Dad was doing. Mom sent out group emails again and again. Most of the time she and Mom stopped answering the phone. When Mom had some extra energy, she sat on the kitchen stool, playing back messages and writing the important ones down.

Terpe decided Mom must have turned off her cell phone. She hadn't heard that special cell ring tone since yesterday. She hoped he had gone forever. He didn't belong in her family, and he knew it.

Zoe left a message saying she'd call back on Wednesday. Terpe wanted the funeral to be over fast so Dad wouldn't stay in her head every minute. If he were buried, she might not think about him. No, burying wouldn't fix it. She'd be sad about Dad for the rest of her life. Mom had already warned her not to lie to herself.

Jacks only wore jeans, work shirts, sweatshirts, and boots. Mom had offered to buy her a new dress, but Terpe refused. Mom said that after the funeral, they should take Jacks to the museum and the big park on the edge of town. He suggested dinner out so Mom wouldn't have to cook after shopping.

Sometimes Mom talked fast and acted jittery, like she was full of energy, but Terpe knew Mom was still tired and nervous. Maybe Jackson hadn't figured out yet that Mom kept trying to make the city interesting for him. It would be cool if he lived in their house, or even in the neighborhood. Jackson talked to her like a grown-up and listened when she talked. He made it easy for her to be super nice to him and even nice to other people besides Zoe. She looked forward to breakfast with him every morning. During their walk to settle their breakfast earlier that morning, she had asked him if she could call him Jacks, instead of Uncle Jackson.

He'd laughed nice and loud, kissed her forehead, and told her, "Sure thing."

Chapter Thirty-Two: Adam

ON MONDAY, THE FIRST DAY of the trip, Adam drove through a few scenic towns. Eager to keep moving, he didn't stop until late afternoon. Leaving the highway, he took a secondary road. He drove along at thirty-five or forty, taking in the trees close to the road, the fresh smells, and four times he crossed little bridges over creeks.

He slowed when he spotted an old motel set back off the road. A freshly painted sign read THE GATEWAY in bold red letters. And another sign on the motel office door. The office was attached to a row of white cinder-block rooms. The doors to the office and the rooms were also painted bright red. Cars sat in the parking lot: two West Virginia license plates, one Florida, and a Montana. This many cars on a secondary road were a good sign.

Walking to the office, he spotted a new Ford pickup parked next to a wooden house behind the motel. A lake with a dock and rowboat stretched out beyond the house. He smelled fish in the air.

A thin guy around Adam's age stood at the front desk. His undershirt showed off muscled arms covered with tattoos. The clerk registered him and gave directions to a diner a mile or so down the road. Adam threw his duffle on the bed in room number three and drove to the diner. So excited to have come to this open, beautiful place, he didn't eat a big meal. He ordered a grilled cheese, a piece of cherry pie, and a Coke. He took the food outside to a picnic table. Fading afternoon light was turning the leaves golden, and the air smelling like pine trees and fresh-cut wood acted as a balm. Gleeful to be out of the city.

This journey marked the first time he'd traveled alone. One trip to DC with his parents when he saw the mammoth and the few summers when they went to the beach for a week. Nothing else. He didn't count the bus trips to other high schools when he played football and basketball.

Joss would be busy with the funeral and people stopping by the house. Papa's funeral? The only part he remembered, he and Mama sat talking in his truck in the church parking lot. He never visited Papa's grave, never even drove near the cemetery. Those places gave him the creeps.

Back in room three, he quickly fell asleep. In the morning he asked the desk clerk which western route had the best scenery and the least traffic.

The clerk grinned. "Morning. My pals call me Easy. You want scenery?"

"Easy, a good nickname. Playing football, the guys called me Adam the Mammoth, because I played center. Thank goodness that name didn't stick. Yeah, scenery."

"Everything around here's worth seeing. When I get time, I take my boat out and throw in a line. Sometimes I just sit on the dock." Easy tore a piece of paper off the top of a pad and grabbed a pen out of a cubby behind him. Adam half watched the lit cigarette bounce in the corner of his mouth while he drew the map, fascinated that the cigarette didn't fall out. One of Easy's arms had a red dragon breathing orange flames running from elbow to wrist; on the other arm, a small black snake wove its way through stalks of green bamboo all the way down.

He finished the map. Adam pointed to the dragon. "Nice tats. Especially the dragon."

"Got these before Iraq, in oh-five. This Buddhist guy I met in a bar had great tattoos and took me to his artist. The Buddhist guy and I became friends, and both of us served in Iraq. Three tours."

Easy's talk seemed confident, and he looked tough. Words just seemed to fall out. He probably charmed all the girls.

Adam laid his room key on the counter and picked up the map. They shook hands. "Have a good trip. Maybe I'll catch you on the way back."

"Thanks." Adam held up Easy's map. "Yeah, catch you on my way back."

Adam drove to the diner, surprised he said he'd stay at the motel on the way back. Usually when he made decisions, he thought about them, but he wondered if that might be a lie he told himself. It sure hadn't happened with Joss. His heart took the lead, forgetting his head could make good decisions.

He pulled halfway out of the lot, stopped, and studied the small house behind the motel. A lonely house on the half-deserted secondary road. But while covering the miles, he wondered if a house facing a lake with a view of the mountains would be fine for him. It wouldn't feel any lonelier than his own city apartment.

Should he get a tattoo? Maybe a small one on his back? No, Joss was the sort of woman who thought only criminals and musicians wore tattoos. How stupid. She wouldn't speak to him again. His stomach clenched. By Tuesday afternoon, he'd called her cell and the landline five times each day. He left messages, but she never answered or left him a message.

The funeral happened yesterday, Monday. Still she could have made a quick phone call.

If he kept dating Joss, he and the kids would need to learn to get along. Geline would be easier. When he saw himself running around in a park chasing kids, he saw different kids, his own two, plus Joss's kids. He saw himself building stuff with them in the sandbox and pushing their swings, but not too high. When he came home from work, he'd give them hugs, first thing. He wanted to teach them songs and read to them. Even when they got older, they'd still do stuff together. He would not lay a hand on them. Not ever.

But kids weren't all fun.

When Joss told him Phil killed himself, Adam thought about why most TV shows bored him. TV characters had problems they could make go away fast, or something fake made the problems disappear. Not like with his drinking, not like with Joss's husband. The TV characters would laugh and say problems always worked out. Did it ever happen that way? Not to anyone Adam knew.

For instance, Morticia, his friend from high school. One of the guys had said she married some other creep, not the one who got her pregnant. This guy hardly worked. Soon she had another baby with him. When Adam's buddy spotted her in the grocery store, she was pushing a double stroller. She turned away and ducked behind a display of cans.

Sunday afternoon before he left town, he'd driven by Joss's house. Lights were off and car in the driveway. He dropped off lumber in Terpe's backyard near the hill to the creek. He attached a note about them building a tree house together. Terpe would find the lumber. He hoped she'd call him and they'd talk about the tree house. He wanted to cheer up the kid. When Joss said that Terpe had finally made a friend at school, he felt bad. A nine-year-old who'd never made a real friend? He couldn't imagine how lonely that must've been.

Chapter Thirty-Three: Joss

JOSS DROVE HOME FROM THE mall at low speed, not wanting to break the mood. Jacks sat in the back seat next to Geline in her car seat. Terpe sat up front and sang along with him. Geline waved her fists, squealing and babbling. When the song ended, Jacks covered his face and in a Donald Duck voice, he chanted, "Peek-a-boo, peek-a-boo," and dropped his hands. Geline screeched with laughter and waved her fists again.

Joss turned into the driveway, laughing and crying. She and Phil used to play peek-a-boo with Terpe.

Jacks took Geline out of her car seat and held her while Joss unlocked the back door.

"Mom! What's that big white thing? Over there, at the top of the hill?"

Joss squinted at the trees. "I'm not sure."

Terpe turned to her uncle. "Come on!"

He handed the baby to Joss and set down his shopping bags. "Duty calls." He followed Terpe across the lawn.

Joss took a baby bottle from the refrigerator and carried Geline to her room, changed her diaper, and sat in the rocking chair with her. While Geline drank her bottle, Joss hummed snatches of songs. Joss put the empty bottle on a table. Geline's breathing changed, and Joss laid her gently in the crib.

Terpe ran back to the patio. "Mom. It's a pile of wood. And this!" She waved a plastic bag. "Something's inside." She opened the bag and read the piece of paper.

"What does it say?" Joss peered over her shoulder. In block letters the note read: "Terpe, I got this lumber. We can build your tree house when I get back. I'll be back soon. Adam."

"Oh my. Wasn't that nice of Adam?"

"Adam's the keeper? The mammoth guy?" Jacks grinned in a sly way.

"What do you think, Terpe?" Joss pursed her lips.

"Don't know." Terpe's face stayed stiff. "I'm surprised. I gotta think."

"Think about it later. We need to be at the church by one forty-five, so go get ready."

Terpe ran upstairs.

Joss and Jacks settled in the living room. "Terpe's been around a lot, so I haven't been able to warn you that I don't get along with Phil's parents. Terpe hates going over there. Her grandmother bosses her around and criticizes her and her husband follows her lead. I agree my child can be sulky, but she's their grandchild, and they don't even know Geline.

"When Terpe turned five, Phil was still pleading with me to stay at his parents for two days, either for Thanksgiving, or Christmas. I refused to go for both holidays. Last Thanksgiving, Phil's mother yelled at Terpe, calling her a spoiled, whiny brat.

"I told Phil's mother off: 'You don't know Terpe because you never took the time. You're a terrible grandmother.'

"Later Terpe said her grandmother acted scared of her. Terpe thought about kicking her grandmother on the leg and crippling the mean old woman. I told her these thoughts were normal when you're hurt. I told her, 'It's okay if your grandmother fears you. You're never staying overnight in that house again.'

"When Geline was born, Phil's parents stopped by for half an hour to see her, and afterward Phil took them and Terpe out to dinner. I stayed home with the newborn. Later that night Phil told me, 'I'm ashamed of my parents. But they wouldn't like anyone I married because they want me to themselves. That's why I whine when I'm sick. It's Mother's fault I'm spoiled.' His mouth drooped. Some truth, I thought, but he missed the part about taking responsibility to stop whining at his own wife."

Jacks grumbled. "Phil's parents. What losers. I sat next to the father at your wedding rehearsal dinner. Nothing but snide comments, the bastard ruined my dinner. Two days later I watched you and Phil dancing. Thinking back, the wedding day might be the one time you two looked happy. And there sat Phil's mother whispering to her husband, pointing at people dancing. Even her smile looked nasty."

"Think about it. Phil grew up alone, with those parents. No brothers and sisters as buffers. I'd been the only person he ever told about his mother slapping him around while his father watched in some kind of fog. Plus their pretenses about wealth."

"Phil didn't try hard enough." Jacks shook his head. "A petty, whiny complainer and a hypochondriac. No wonder he screwed every woman who glanced at him twice. Too bad he's already dead. I'd like to put my hands around his scrawny neck and squeeze."

"You don't mean that."

"Yeah, I do. That man ran you into the ground. I don't want nobody messing with my Sissy."

Her voice rose. "Phil did defend me to his parents. He tried and tried. When Phil killed himself, he contrived the ultimate get-back."

"You hear how crazy that sounds? Killing yourself to get back at your parents is a teenage move. You're better off without him." He faced her. "I'm serious. Better off."

"You're right about that part."

He sighed. "Sometimes I'm relieved I live alone, sometimes I don't like it. I've been dating someone, but it's only been a couple months."

He sounded forlorn. He defended her now, but he hadn't expressed much concern about her marriage when they emailed or talked on the phone. Well, she probably hadn't revealed much either.

A sudden image of Jacks when he was about Terpe's age. One afternoon, just home from school, she lingered in the kitchen with Sally, but Jacks ran upstairs. A few minutes later strange sounds came from his room. She hurried upstairs, listened at the door, and opened it a crack.

He sat on the side of his bed, his head hanging down, his body rocking.

"What's wrong?" She moved toward him.

"Get the fuck out of my room!" Jacks jumped up, pushed on her chest, shoved her out, and slammed the door. Her heart thudding, she paced the hall. She hadn't seen her brother cry since he was five. She didn't know how to help him.

Down in the kitchen, Sally's radio was playing loud music, which meant she'd be rolling out biscuit dough. Joss went to her own room, inspected the colorful flowers on her wallpaper. Now the stupid flowers struck her as dull and flat. Tears leaked down her cheeks. Her brother pushed her out of his room, something he'd never done. Remembering, the incident still hurt.

"Remember when you got upset after school and wouldn't talk about it?" She fiddled with her fingers.

He grimaced. "That time I slammed the door so fast I almost smashed it in your face? I got scared after I did that. I felt terrible. Yet I can't even remember why I got upset."

"I stayed mad at you and Daddy mostly because I couldn't come with you all to the races. Now you're here, and I'm so glad." She stretched. "I've got to get ready now."

"The shopping wore me out." He laughed. "First time I've been inside a mall in years."

Joss dressed quickly and tended to the children. Last night she had decided not to take Geline to the service. Church wouldn't be a good place for a small child, unless the child slept a lot. Mrs. O'Toole had offered to keep Geline, and Joss had agreed.

She, Terpe, and Jacks entered the church late, only two minutes before the service began. All the way to church, Joss told herself they should sit with Phil's parents. Try to act like a close-knit family? Would anyone even believe that? Joss led the way to the front, but at the last second turned and steered Terpe across the aisle to the other front row reserved for family. Jacks followed.

During the first hymn, Terpe fidgeted and turned to face the back of the church. Sounds of heavy rain wove through the minister's words. Basic elemental rain. Phil in a wooden box, under grass and mud, marked by a stone. His spirit wouldn't go anywhere. Nor would anyone else's. He had ended his one precious life.

No one went to the pulpit to talk about the great guy Phil. Joss dreaded platitudes and felt relieved the service would be short. During the recessional while the crucifer passed, Terpe elbowed her. "Quick, turn around. Wearing a big black hat, she's with people from Dad's department."

Vivienne, dressed in black. A pretend-widow slut.

Joss felt her stomach churn. Jacks put his arm around her shoulder and whispered, "Hang tough. It's almost over." Joss wondered if the woman would be arrested as an accomplice to arson. At this point she wanted to get on with her life and wouldn't dwell on the past.

Joss tried to stay aware while they walked through the graveyard behind the church. She handed her umbrella to her brother and lurched along, pulling her shoes out of the mud between flagstones. They left the flagstones and walked on soggy grass to a dirt pile next to three or four headstones engraved with the name Montgomery.

Terpe grabbed her hand. "Mom, that woman's over there, she's by that big tree."

Jacks pulled Terpe close. She leaned against him, and Joss heard her whisper, "You're my Jacks, too."

Joss kept her gaze lowered while they walked out of the cemetery. What might she do if she came face-to-face with Vivienne? She imagined screaming and pounding her face. No. She wouldn't make a scene.

When they made it back in the car, Joss said, "I can't go to the Montgomerys' and make vapid conversation and eat potato salad off a paper plate. It's the proper thing, but I can't do it."

"You think I care?" Jacks laughed. "If the rain stops, let's walk along the river. I wanna see how your river stacks up against Sitka's."

"I don't wanna go to their house either," Terpe said.

"My heels are coated with mud. Let's change our clothes. I'll run next door and check on Geline."

"Excellent plan, Sissy. I'll get out of this suit and tie, which I probably won't wear again."

"Wear suits every day." Terpe patted his back. "You look handsome." She giggled.

Chapter Thirty-Four: Adam

FOR HIS FIRST HIKE, ADAM took the Cedar Falls Trail. The path started out wider than he expected. Halfway up the trail, he stopped and searched his pack for the ham and cheese sandwich and a big orange, but found no food. He wouldn't turn around. The distant roar of the falls called him, and he stood amazed at the rushing water and deafening roar. He took off his shirt and dunked his head in a pool below the falls. Stunned by the cold water, he figured it must be snowmelt. He filled his canteen, found a flat rock, and sat in sunlight. Water sounds soothed him.

Thoughts of Joss crept in. To distract himself, he picked up pebbles, tossed them in the water, and watched them land. Since starting on the trail, he'd caught himself glancing around every few minutes, scoping the area. He didn't feel quite safe and worried about what to do if some animal ran out of the woods, coming after him. Embarrassing that a jock had to stay on a well-marked trail because he didn't have a topo map and couldn't read one if he had it. No one knew he was out hiking; if he were attacked by a bear, he could get slashed with a claw and bleed to death.

The dusty trail showed footprints, but so far he hadn't seen any hikers. He put on his shirt and headed down to the trailhead.

Every inch of his body felt alive, relaxed, even though his legs shook a little with the strain of going downhill. At the trailhead, he greeted his truck like a good buddy. When he opened the door, a blast of heat and a strong smell of oranges hit him. The runny ham and cheese sandwich and warm orange on the front seat made his stomach clench, but he ate them anyway.

By the time he parked in the town of Brown's Mill, the sun had dropped behind the buildings. He ambled along the main street, looking into window displays at a small department store, a hardware store, and a drugstore. In the second block, he spotted a sign for Slater's Restaurant across the street. Through the plate glass windows, he saw lights and people. On the curb, ready to cross the street, he suddenly heard high-pitched screams.

Adam ran toward the sound. Two figures were fighting in a lot between buildings, a small man, no, a kid, and a big man. The boy fell, and the man stood over the child, swinging a stick.

Adam plowed into the man, knocked him to the ground, and slugged him in the face. Confident the man would be slow to rise, Adam grabbed the child's arm and said, "Come on."

They'd gotten as far as the sidewalk when the man came after them, cursing. The man knocked Adam to the ground. Something cold splashed along his leg. With a crazy laugh, the man flicked open a lighter, grabbed Adam's leg, and set his jeans on fire.

Adam jumped to his feet and aimed his fist at the man's face, but the man turned. His blow glanced off the man's ear.

The kid grabbed Adam's arm. "Let's go!" They sprinted down the sidewalk; the boy shoved open a door and yelled, "He's on fire!"

The room erupted. Men slid off barstools and leapt from chairs. People eased Adam to the floor and threw a coat over his legs. A ceiling fan spun overhead and the floor rotated.

Adam turned his head and threw up. His leg burning and his own yells.

The boy stared down at him. Adam tried to rise, but he couldn't. He mumbled, "What's your name?"

"Willie."

He tried to grab the boy's arm.

Loud sounds, maybe sirens. His body rose off the floor. An island dream sled slipped underneath him. The sled rolled into a dark space lined with blinking lights. An airplane inside a cave? Ice caves were all over the island, and he'd always suspected airplanes were stored in some of the caves. Maybe the red horse lived in this cave, too. Despite all the ice, Adam's body felt like fire. The sled flew out of the cave. All around him some animal wailed and wailed.

Wild animals were chasing him. The wind at his back. He slid across a sheet of ice and floated onto another sled. This one bumped along with people talking all around him. Bright daylight burned his eyes.

His body floated inside a white room. His sled had stopped and landed somewhere and hands were touching his body all over.

Later, his head hurt. Someone still touching his body.

He half opened his eyes. Out the window, mountains.

The person was a woman wearing a blue uniform. She stood over him, smiling; she kept talking until he could keep his eyes open. Her name tag said "Martha." She put a tight cuff on his arm and squeezed, and after she took it off, she helped him sit enough to drink a glass of water.

"A hospital? How long have I been here?"

"Since last evening. Your leg got burned, but you're going to be fine. We're giving you fluids and medicine through that tube." She pointed to a bag on a pole.

"A man threw gas on me and set my pants on fire. I fought the man beating a little boy."

"Two policemen came here to talk to you, but you were sleeping. The boy stopped by to see you and he talked with the police. Apparently there were quite a few witnesses. The police caught the man and took him into custody."

"Could you find my cell and wallet? I need the motel business card."

"They're locked up in the nurses' station. I'll get them for you."

He wouldn't call Joss. She hadn't answered her calls because she felt done with him. Maybe he could leave the city and live out here. Mom's idea of country living, maybe that could be a good plan after all. Even his own relatives didn't seem scary now.

He dialed his mother's number and her voice came on her machine.

"Sorry I didn't call sooner. I'm still in West Virginia, hiking and swimming. It's beautiful here. I might not make it any farther west. I'll bring you out here sometime. I think you'll love it. I'll call again, love you. Bye."

The nurse gave him a shot for pain. He thanked her, drank more water, and held his phone. Maybe he'd call his buddy Freddie, or someone. But if Adam mentioned where he'd gone, any one of his friends would ask the same question: Had he been drinking? He'd say no. But unless they hung out with him, they probably wouldn't believe him. To hell with their suspicions. This stuff made him mad at himself since he'd created their suspicions. All his fault.

The pain shot kicked in. With the phone resting on his stomach, he dozed.

Someone came in his room. He opened his eyes. Someone small moved toward his bed. Oh, the kid from the fight. Adam struggled to sit, but he felt too weak. "Come on in. How you doing?" His name? Adam had no idea.

"I'm okay. Mom's down the hall in the waiting room. I wanted to see how you were doing. And to say thanks. Also, my mom, she says to tell you thanks a lot."

"Glad I happened by. No worries, I'll be out of here in no time. There are real nice people here."

"I hope they lock up Pop for good. This time Mom pressed assault charges."

"I figured the man was your father. Tell your mom to keep pressing charges. It's better if she kicks him out, for good. Don't let that man ruin your life. What's your name, I can't remember."

"Willie Bradshaw. Man, you're tough. You a wrestler?"

"Nope, I played center in football, also basketball. Thanks for stopping by, and good luck to you, Willie."

"Yeah, you, too." The boy turned to leave.

Adam remembered something. He fought to raise himself on one elbow. By the time he rearranged his body, he started yelling to the empty doorway. "Remember Willie, it was never your fault. Remember, it's not your fault. Not your fault. Not your fault!"

Chapter Thirty-Five: Joss

THESE DAYS JOSS DIDN'T ANSWER her landline or cell until she checked caller ID. She didn't want, or need, to talk to Adam. Three weeks had passed since Phil's funeral. That morning the urge came over her to clear out Phil's clothes. Jacks would help pack his books and papers. Whatever Phil's department didn't want, she'd donate to the historical society. Phil wore nice clothes. A donation truck could come get them, but this chore could wait a few days.

Today she must write Adam a letter. That could not wait. He might be driving home today. She wanted her letter to be at his apartment when he got home. What to say? His attention had taken her mind off the crisis with Phil. A gentle man, she liked his kindness and stability, until she met another side, when he took off like a scared teenager. For someone with no experience with children, he'd made a good effort in a hard situation. A kind man who had helped her through a bad time. The truth. She wrote the words on a piece of stationery, tucked it in an envelope, and wrote his address. The letter would go out today.

The next thing. Call the man who owned the SUV. She had already alerted her insurance agent about hitting his car. She phoned the man and left a message apologizing for not calling earlier. Said she'd been at a funeral. She gave him her insurance company's name and number, finishing her business for the day.

She had begun rereading old journals, thankful she'd dated each entry. She paid special attention to her teenage years, the ones before and after her mother died. Her pattern of going along with people to keep the peace seemed to have started in middle school.

One day while reading an entry, a truth struck her. She had to act nice, because if she accused her mother or father of anything big and serious, both of them might leave her and Jacks alone in the house. What if something happened to Sally? What if her parents left them completely and never came back?

Furious with her mother, Joss knew she'd always judged her severely. Never any slack, she never tried to see through her mother's eyes. As a kid, Joss felt sad mostly because Mother wasn't home. Not to talk with, not to have an adventure at the zoo, not to go out to eat, just the two of them. They rarely did things together.

Daddy had basically left the marriage years before Mother died. She had filled her life with activities, not her own children.

Joss needed to figure out if she'd done the same thing. When she met Phil, he felt different from Daddy. Yet if Phil had grown up with money or married a wealthy and socially connected woman, he could have acted like her father. So, Phil had affairs, and in his own way he left the marriage. Had she guessed that he might start leaving their marriage? She sat at her desk, staring out the window, letting tears come without stopping them. Finally she grabbed a tissue and wiped her face.

Jacks had dealt with their parents by rebelling. As soon as he left home, he had pushed against Daddy's training. Their father would be appalled to know his well-mannered, well-educated, well-dressed son was wearing jeans and living in a cabin in Alaska, making a living as a fishing guide and giving nature talks on a ferry full of tourists. Proud of her brother making his own way, Joss smiled.

She closed the notebook. Enough insight about her early life for one day. She and Jacks had planned to go to her favorite coffee shop. Geline would be in day care, and Terpe would spend the day at Zoe's house. Joss planned to talk about money, her children, and the future. She also wanted to tell him about reading her old journal entries and what she'd discovered about their childhood while looking back.

Jacks could stay as long as he liked. But she knew he'd leave soon. From his vivid descriptions and the photographs he sent her, she understood Sitka had become a place where he could live simply and make his own schedule.

The same thought popped into her head again: she could cut expenses and live more simply, like Jacks. She could get by on tutoring students in Greek and French. She wouldn't have to get some big university job. Since Phil had gone into the hospital, she'd been thinking about divorce and moving. Her research and writing were portable. She couldn't be sure yet, but maybe she and the girls would move to Sitka.

Chapter Thirty-Six: Adam

HALF-AWAKE, HALF IN A DREAM, Adam lay in bed watching the shape of the mountains change with the angle of the sun. Mountains calmed him. If someone had asked where he was, he couldn't have answered or even said the name of the town. He felt surprised he didn't care.

A nurse took the IV out of his arm and gave him pills. She said, "You're healing well."

"What day is it?"

"You came in Tuesday evening. It's Thursday afternoon."

"I have to leave tomorrow." He opened a drawer in his bedside table and took out his cell, but before he could dial, he fell asleep. When he woke, the mountains were indistinct. He squinted to keep them in focus, but couldn't fight against the darkness. That felt okay because he'd see them again tomorrow.

Friday morning, his leg felt okay, but that morning the doctor told him he needed one more day in the hospital.

Adam said to the nurse, "I've walked up and down these halls a lot. I'm in shape."

She said, "You only walked up and down twice yesterday. Each walk wasn't very long."

"I'm getting restless. I came for the outdoors. Just give me the antibiotic pills and whatever else I'm supposed to take. Show me how to change the bandage. I'll be on my way after lunch."

The nurse pulled off the dressing, which hurt, but he gritted his teeth. She put on a clean dressing while he watched. "I'll give you another bandage, change this one in a couple days. Try not to get it wet. Cover it with plastic bags when you shower. You can buy gauze and such at a drugstore. If the burn starts hurting or gets red around the edges, come back. We have an outpatient clinic in the building next door. Take every single one of the antibiotics the pharmacy gives you, at the time of day that the bottle says. You'll get some pain pills for when you need them, but no refills."

"Okay, okay. Thanks very much for your help. Everyone has treated me great."

He took the Gateway business card out of his wallet and dialed the number.

"Gateway Motel. Easy speaking. May I help you?"

"Hey, Easy. Adam, here. Remember me?"

"Course I do."

"Do you have a guest room available later today?"

"Lemme check. Nope, nothing tonight, but I got a room on Saturday, check in is two in the afternoon."

"Okay. Put me down for tomorrow at two."

"You sound bad. Groggy."

"Some guy set my leg on fire a few days ago. I'm in the hospital near Brown's Mill."

"Oh, man. You were drunk?"

"No, not a bar fight. I fought this guy in an alley."

"I got an extra room in my house. It isn't big, but the bed's comfortable."

"You sure?"

"Yep. Come on ahead."

"Be there in about an hour." Adam fumbled to dress himself. He had to sit in a chair to pull on his pants over his leg. Luckily one of the pant legs was burned and shredded, so it fit better. When he finished dressing, he waited until the room stopped spinning. He didn't know what he'd do if he couldn't find his truck.

The nurse told him Slater's Restaurant was about a mile away. She'd call him a cab. "You shouldn't be walking that distance. It's hot, and you haven't healed."

"No, thanks. I'll take it slow. The exercise will do me good. I got a place to stay."

She shook her head. "Not a smart idea."

He gave her his best smile and hobbled to the elevators. He picked up his prescriptions in the basement pharmacy. He'd taken his medicines about an hour ago, so he should be fine to walk.

The glare on the sidewalk gave him a headache right away. He patted his pants, hoping to find his sunglasses. They must be in the truck. He squinted and walked slowly for about two blocks. His back and armpits were already sweaty. People walked by him, their voices all muffled. Some people noticed his jeans. He ignored them because he couldn't do anything about the burned-off part or about his limp.

The street rippled. He halfway fell and grabbed the door handle on a car, then sprawled out on the car's trunk, panting. God, he was thirsty. Waves of nausea hit him. He leaned over and gagged. He tried to slow his breathing, but it sped up. Desperate, he looked around to hail a cab. But this place wasn't a big city. Where could he even find a phone for a cab?

The nausea passed. A restaurant, something cold to drink. Nothing in this block. *Okay, go slow and rest about every fifteen steps.*

A drugstore. He grabbed onto a street sign and waited for the light to change. He hobbled across the street into a drugstore. At an upright refrigerator, he grabbed a bottle of water and a bottle of Pepsi. His hands shook when he paid the cashier. Leaning against the counter, he gulped down half the water. He didn't want to leave the air-conditioning.

Back on the street, he remembered sunglasses. The drugstore sold glasses. Stupid. No, he kept hurrying. His glasses were in the truck. He only needed to walk another block or two; soon he'd spot his Ford.

Afraid of falling, he walked close to parked cars to hold on to. Nausea hit him again. He leaned over the curb and threw up into the street. Vomit splashed onto the grill of a car. He wiped his mouth as best he could.

Up ahead. Maybe his truck? Yes. Not even a parking ticket? He moved slowly toward a blue truck. Yes, his. He leaned against it and felt around for his keys. He hauled himself into the truck, started it, revved up the engine, and cranked up the air-conditioning. With closed eyes he enjoyed the feeling of the moving air slowly cooling him.

With a rag from under the seat, he wiped his mouth, took a swig of water, and swished it around. He opened the door and spit onto the street. Using more water to wet the rag, he wiped his mouth again. As soon as he closed the door, he spotted parking tickets on the other side of the windshield. He sipped the rest of the water, got out of the truck, and inched along, holding on to the hood. With three tickets in hand, he hobbled back to the driver's side. His sunglasses were in the glove compartment and he slid them on. By now the truck cab had cooled.

The nurse didn't think he could walk a mile, and halfway here he'd been agreeing with her. His leg throbbed. Probably he'd made a mistake walking.

But he hung in there, and he made it! That made him feel strong and good.

Would the Pepsi stay down? He waited a few minutes before pulling out of the parking space. He drove forty miles an hour, using the same route back to the motel, and feeling grateful for his truck and for his life.

Easy was sitting near the desk reading a book when Adam arrived. He gave Adam a house key. "You look terrible. We'll talk later. The spare room's off the hall, on the right. The sheets are clean."

"I appreciate this. Really." Adam walked slowly to the house. The bedroom walls were plain. An oak dresser had a mirror, and the double bed was covered with a white chenille bedspread. The bedspread and pillows smelled clean, faintly of laundry soap. Faded green curtains covered a large window on one wall. He intended to open the curtains and check out the lake. With his duffle leaning against the wall, he took off his shoes and headed to the bathroom, splashed water and soap on his face, and brushed his teeth. Not bothering to pull down the bedspread, he fell on the bed and slept.

When he woke, he stared at the lit hallway. Noises and frying smells drifted from the kitchen.

A struggle to put on his shoes. He gritted his teeth as he hobbled down the hall.

"How you feeling?" Easy stirred something in a pan.

"Better after the nap. I only walked a mile back to my truck, but that took it out of me."

"A guy set your leg on fire?"

"I was minding my own business, walking down the street looking for a restaurant. A kid hollered—the screams came from this vacant lot, so I ran down the block. A man was yelling and beating this kid, so I punched the guy and knocked him down. The kid and I were running away, but the guy rose up like some swamp monster. He threw a can of gas on my pants and used a lighter to set me on fire. It all happened fast.

"The kid helped me get away. I only remember bits and pieces after that until I woke up in a hospital bed."

"You're a hero, man."

"Nah. I did what anyone would've. Stop some asshole beating on a kid."

"People walk away all the time. What did you think when you heard the yelling?"

"No thinking. Something clicked. I did it." Adam's stomach felt empty. "You cooking?"

"I'm frying some pork chops. I cooked up green beans, and the fried potatoes and onions are done and warming in the pan. You hungry?"

"Yep, the chops and onions smell great. Makes me more hungry. Who's watching the desk?"

"My cousin Harry works every other weekend. Friday evening till Sunday night around nine."

"This your motel?"

"Harry and I inherited it, this house and twenty acres. Harry owns half the motel. I own the other half, plus the house and land because I agreed to be the live-in manager. About nine months out of the year, someone should stay on the property. Fall, spring, and summer, some folks show up after midnight. I close up December, January, and February when the roads are the worst."

Easy filled the plates with food and set them on the table. Adam waited until Easy was seated before he started to eat.

"Dad and Uncle Jerry died in a hunting accident a few years back."

"My father died suddenly, too," Adam said. "A heart attack at fifty-four."

"When people go real fast like that, it's damn hard to digest. Want ketchup?" He picked up a ketchup bottle off the counter and put it on the table. "I get good TV reception, though you wouldn't think it. Wanna watch TV after dinner?"

Adam didn't want to watch TV, but he nodded yes. They talked about restaurants in the area.

Adam finished eating first. "Best meal I've had in a long time."

"A beer goes good with TV." Easy headed to the refrigerator.

"No beer for me, thanks. I'm still on pain pills, and I'm in AA."

"Got it. Coffee?"

"Decaf? Don't I sound like an old man?"

"You sound like a guy right out of the hospital. Let's catch some breeze."

Adam settled in a wooden rocker on the porch. Easy set his mug on a peach crate, stretched his legs, and knocked out twenty-five leg lifts. "The doc said I gotta exercise this leg."

A half-moon slid over the lake, and a breeze rippled the dark water. The air filled with sharp squeals from creatures scurrying through brush. Not a single car went by.

"I'm a city guy. I've never fished, but I wanna learn. If you have time, can you show me some basics, or tell me where I could get a lesson?"

He chuckled. "No fishing lessons out here. But at the hardware, we'll pick up a pole that feels good in your hand. I've got plenty tackle. We'll fish off the dock or take my boat out. I'll show you."

"I also want to learn to read topo maps. I've been in these mountains only two weeks, and already the idea of living in this country is growing on me. If I don't leave the city, I'm afraid I'll get stuck in my old neighborhood forever."

"The hardware sells topo maps." Easy yawned. "This place ain't perfect, but it grew on me. Until Dad and my uncle died, I'd been training to be a park ranger. But when Harry and I talked about this place, we couldn't let it go. Someday I'll spruce up the motel, do some marketing. Maybe finish ranger training."

"What does Harry do?"

"Insurance. He's got an office in town. We never fight because we're different. For example, he's Methodist. I'm a Buddhist. Zen."

Adam turned to Easy's voice. "Zen?"

"Yep, that's a whole other story. Harry's getting married. He found somebody to keep him from dying of loneliness. He's a nervous guy and hates living alone. I tolerate it better because I enjoy my own company."

"Guess I'm more like Harry," Adam said. Easy could probably puzzle out people, figure out why they did this, or that. A relaxing guy to hang with.

Adam stared at the crate. "Papa kicked me and beat me with a broomstick from when I was twelve, and for about a year, until I told Mama. By sixteen I had muscles from football and weights. One night I came home drunk and picked an argument, itching to send Papa to the ER. Mama ran into the bathroom and locked the door. Papa slipped out. I didn't chase him.

"I didn't care if he slept in his car in zero degrees. A few times I chased him out of the apartment. Mama never called the cops. He'd beat her, if she called.

"Finally, Papa feared me. That felt good."

Easy sipped his beer. "Nobody in my family got physical. Usually."

Adam's leg was throbbing again. "Time for bed. I'm running out of steam."

Easy stood. "I'll get up early. I got some electrical and plumbing problems in the guest rooms down at the end."

"You're in luck. I'm an electrician."

"I am in luck. Electrical gives me the creeps because I don't half know what I'm doing."

"Thanks for dinner. See you in the morning." Eager to climb into bed, he took his pills, then pulled back the bedspread to find a black-and-white Guatemalan blanket and red flannel sheets. Under the heavy blanket, he sank into comfort. He read a few pages of a thriller before turning out the light. With fresh mountain air, he assumed he'd sleep well, but one dream collapsed into another. Shaggy creatures plodded next to him, and steam engine trains crept over frozen plains. He and Joss galloped away on the red horse, her hands tight around his waist, her warm mouth against his neck. Something fell on them, gritty like dirt. Joss disappeared. He rushed down endless empty city streets. Tall buildings and trash blowing, like a hurricane coming. Breaking glass. Mannequins blew out of department store windows and moved toward him, stumbling like zombies, green faces dripping, but their moaning and weeping scared him most.

He sprinted to a tall apartment building, but the building didn't have doors. High up, a figure lay in a store window. He climbed up the side of the building and crawled through the window. Joss lay in his bed from childhood, nude and waiting. He stroked her lovely back and kissed her neck. She rolled over and threw a can of fire in his face.

When he woke, his leg was throbbing. Five thirty, with millions of birds making a racket. He opened the curtains to the light, the lake a rippling dark blue. Would Joss try to hurt him? No, she had dropped away, which hurt bad enough. His fault, or maybe not his fault, nor hers. If they'd only made something deeper and stronger, if they'd met each other after Phil died, perhaps. They did have some fun times.

He found three plastic bags in the kitchen to cover his bandage, showered, found the real coffee, and made it strong. From the porch, he watched the rising sun throw sparks over the water. Time vanished into air, sky, and lake. When he became aware of Easy moving around in the kitchen, he opened his eyes. They ate breakfast on the porch.

Adam said, "I have tools in my truck. I'll take a look at those rooms."

Easy unlocked the doors to two rooms at the end. The wiring looked old and frayed. Humidity from clogged air conditioners had ruined the paint. The walls needed to be scraped and sanded before they were painted. Adam set to work on the wiring. About an hour later, he finished.

Easy banged away on a nearby pipe.

Adam followed the sound. "The wiring's done. The back two A/Cs are struggling. They need new filters, or better yet, replace them. I'm guessing all the rooms need new filters. Excess moisture has ruined the paint in those back rooms. Got a sanding machine and enough paint? I could help. Best to scrape and paint the back rooms now, before summer is in full swing."

"Not enough paint on hand." Easy surveyed the parking lot. "Everybody's gone out for the day, let's check the other rooms."

He followed Easy, and they checked each room, working their way back to the office. Some rooms smelled moldy when Easy opened the door.

"Maybe you've just gotten used to the smell," Adam said. "But I wouldn't stay in those rooms. It's not healthy."

Easy nodded. "Okay, you're right. Two new air conditioners. New A/C filters in every room, sanding and painting the end rooms. Those back rooms aren't usually booked. Harry and I have been slacking."

Adam took a breath. "You'd probably book them, if they looked better and didn't stink. Give me directions to a hardware store. What color paint you want?"

"I'll drive. I'm familiar with the route. We'll take the scenic way. Lemme tell Harry and grab my wallet."

Easy's new Ford ran smoother than Adam's replacement truck. Easy drove fast, navigating each turn on the winding road with skill.

"You got a girlfriend?" Adam assumed Easy would say yes.

"Nope." Easy said. "What about you?"

"Right around Christmas, I met this beautiful woman when I did her electrical work. We talked and got along, and then we had great sex. But now she's finished with me, partly because I left to come on this trip. When I met her, she had separated from her husband, and later the guy killed himself. She's got two kids. I suspected it wouldn't ever happen with us. I'm getting over it, but I miss her."

He didn't reveal his promise to himself not to hate Joss, but he might. Did his dreams tell him that? She couldn't help being who she was. But he hated her for being rich and knowing a lot more about the world than he did. Despite their great sex, soon he'd bore her. He felt ashamed.

"Suicide. A vet?"

"No. A head injury made him crazy, and he never came out of it. My mama is smart about people. She warned me, told me to let Joss go. I aimed too high. Before I left on this trip, I bought books about myths, because Joss likes them. Something for us to talk about. But after reading a few pages, I stuck the book at the bottom of my duffle. I've been reading a thriller." He laughed.

"These days I mostly read Buddhist books. I meditate," Easy said. "Iraq turned my head upside down, and I was halfway nuts by time I got home. Trouble sleeping. I had to stay home to keep from getting in bar fights or losing my driver's license. Out here everyone does a fair amount of driving. Half-drunk and alone one day when my old buddy called. He asked me please to visit him in rehab.

"His family came here from Vietnam. He grew up in California. While we were in Iraq, back in oh-six an IED got him. Took off most of his leg. He got airlifted out. Since then he has had a few surgeries, but finally he's doing real good. Learning to walk. When I have some time, I go to DC to visit him.

"He struggles across a room, but he's determined. I envied him. Here he had a fake leg, thick scars all down one side of his face, and usually in pain. Yet he's grateful. I asked if he'd teach me how. He said Buddhism helped him learn about his own mind. I'm reading a book about the three poisons."

"The what?"

"Greed, hatred, and delusion. Hatred's anger, which I still got plenty of. At first I stomped around hating everyone who hadn't gone to Iraq. Delusion means messed-up thinking, not knowing the truth and lying to yourself. Greed's obvious. Every kid on a playground knows about greed."

"When I drank," Adam said, "I was a jerk, starting fights and hollering at neighborhood kids. I lied. I've hated Papa since I turned twelve. I'm used to it."

"No, you aren't used to it. You carry it around." Easy lowered the gear and the truck climbed.

Looking out of Easy's window, Adam took in a valley that resembled a postcard. For a couple of minutes, he closed his eyes against the sun flickering through trees, worried he could get another headache. Since his leg got burned, he'd gotten hangover-type headaches. Maybe he'd banged his head fighting that guy, but nobody at the hospital said he had a concussion.

"Is there someplace to meet women? Not a bar, where all I could do is drink. Someplace like a restaurant?"

Easy nodded. "Yep, there's a dance club. I'll take you, though nothing there interests me."

Adam thought about Easy's house. No pictures of women or even family, at least none he noticed. A guy as outgoing as Easy didn't act like a loner. Easy drove a showy truck, a new Ford-250, like what Adam wanted, but couldn't afford, not if he wanted travel money.

The road grew steeper, the trees grew closer together, edging the road. The leaves were turning bright green. He loved the clean tree smells. His leg didn't hurt.

Easy turned on the radio and hummed to a country song Adam didn't recognize. When the song ended, Easy said, "I know what you're probably thinking, but don't worry, I never make a move unless the guy gives a signal. I know plenty of guys."

Signal? Easy's voice sounded casual. Had he missed something? In high school, gay boys stood out, a few skinny boys in tight jeans who hung together at lunch. Some of Adam's friends yelled insults, but Adam never did. Busy with girls and sports, he paid little attention. But Easy didn't act like those high school boys.

"I hung out with jocks." Adam watched for Easy's reaction.

Easy laughed. "You think none of the ball players were gay? Never been inside a gym? Gyms are full of gay guys."

"I go to the gym, work out, and leave. For me, a gym isn't social." Adam looked out of his window.

Clouds blocked the sun, and wisps of fog drifted across the road while they gained altitude. Adam said, "I've never ridden through clouds. Like visiting another country."

"Tourists say that."

This gay thing was another world. Different from Joss, but something new. Adam's neighborhood had been a small town inside a big city. He remembered he and his buddies were toughs. Fistfights, liquored up and smoked weed, every now and then, other drugs. Some of the girls put out. By sixteen, he'd become a sweet-talking drunk. He'd bedded at least three girls. The team wouldn't booze it up in football season.

Adam decided he wouldn't tell all this stuff to Easy. He wouldn't be interested.

He should move out of Easy's house. Except he liked the guy. Maybe thank Easy for the bedroom and say he decided to move over to the motel since he could pay. Plus his leg felt better, and that was the truth. He'd tell Easy he had to get used to this idea he didn't go with girls. But he didn't want to hurt the guy's feelings. They had fun talking. Maybe they could become friends.

Adam's mind raced with these new situations: beating up a man to rescue a kid, getting his leg burned and waking up in a hospital, his first time in a hospital. Visiting this beautiful place, the waterfalls and the lake and Easy.

Surprised, he felt okay, better than okay, and curious about what might happen next.

When they got to town, maybe he'd look for a bar. Bad idea. Beer never cleared his head. How long would it take to stop thinking about alcohol? After the hardware store, they'd find a diner and have lunch. He'd order a Coke or maybe milk.

"I got plans tonight," Easy said, "but tomorrow night, I'll take you to the dance club."

"Didn't you say you were on the front desk?"

"Maybe Harry will cover another night. Or I'll put a sign on the door."

Easy turned up the radio. "Know this song? It's an old tune from *Porgy and Bess*? 'Summertime.' Remember that big splash we heard last night when we were sitting on the porch? A fish jumping. They can jump way out the water."

Adam smiled, maybe jumping was what he felt. Jumping out the water.

Easy hummed along like he'd heard the song a million times. "Fish is jumpin', and the cotton is high. Your daddy's rich and your ma is good lookin', so hush little baby, don't you cry."

Adam didn't know the song, but never mind, the music sounded fine. Out of his window, the tall trees swayed and roared, and even when he leaned out as far as he could, he couldn't see the tops of some trees. He thought about saying something, but Easy lived here and already knew how trees looked. Maybe Easy even knew some biology. Adam kept looking out his open window and breathing mountain air.

Chapter Thirty-Seven: Terpe

TERPE WORRIED ABOUT MOM, WHO walked around the house with a serious, sad face that looked even worse since the funeral. She and Jacks had tried to get her laughing. They acted silly, making faces at her and singing stupid songs. Mom sometimes forced a tiny laugh and then back to looking sad and still jittery at times.

Terpe put Geline in her stroller. She and Jacks took a walk around the neighborhood to give Mom some peace and quiet.

Terpe wanted her uncle to stay forever, but deep down she knew he wouldn't. She tried not to think about him leaving. When she did, she got scared. Since Jacks was a grown-up, she didn't know how to make him stay. Nothing she said could make him stay.

One good thing, the fire had made her a nicer kid. Sometimes she even wanted to be kind. What her parents had tried to tell her. But Mom didn't tell her to apologize to her classmate, Caroline. Terpe did that on her own.

Even though she'd stuck the note in Caroline's desk a while ago, Terpe hadn't forgotten that mean thing she did. When she saw Caroline in the halls, she felt bad and turned her head. A few weeks after Apology Monday, she found Caroline at recess and said she wanted to talk. Caroline followed her to the water fountain. Terpe moved in front of her, so she had to listen, so she couldn't run away.

"I'm sorry I put that note in your desk. Later I figured out that I wasn't even mad at you, but mad at something else. I'm sorry I acted really mean." She said the words fast, but she meant the words.

Caroline stood like a statue in her ruffled, yellow dress. She faked a smile. "Oh, that's okay." She pushed past Terpe and ran across the playground.

Terpe leaned over the fountain and splashed water on her hot face.

How Caroline acted helped her understand something. The girl acted, put on fake nice. A sort of blah girl. Who could play at recess wearing ruffles and shoes with slick soles that made you slip in the halls and while climbing up the sliding board? Her apology wouldn't make them friends. But she thought she wouldn't have to be somebody's best pal to be nice.

Zoe was still her best friend. They ate lunch together and other girls sat at their table, too. They made up a lunch game: everyone opened her lunch bag and lined up the food. The trading began: a hard-boiled egg for an orange, a peanut butter sandwich for a donut. It went on until everyone made a new lunch, even if they didn't get what they wanted. They laughed and screeched, telling each other what their mothers would say if they found out.

After dinner Terpe usually called Zoe and one or two girls. Her phone rang now, too.

The Saturday after Dad's funeral, she spent the night at Zoe's. On Sunday morning, she told Zoe more about her dad, mostly good memories. She sang her silly song he made up for her.

Zoe said, "Good song. Okay, now stop crying. Listen! You'll miss him forever. That shows how much you love him. That's what happened with my grandma. I still think about her and want to tell her what's happening at school and other things. Sometimes I make a list, but there's no one to hear it, so I put it in my desk drawer with the other stuff I've written."

"Mom told me I'd miss him forever. But it hurts. I hate it."

"Let's go ride bikes." Zoe jumped off the bed. "Come on, lazybones!"

Terpe followed.

Back at home, Terpe thought about Benjy and Declan. She never saw them down by the creek anymore. Sometimes the boys came into her dreams, and sometimes in the early morning, she'd shut her eyes and imagine all three of them running through the woods. Except now their bodies were shaped like mist spirits.

Her life felt bigger, with school and friends, Mom, Geline, and Jacks. She loved her imaginary friends and their adventures, as much as she loved her stuffed animals. The creek remained one of her favorite places. She walked along the bank, alone, and sometimes she whistled and scanned trees, searching for a good spot for a tree house.

Since Jacks had come, she didn't fear the house would catch fire, didn't fear smothering in an elevator or being attacked by a stranger driving along the curb trying to grab her and hurt her. A proud feeling came when she guided Jacks through the mall. He walked slowly, fascinated at the difference between East Coast malls and Alaskan stores. Mostly he didn't want to go into these stores. When he pointed to some stupid kitchen gadget and asked her what it did, she laughed and admitted she didn't know. Sometimes she made up something impossible to make him laugh.

One night he asked her to help him wash the dinner dishes. He didn't like dishwashers and said he wouldn't own one. They got into the habit of cleaning up after dinner. They chased each other around the kitchen, laughing and swatting each other with dish towels.

Jacks kept the kitchen radio playing, and they sang along with the songs. That radio, an old-fashioned brown box, sat in an alcove. Jacks told her that radio was so old it had been in the kitchen of the house where he and Mom had grown up. Somebody named Sally had listened to the radio all day long. Jacks smiled. "I loved Sally, and she loved me and your mom. She took care of us."

One evening after they finished putting away the dishes, he asked if she thought tomorrow would be a good day for them to get going on building her tree house.

He laughed when she shouted, "Yeah, Jacks, heck yeah!"

Acknowledgments

I'VE HAD MANY TEACHERS AND opportunities along the way. The Virginia Center for the Creative Arts (VCCA) for awarding me two fellowships. Gifts of time and support.

Blackbird, Online Journal of Literature and the Arts for the opportunity to work on a wonderful journal and learn from editors Mary Flinn, Gregory Donovan, Michael Keller, and Randy Marshall; to the Fine Arts Work Center, Provincetown, Massachusetts, for workshops led by inspiring teachers Marie Howe and Victoria Redel; and to Elizabeth Cox at Bennington Summer Writing Workshops, for her encouragement.

The Rappahannock Fiction Writer's Workshop and my teacher, Bob Olmstead, who pointed the way to writing my first novel.

To wonderful teachers: Sally Doud, Gloria Wade Gayles, Jamie Fueglein, Susan Hankla, Elizabeth Hodges, Paule Marshall, David Robbins, and Leslie Shiel.

Brooke Warner, Shannon Green, Jennifer Cavin, and Samantha Strom of She Writes Press. I've appreciated their accessibility and kind guidance through my first novel, and my second, *Other Fires.*

Thanks to my editor for *Other Fires*, Randy Marshall, Associate Literary Editor at *Blackbird, Online Journal of Literature and the Arts*. He worked with me editing my entire book. And thanks to editors Jamie Fueglein, who got me started, and Susan Breen for her useful feedback and expertise.

And the writers: Ron Andrea, Helen Foster, Jean Huets, Laura Jones, Danny Cox, Chuck Cleary, Karla Helbert, Megan Holley, Taigen Dan Leighton, Cheryl Pallant, Pam Webber, and Anne Westrick.

My friend Jill Wilson, a literature professor, who listened and gave smart suggestions. My friend Chris Reid for her academic writing. My daughter Sasha for my photo and my grandson Cy, who reads, draws cartoons, and writes stories. His enthusiasm inspires me.

About the Author

LENORE GAY is a retired Licensed Professional Counselor with a master's in sociology and rehabilitation counseling. She was an adjunct faculty at Virginia Commonwealth University's Rehabilitation Counseling Department for thirty years. She has worked in several agencies and psychiatric hospitals, and for ten years worked at her private counseling practice before becoming Coordinator of VCU's Rehabilitation Counseling Department internship program. Her debut novel, *Shelter of Leaves*, was a finalist for the Foreword Book of the Year award and a finalist for an INDEFAB award. For three years, Lenore has served on the Steering Committee of the RVALitCrawl, which has been featured in *RVAMag*, *Richmond Family Magazine*, and *Richmond Magazine*. She is an active member of James River Writers. She lives in Richmond, Virginia.

Author photo © Sasha Gay-Overstreet

SELECTED TITLES FROM SHE WRITES PRESS

She Writes Press is an independent publishing company founded to serve women writers everywhere. Visit us at www.shewritespress.com.

Shelter of Leaves by Lenore Gay. $16.95, 978-1-63152-101-0. When a series of bomb explosions hit on Memorial Day, Sabine flees Washington DC on foot and eventually finds safety at an abandoned farmhouse with other refugees—but surrounded by chaos, and unable to remember her family or her last name, who can she trust?

As Long As It's Perfect by Lisa Tognola. $16.95, 978-1-63152-624-4. What happens when you ignore the signs that you're living beyond your means? When married mother of three Janie Margolis's house lust gets the best of her, she is catapulted into a years-long quest for domicile perfection—one that nearly ruins her marriage.

Play for Me by Céline Keating. $16.95, 978-1-63152-972-6. Middle-aged Lily impulsively joins a touring folk-rock band, leaving her job and marriage behind in an attempt to find a second chance at life, passion, and art.

The Geometry of Love by Jessica Levine. $16.95, 978-1-938314-62-9. Torn between her need for stability and her desire for independence, an aspiring poet grapples with questions of artistic inspiration, erotic love, and infidelity.

Arboria Park by Kate Tyler Wall. $16.95, 978-1631521676. Stacy Halloran's life has always been centered around her beloved neighborhood, a 1950s-era housing development called Arboria Park—so when a massive highway project threaten the Park in the 2000s, she steps up to the task of trying to save it.

Center Ring by Nicole Waggoner. $17.95, 978-1-63152-034-1. When a startling confession rattles a group of tightly knit women to its core, the friends are left analyzing their own roads not taken and the vastly different choices they've made in life and love.